BOOK 2
OF

The River Quintet

YOUNG LIVES IN A CHANGING WORLD

Laughing Rain and Awakens Corn

LOOK-THE-SAME GIRLS IN THE LAND OF THE CLOUD-SPLITTER

Ray E. Phillips

Quill Publications | USA

QuillPublications.com
Cover Illustration by Sophie D. Seypura

ISBN: 979-8-9899062-2-2

Typesetting by C'est Beau Designs

Preface

Have you ever had mixed emotions about whether to do what is expected of you or to follow a more adventurous path? Such a mental tug-of-war plays out in this book. Here, the struggle is between twin girls—identical in every way except for one small difference about each one's opinion on duty versus desire.

There may seem to be but a hair breadth's difference between identical human twins in appearance or thoughts. Yet, such a tiny difference can create a long-simmering problem. Such is the case of the adolescent girls in a story that takes us back four centuries. An innocent comment by one of the girls about their future is wholly rejected by the other. This difference smolders and slowly expands until it becomes a force that defies resolution; it eventually drives the girls apart. Each seeks solace in a different way and, for one, it leads to near disaster.

This story begins with the departure of the twins' older brother, Tail Feather, on a long journey in early spring. It ends with his return in the summer. Whereas the story of their brother in the first book is nearly all a descriptive narrative, the second book—*Laughing Rain and Awakens Corn*—is mainly conversation between the inseparable sisters as they chat incessantly about everyday events. For fun, they even go so far as to invent their own language and to play identity tricks on unsuspecting visitors to their village.

A differing attitude about one aspect of the twins' view of their future becomes a spider-web that weaves throughout the book. A hint of meaningful resolution, however, is eventually found in the web.

The story portrays everyday lives and the expectations of women in an Indian village. It explores attitudes concerning religion, family life, work ethics, marriage, the healing arts, warriors, and personal values. It recalls the legend of Hiawatha and the founding of the Iroquois Confederation. The Story of Creation is told by the fireside. A surprise visit by a missionary causes an astonishing distraction. In addition, Book Two delves into the psychology of growing up. You may find that the struggle between the Look-a-Like girls is at times like a conflict within yourself.

You will notice superscript numbers throughout the story. These refer to Part II: Notes About the Story, which put the story in context with details about history, anthropology, and the natural world.

—R.E.P.

Special Thanks

A note of heartfelt thanks to all those people who have contributed their advice, assistance and constructive criticism to the creation of The River Quintet:

The late Kenneth Little Hawk, Mi'kmaq-Mohawk storyteller
William "Chip" Reynolds, (formerly) Captain of the *Half Moon* Replica Ship
Janny Venema, author and (formerly) Dutch translator and Associate Director, New Netherland Research Center, Albany, NY
Walter Woodward, Connecticut State Historian
Stefan Nicolescu, Research Scientist and Collections Manager, Division of Mineralogy and Meteoritics, Yale Peabody Museum of Natural History, New Haven, CT
Barrie Kavasch, author, Institute for American Indian Studies, Washington, CT
Teachers at the American School for the Deaf, West Hartford, CT
The late Frank Kozelek, Tarrytown, NY
Research staff at various libraries, including those at Kent Lakes, Corinth and Glens Falls, NY, Windsor, CT and Shepperton, England
Joan G. Sheeran and Wendy Phillips Kahn, editors
Sophie Seypura and Arturo Aguirre, illustrators
and Patrick Seypura, digital publisher and website manager.

—R.E.P.

This reissued and corrected version of Laughing Rain and Awakens Corn *was prepared and published following the death of Ray Phillips in July, 2021. The editors have made minor changes and proofreading corrections and now offer this edition in loving memory of the author. Throughout the writing of The River Quintet, Ray Phillips devoted himself during his last decades to bringing history alive with accuracy and compassion.*

—Joan G. Sheeran and Wendy Phillips Kahn

Contents

PART I

The Story of Laughing Rain and Awakens Corn

CHAPTER 1

The Secret

Two girls, lost in thought, stood silently in the dappled sunlight. The ever-changing streaks of early sun breaking through the treetops tempted them to linger along the stream. Their gaze flittered aimlessly upon flashes of light that played on the smooth, wet rocks lying among the ripples. All was quiet save for the murmur of the wind in the pine boughs above and the splash of water in the rippling brook below.

Slowly, and at the same time, the girls turned away. They began to walk, hand-in-hand, along the pebble-covered lakeshore that led to their village. After every few steps they hesitated. They looked back to where—between rocky ledges—the lake gave up its water to form a roaring swirl.[1,2]

Not so long before, at first light, the whole village had come to see eight paddlers in four canoes. The paddlers had just pushed off and were quickly out of sight. Their travels would take them to places far away. All but the look-the-same girls had left to return to their village.[3] From time to time, the girls heard a howl above the splash. It came from far downstream. They knew that mournful howl, and it saddened them.

Laughing Rain and Awakens Corn soon came to Big Turtle Rock, the great boulder that lay half in the lake and half on the shore. A mound of snow still clung to the side that was away from the sun. Here, a narrow but well-trodden path veered from the lake and followed along a trickling brook. The path brought them through a bog of shoulder-high, yellowed marsh grass. Pleasant chills ran up and down their bare arms as they brushed against blades studded with sparkling dew drops.

By now, the upper rim of the sun peeked above the dull green treetops. Their glances sideways from time to time rested on the splashes of pink that spread across the jagged horizon. Ahead, in the far distance, dazzling whiteness formed a great dome. The girls were not sure where the snow-topped mountain ended and where the passing clouds began.

Suddenly, Awakens Corn stopped, reaching to hold her sister back with a gentle tug on the elbow. Together, they watched a sight seen a thousand times before but one that had never become tiring: the clouds across the mountain slowly drifting upward so that the mountain seemed to grow higher with each breath. Then, as if by magic, the top of Cloud-Splitter broke free of the clouds.[4] The sight brought a hint of smile to both. Soon after, the girls turned to take one last look at the lake. There, a delicate mist rose from the still, black water and curled slowly skyward. There was a long space in time before the trek homeward started once again.

Laughing Rain, at last, broke the silence. "Why do you not speak?" she asked with a gentle tease. "It is not like my sister to be quiet for so long."

Half-whispering, Awakens Corn answered, "Ah." There followed a drawn-out, thoughtful pause, "I... was,... I was thinking." Another pause.

"You cannot speak your thoughts?" chided her sister playfully.

"Hmm," Awakens Corn began once again. "In my quiet..." There came another pause but only for a moment. "In my quiet way I think of Tail Feather starting out on his long journey."

"Are you happy for our almost grown-up brother, happy that he is paddling to Water-With-No-End? Paddling with Father and the other men?"[5]

"Yes. My words do not tell the happiness in my heart."

"I am glad, too," replied Laughing Rain. "He did not say much about traveling the long river. Yet I know he was thinking happily of the journey for a long time."

Awakens Corn added, "All through the Long Cold and then the Earth Thaw, there was a faraway look in his eyes. He could not hide his dream to go to that place."

"Still, I will miss him," Laughing Rain said, "He is a kind and gentle brother. He listens to what we have to say. He helps us carry the heavy things. He brings us flowers from the forest. Everyone spoke of the way he helped repair the longhouses after the winter's thrashing. Yet, I feel uneasy to see him paddle away on so long a journey."

"For me," her sister answered, "The saddest part was watching KyKoo run through the cold water trying to catch up with the canoes."

"I, too, feel sorry for KyKoo" Laughing Rain agreed. "If only KyKoo understood that there was no room for a wolf in the canoes."

The voice of Awakens Corn brightened, "But think of all the wonders that Tail Feather will see along the way!"

"Oh, I have been thinking about them. He will see new lands along the great river, strange animals, people with ways quite different from ours, and a place where there is water as far as you can see. I close my eyes and try to imagine the things that our brother will see. What do you imagine?"

"Me?" Awakens Corn halted, her head turned down as if in deep thought about her feet. "Oh, I imagine many things," she replied in a quiet voice.

"Tell me, what things?" Laughing Rain persisted.

"I imagine all the wonderful things about the long river that are told in the night stories. There is not enough room in my head for all of them."

"Do you think Tail Feather will see any of them?"

"Yes, I know he will. For Tail Feather, these stories will come alive. It was a great honor, you know, for him to be chosen to go. He is so young for such a journey."

"At the same time," Laughing Rain worried aloud, "Tail Feather will be cold and hungry most of the time. He must paddle all day, every day. At night he will sleep on the wet ground. There are many dangers, too. Remember, he is only a boy."

"Ha," replied her sister. "He will come back a man. I know Tail Feather will be safe." Awakens Corn tried to ease her sister's mind. "He knows how to take care of himself. BaBa taught him as much as a grandfather can about the rivers and the forest. Boys must learn all those things, even when they are very young."

Laughing Rain squeezed her sister's hand more tightly. "Grandfathers are the best teachers. BaBa told us that himself. Besides, Father will be with Tail Feather all the way."

By now, a slit of sky appeared between the lower rim of the sun and the tree line. The sky pink soon gave way to bright blue while the conifers that filled the landscape took on a brilliant green. The slow-flowing, misty images of dawn were replaced by the sharp reality of lake, trees and marsh grass. The day was the beginning of a great adventure for the brother of the twins. How could they know that on this same day a great change in their own lives would begin as well?

The pair continued to stroll lazily along the soggy pathway that wound through a field of high grass and cattails.[6] There were many steps without a spoken word. Suddenly, Awakens Corn spun around, long braids flying, to face her sister, sending showers of dewdrops in every direction, a string of seashells swirling around her neck. She walked backwards in a comical, duck-like waddle, now grasping both of her sister's hands and drawing her along. A playful grin spread across the high cheek-boned face. Her acorn-shaped eyes glowed with excitement. The red leather band across her brow lifted a trifle. Awakens Corn chose her words carefully, "Laughing Rain, I must tell you something. What I am going to say is—for now—for your ears only." In the excitement of the telling, her backwards stepping got faster.

"Are we not all by ourselves?" questioned Laughing Rain with an amused, scowling face.

"But you must tell no one," Awakens Corn pleaded. "Do you agree?"

"Only for my ears? Do porcupines fly?" Laughing Rain asked. Not waiting for an answer, she added, "I always keep our secrets! You know that. Why must you ask me something so strange?"

"Because, this secret is the most secret ever told. You must never breathe a word of it, not even to Mother. Not now, anyway."

Laughing Rain, showing a half-smile and pulling her hands in, blurted out with both intense curiosity and at the same time a bit of uneasiness: "What is in your head, Awakens Corn?" She nervously untangled a branch of briars that had caught on her buckskin smock. "Always, just when life becomes too serious, you tell me something to make me laugh." She paused for a moment, her head down but her eyes turned up to look directly into her sister's. "You are a fun-maker. True, you are a coyote.[7] That is your way. Your queer ideas, I will say, always cheer me up."

Awakens Corn seemed not to have heard her sister's words. She went on speaking, now in a hushed manner although there was not a soul nearby to overhear. "If you promise not to say a word, I will tell you what I am going to do. Someday I am going to ..."

At that moment, a big brown-gray ball of wet fur burst through the waist high grass and charged between the girls. Yelping frantically, it lunged first against one and then against the other, thrashing so wildly that the girls struggled to stay on their feet. Dripping and muddied, its long and sharp teeth fully exposed, the animal panted breathlessly. Then, it shook itself. Water droplets sprayed all over the girls. They jumped back, laughing, eyes squinted, and hands held up against the muddy splatter.[8]

"KyKoo!" Awakens Corn cried out. "I knew you would come back. Eeee! Look at you! Sopping wet. Covered with mud." She looked into the wolf's golden eyes, then at her sister. "Laughing Rain, do you see her sadness? She is thinking, how could Tail Feather go away without her?" Then turning back to KyKoo, she cooed, "Tail Feather will be away a long time, but he will come back to you. Yes, yes, he will."

For the moment, four hugging arms softened KyKoo's whimpers. Awakens Corn added, "You will have to wait for him, just as we must wait. I promise, Tail Feather will be back before the leaves on the maple trees turn red."

Laughing Rain, bent over, tugged playfully at the long snout, "Tail Feather felt terrible about leaving you behind, KyKoo. But his canoe was too filled with important things to stuff a wolf in, too. Now, you will have two good friends." She stroked the coarse hair on KyKoo's back and tweaked her one ear. "Life with us may not be as exciting as it was with Tail Feather. Still, we will have good times together. We will look after you. We give you our solemn word. Do you agree, Awakens Corn?"

"Oh, yes. Laughing Rain speaks true, KyKoo. You can spend all day, every day with us if you like." Her sister added quickly: "We will see that you always have much to eat. Soon you can go strawberry-picking with us."

The girls started off again along the footpath, this time with their hands clasped together. KyKoo, still panting, tagged along a few steps behind, her head sagging and her bushy tail limp.

Laughing Rain could wait no longer, "Well?"

"Well, what?"

"Well, are you going to tell me what is only for my ears?" The corners of her mouth lifted slightly with anticipation.

Awakens Corn replied, "I did not hear you say that you would promise."

"Promise what?"

"Promise to keep a secret."

Laughing Rain stooped to give KyKoo a few soothing pats. She answered, looking up toward her sister with growing, questioning impatience, "Yes. Yes, I promise."

Awakens Corn began again, "Someday—this is what I want you to know—someday I will paddle to Water-With-No-End, just as Tail Feather paddles now." With the secret now in the open, her voice sped up, reaching a higher pitch. "I will see all the wondrous sights and talk to all the people along the way. Everyone will know me as a great traveler."

Startled by such a brash notion, Laughing Rain held her hands before her taut face and gasped. Then the hand came down slowly, and the face relaxed. She allowed a little chuckle to come through. "Sometimes, my sister, you are just silly. But what you say always makes me think, even when you say things that can never come to pass."

"No! No, Laughing Rain." The voice of Awakens Corn turned sharper. Each word came out separately and with uncommon certainty. "You—must—believe—me. I speak from deep within myself."

"But... but... you cannot leave the village. Long journeys are for men. Women are needed here. It is always the way."[9]

"Fish feathers! Is it that only men can go to far-away places? Hah! Should women not see the same things?"

"Believe me, Awakens Corn," returned her sister. "The elders will say 'No.' Mother will speak the words of the elders, 'No.'"

"Ah, hah! I will find a way, Laughing Rain. Tail Feather did! You saw how hard he worked all the time, bringing firewood and making a canoe with Baba, how he won foot races, became the best at snow snake, and spent days in the forest with KyKoo. People even called him the Boy-Like-Beaver."

"Yes, but he is a grown boy. Everyone will laugh at a girl who thinks like a boy. Then they will say, 'Such a foolish girl! She will never get a husband.' Ah, you must forget all about taking a long journey."

"Laughing Rain, I cannot forget about going far away. It is always on my mind," Awakens Corn confided. "Why should we always stay in the village? Travelers tell us about the River-That-Flows-Two-Ways and the Sparkling-Face-in-The-Mountain." Her voice picked up speed, "We have heard about a Fish-Bigger-Than-A-Man and the Rocks-That-Look-Like-Trees." Nearly breathless, she said "At the end of the long river, the mountains all turned into water. Just think of that!"

Awakens Corn paused, then spoke slower and more carefully. "I want to visit other villages. Most of all, I want to see the one at the river's end where the People-Like-Birds make beads out of seashells. I must see all these things for myself."

"My dear, dear sister," Laughing Rain appealed now with a wisp of tremor in her voice. "We listen to the telling stories night after night about all these strange places and about the curious people and great fish along the way. We can see them in our minds."

"What you say is true," returned her sister. "We have listened to these stories since we were tiny children. Only now, the stories are not enough. Of course, I want you to go with me."

"Awakens Corn! Stop this talk!" Laughing Rain reached over and put her fingertips over the mouth of her sister. "It can only cause trouble."

Awakens Corn mumbled through half-closed lips, "I can stop talking about it but cannot stop thinking about it." The hand of Laughing Rain drew away. Awakens Corn added, "You will see how strong-minded I am, even if it means..."

KyKoo's whimpering began all over again, begging attention. Laughing Rain was grateful for the interruption. "Oh, sad KyKoo. If wolves shed tears, it would be raining now." Her cuddling and cooing words soon comforted Tail Feather's left-behind friend.

Laughing Rain, however, was not long distracted, "Awakens Corn! Listen to me. Women are satisfied with their lives as they are, even if they would like some changes. Look at us; we have a good time. It is true, we work hard. But we sing with the other women. We listen to all the gossip. We laugh most of the time. Think of the fun we have picking strawberries in a sunny meadow. We always find moments to play children's games." There was a thoughtful gap in her words before saying, "Remember, too, Sky Flower is just a baby. She needs us. Also, you cannot forget that men who go on long journeys suffer terribly. They take great risks for our people. No one does it just for fun, just to see new things."

"I know of all you speak," Awakens Corn made clear. "But listen to me. Every day from now on, we will be scraping hides, sewing moccasins, planting seeds, pounding corn, and cooking. Pot-making and stirring the cookfire never ends. Just boiling sap for maple syrup takes many cold and sticky days when I cannot separate my fingers. Then, there are always babies to take care of. She sighed, "And surely not many winters from now, there will be husbands who need us. These are good things, but only these and nothing more for the rest of our lives? I cannot bring myself to think so."

"No more of such talk!" her sister broke in. "We always find ways to make working more fun. And we are always together, no matter how tiresome our work may seem."

"Ah, you speak true, Laughing Rain," was the quick reply. "But I want to have one—just one—great adventure to remember when I am old, just one real story to tell my children's children. Is that too much to ask for a lifetime of grinding duty?"

"Awakens Corn!" Laughing Rain spoke while turning away from her sister with a shrug. "You must come to your senses. Remember Yellow-Moon-Clouds?" she asked. By now a hint of despair had crept into her voice. "You know what happened to her."

"We should not speak of Yellow-Moon-Clouds. You know that."

"I will speak of her. Now I speak only for your ears. Yellow-Moon-Clouds left our village so that..."

"That was not the same," interrupted Awakens Corn. "Yellow-Moon-Clouds chose to live in another clan. It was during the Time for Planting. Hunters told her that life would be easier for her in their village."

"True, but the people there behaved badly toward her. Do you remember the snowy night she came back to the longhouse of her family?"

"Yes, I remember that night," her sister interrupted. "How terrible it was."

Laughing Rain continued, "Her family would not take her back. We listened to the cries of Yellow-Moon-Clouds all through the night. Came daylight, and she was gone. New fallen snow covered her footprints. Now, no one even dares mention her name."

Awakens Corn stopped short, turning her back toward her sister. She stamped one foot into the muck. The splatter sent black mud flying. She stood with arms folded in front with half-pretended bravado. KyKoo looked on inquisitively. "No! I will never live in another village. No. Never! And I do not want to leave you, not even for one day. I only want to feel free by traveling far away, just one time."

Laughing Rain covered her ears with her hands pressed tightly. She stood stiffly as if braced against a cutting wind, shouting, "You can dream, Awakens Corn. Yes, dream of faraway places. But real life is not like a dream. No. You cannot go." Even with words as strong as she could make them, Laughing Rain felt they were not strong enough.

At the same time, Awakens Corn felt her own spirit, just as her feet, slowly sinking into the mud.

Awakens Corn pulled her sister's hands away from her ears. "Only one time!" said she, in a loud but strained voice as she placed her hands around her sister's waist. The hands of Laughing Rain fell on her sister's shoulders.

The look-the-same girls stood together wordlessly in this way as if frozen in time, then, slowly, stepped away from the mud. When they did, Awakens Corn felt the cold ooze gush up between her toes. Looking back, she saw a moccasin stuck in the black mud among the tall marsh grasses. The twins' eyes met once again. For an instant, they shared a laugh out loud before Awakens Corn squished her way back to fetch her moccasin.

Finding inner strength reborn, Laughing Rain tried to reason one more time. "Mother tells us that we are looking more like women every day. You can see the changes yourself. We are not children anymore, Awakens Corn. Now, we will have more grown-up things to do. For us to daydream about journeys to faraway places is wrong." Her words were now spoken with measured emphasis, "I beg of you, my dearest sister and my life-friend, get this thought out of your head."

"We are fast changing. I know that," Awakens Corn nodded. "I like the feeling that it brings to my body. This morning before the canoes left, as you stood beside Mother, I saw that you are a little taller than she is. So, I must be a little taller, too. I accept the duties that come with growing up. You know that I am a good worker, almost as good as you. I will be a good wife, too. But I also need to be without a woman's burden one time in my life. I will be the Woman-who-Travels-Far. We could..." She did not finish speaking her thought.

Once again, the girls became mindful of KyKoo's fretful cries. Awakens Corn, crouching, spoke in a low, voice, "Oh, KyKoo. Have we forgotten you already? We know that you have never been away from Tail Feather since you were just a little ball of fur. You are his best friend." With renewed attention, the wolf became a bit calmer, and the small procession moved forward.

By now, the twins had crossed the marsh. They came to the dark edge of evergreens where the heavy, musty odor of the wetlands gave way to an aroma sweetened by pines and spruce. There, a well-worn pathway that made a soft, crunchy sound underfoot twisted through the deep-shaded forest. Patches of snow glistened here and there.

At last, Laughing Rain formed some sort of reply for her sister. She voiced newfound confidence, "Let us not quarrel about something so impossible. We have quarreled about many things, always little things even when we thought they were big things at the time. You should know, I have always loved our quarrels; they make me reach deeply into my own thoughts. Do you remember the story about the geese: why do they fly one way before the snow comes, and the other way when it melts?"

"I do remember," Awakens Corn answered with a faint chuckle. "We did not believe what people said: that the geese turn into beavers when the weather turns cold, and back to geese when it warms again. How we giggled about that story. Each of us made up different reasons to explain the flying geese, most of them foolish reasons. Which one was right? We bickered about every one of them."

Laughing Rain reminded her sister about another quarrel for fun, "Do you remember the braids? About our game?"

"Of course, everyone wanted one of us to always wear one braid and the other, always two braids. That way, people could tell us apart." A mischievous smile came upon both faces. "We pouted for days because both of us wanted to wear two braids—or was it one braid? I have forgotten now. And so, we agreed to change each day to confuse people. Sometimes, we changed a few times even in one day. Only Mother was never fooled. I am sure that she played the game with us."

"It did not matter who won our squabbles," Laughing Rain chuckled. "We always went to sleep as friends. But this time, what you say frightens me. I will make believe we did not talk that way. Come, we must hurry home. Meadow Bird Singing will be looking for us. She has a fresh deer hide for us to scrape." She glanced behind to make sure that KyKoo was following along.

The girls took the shortcut back to the village. They were careful to step over bare gnarled roots that gripped the rocks and to find solid footing on tippy stones. At times, they climbed on all fours across slippery wet boulders and stepped cautiously through narrow deep footpaths between ledges. In such places, KyKoo led the way. "Oh, Wa! For you, KyKoo," one said, "it is all so easy." Soon, the three came to a high ridge. From their viewpoint, the high peak of Cloud-Splitter loomed ahead as if it were a whole universe by itself.

"You will not ever forget your promise, Laughing Rain, will you? The promise about my secret?" With one arm hooked around her sister's elbow, Awakens Corn added "Will you?"

"No, I will never tell anyone. You can depend on that. You always know me as a trusted sister. But you must promise me something." A faint wavering in her voice did not betray the firmness with which Laughing Rain spoke. "You must promise me that you will never speak of impossible travels again,... never again." The words spoken, there followed a face as hard as the stone on which they stood.

In reply, "As much as I care about you, Laughing Rain," Awakens Corn said, "I cannot make that promise." She struggled to find words. "Try to understand me. For now, that is all I ask of you." The face of Awakens Corn also hardened.

The path nearing the village leveled off. Walking closely one behind the other with KyKoo loping along at their heels, the girls came to an opening in the high wall of saplings with intertwined branches that encircled the village.[10] Suddenly, unexpectedly, a great wall, for the first time in their lives, had come between Laughing Rain and Awakens Corn. It was a different kind of wall from the one that protected their village. There seemed to be no opening. Their wall felt thicker than the briars and brush that were stuffed in between woven saplings. Theirs, instead, was not a wall that could be easily climbed over or crawled under. It was a wall that left each of the twins feeling unprotected on the inside.

CHAPTER 2

Time of the Squirrel's Ears

THE AWAKENING OF the earth after a long winter's nap comes in changes that unfold slowly and expectantly. First comes the melting of snow on the hillsides facing the sun. Then mountain streams quicken. Soon snowdrops blossom in sunny areas where they are sheltered from the wind and warmed by high-standing rocks. Later the song of the robin is heard in the meadows. Tiny buds on trees appear and, in a few days, become blossoms, just as the caterpillar becomes a butterfly. As it does every season of the Earth Thaw, the high grass along the lake turns from brown to green.

The people who live alongside the forest know when it is time for planting. First, comes the toil of breaking the soil. Then comes the chopping of girded trees along the edge of the garden. Finally, there is planting of seeds of the life-giving Three-Sisters: corn, beans, and squash.[11]

The Earth Thaw starts a season of backbreaking work. But the workers in the fields always go about their labor cheerfully. There is always singing and laughter among the women. The children who help them join in on the fun. And no matter how hard the work, it is a welcome relief after the Long Cold spent in crowded, smoky longhouses.

But before any work can be done in the field, the village always holds its Celebration for a Good Harvest. It is a daylong festival to honor the miracle for giving life. The whole village crowds together around the meeting circle. Before them stands the leader of their village, Chief Red Sun.

At this Celebration for a Good Harvest, the chief had put on all the finery of his position: a headdress of deer antlers and a full-length robe made of turkey feathers that shimmered with many colors in the early morning sun. He held strings of wampum in both hands. His moccasins, which were decorated in threaded quills of red, blue, and white, tread in slow, stately steps.[12]

The wide-spreading limbs of an oak tree put all the gathered villagers into patches of dappled sunlight. In a deep and solemn voice that could be heard throughout the longhouses, Chief Red Sun spoke. "By the leaves on this great tree, the Great Spirit tells us that the Season for Planting has come. When the leaves of the oak are as big as a squirrel's ears, the earth is warm enough. Just as the Youngest-Of-All enter our lodges and slowly grow to serve our people, so will the seeds of our Three Sisters: Corn, Squash, and Beans. The corn will grow tall and the beans will climb up along their stalks, just as the Good Twin of Creation had meant. The squash will cover the ground with their broad leaves to keep moisture in the soil. Their leaves will hold back the weeds sent up by the Evil Twin. Just as the Three Sisters work together, so must we join in labor to help the Creator make them grow."

These words said, Chief Red Sun sprinkled shredded tobacco leaves on the ritual fire.[13] With a crackle the bits burst into flame. "May the smoke from these sacred leaves carry these words skyward to the Creator. We give thanks for the return of the Season for Planting. We ask that the Great Spirit continue our bounty. May the Creator provide a plentiful harvest to nourish our people through the Long Cold."

With this prayer, the Chief turned to those waiting to be honored first: the babies born since the last Celebration for a Good Harvest. There were six babies, each held by its mother. The youngest among them was Sky Flower, the sister of Awakens Corn and Laughing Rain. She snuggled in the arms of her mother, Morning Blossom.

"Now, we give thanks to the Great Spirit for our smallest children." With these words, Chief Red Sun took the basket of seeds, placed it over one little head, and swirled it ever so gently. He lifted his head skyward, and while extending his arms, and prayed, "Oh, Creator of All, let earth, sun, and rain join with these sacred seeds so that our Three Sisters, like this newborn, will grow healthy and be filled with the gift of life." The basket then touched the infant's head ever so lightly. Five more times, the ritual was repeated, once for each baby.

When the turn of Sky Flower came, the glow from her big sisters rivaled that of the sachem's turkey feathers. Throughout it all, the people chanted the "Song for Plants to Grow," a traditional prayer always sung at this time of year as far back as anyone could remember. Within themselves, the singers could hear the echoes of their ancestors blessing the future of their crops.

After the Blessing of the Seeds, all the women of the clan, both young and old, gathered in a big circle around the oak tree. It was time to praise those who bore children. Again, Chief Red Sun spoke, "Oh, Great Spirit who blessed women with the power of giving birth, give them the power to bring life to these precious seeds."

These words said, the women formed a hand-holding ring. They began the Circle Dance for a Good Harvest, slowly shuffling around the central basket of seeds. Their feet fell softly on the kindly earth as the ring of women swayed to the throbbing pulse of many soft-speaking water drums.

It was evening when everyone in the clan came together again. They gathered around a single fire that burned in the center of the council longhouse. This building was not like those of the other longhouses. It was not broken up into many compartments, one for each family, but rather was open throughout its length. With sparse furnishings, the inside seemed immense. In it, all the people of the village could meet for occasions of great importance. On this day, after the Celebration for a Good Harvest, they had gathered to hear the telling of the Story of Creation. The telling always came at the beginning of the Season for Planting.

The longhouse filled up quickly. Yet, the crowd was quiet and respectful of what was to come. Those in front, mostly children, sat or kneeled while a host of people stood behind. The fire cast a flickering shine on every face. Its smoke gathered in a gray cloud at the roof before finding its way through the smoke hole.

Little Moose Running, the storyteller, stood close by the fire, leaning slightly toward it. Ash-colored hair, deep wrinkles and chin whiskers made known his many years of life. His raspy voice began, "Now, I will tell you the story of how the world came to be. My father told my sisters and me this story just as his father had told him. All the fathers before him told the same story to their sons and daughters. You will hear it as I did when I was a boy."

The voice of Little Moose Running wavered at times. Even so, the words carried throughout the longhouse. Not one word was missed by anyone.

"When the earth was new, a man and a woman with strong powers lived in a longhouse in the Sky World. Each day, the woman tended the man with great care. Although she faithfully combed his long hair every day, he soon became ill. Despite her ceaseless efforts to restore his health, he died. At the time of his death, she gave birth to a girl. The daughter grew up having to endure the constant weeping of her grief-stricken mother. Yet, the spirit of her dead father continued to visit the daughter, and he taught her many things."[14]

All through the story, the aged storyteller paced slowly around the fire, looking across a forest of faces in all directions. His sparkling eyes seem to fix for a moment on every one of the flickering faces.

"Who knows the name of the daughter?"

One small child in front stood up boldly, hands to his sides. "I know."

"Good," said the aged storyteller. "Tell us. What was her name?"

"Sky Woman."

"Well spoken. Now, the Spirit Father directed Sky Woman to take a long and dangerous journey. In time, she would meet her future husband. She found the man, but he was sick with a long illness. Now, her Spirit Father told her how to make soup that would cure him. The medicine soup proved itself powerful. The health of the husband-to-be of Sky Woman was restored almost overnight. They soon were united in a special ceremony."

As the story continued, the only sound heard in the longhouse—besides the voice of the storyteller and the sputtering of the fire—was a cough or a stifled sneeze from time to time. Sometimes heard, too, was the rustling of children as they shifted their stiffened legs.

"In time, Sky Woman came to realize that she was to bear a child. When her husband learned of this condition, he became angry, thinking that another man had caused this to happen. He fell ill again, and this time he dreamed of looking through a hole in the earth and seeing the world below. He awoke to find that such a hole had formed overnight where a giant pine tree had toppled over. The husband and his pregnant wife stood at the edge of the gaping hole, peering into the emptiness below. In his jealous rage, the husband reached out and pushed her down into the great hole."

At this point in the story, the storyteller stopped his pacing. He stood directly in front of a young boy. He leaned forward so close that their noses nearly touched. "And what do you think happened next?"

The startled boy drew back. Instead of words, his shoulders answered with a shrug.

"Then, I will tell you," the quivering voice of the old man went on. "Sky Woman fell into the endless space below. Suddenly, a great flock of ducks from deep inside flew up to meet her."

The storyteller brought the boy to a stand. Then he lifted the boy's arms out until they stretched way out to his sides as if they were wings. Then he brought his own arms gently down on the boy's arms. The storyteller did it in such a way that the boy seemed to carry his own weight.

"And so, Sky Woman landed softly onto the outstretched wings of ducks." The fearful look on the boy eased. The firelight also gave away a hint of pride on his being the chosen one to show Sky Woman's safe landing.

Little Moose Running then stood upright and continued his slow talking circle. "A giant turtle swimming at the bottom of the great hole offered his back on which Sky Woman could rest. Because the turtle's back was covered with water, Sky Woman could not rest properly. Water animals and diving birds went deep below the surface to bring up soil from the bottom. They all failed except for one: the muskrat. Diving many times, this strong swimmer brought up enough mud to spread over the turtle's shell. In time, the mud became the sacred earth on which all creatures live."

"Time passed," he said. "At last, Sky Woman gave birth to a baby." The story stopped for a while as the teller worked his way in short, soft steps all around the meeting fire. The pause gave some moments for the listeners to think about what was about to come.

Here is how the story went on: "The child of Sky Woman was a girl, Tekawerahkwa. When she grew to be a woman, she, in turn, found herself expecting a baby. The Spirit of the Wind was the father. In due time, Tekawerahkwa gave birth to twin boys. But the occasion was not a happy one. The first twin was born in the usual way. The other twin could not wait to be born, and he pushed out of the mother's side. In doing so, he caused his mother's death."

It was always at this point of the story that the listeners began to stir restlessly. They knew only too well that the conflicts of the Universe were beginning.

"The mother of the twins did not die in vain," went the storyteller, "for Sky Woman found a good purpose in her daughter's death. Her body provided things so that people could live on the earth. From her hands grew squash; from her fingers grew beans; and from her hair grew corn. Sky Woman turned her daughter's head and body into the sun and the moon. In all these things, the Spirit of the Turtle lived."

The voice was getting ever more whispery. Words came slower.

"Sadly, the twins did not grow to become friends with each other. Instead, the brothers quarreled constantly. The one who caused his mother's death was evil-minded. He became known as 'Flint' for he was hard." The listeners began to hear an agitation in the voice of Little Moose Running. "Flint deceived his grandmother into favoring him and into abandoning his brother. Only with the help of their spirit-father did the good-minded twin survive. Because he was gentle, his name became 'Sapling.'"

Awakens Corn leaned toward her sister and whispered, "This is the part of the story that I do not like to hear."

"Nor do I!" replied Laughing Rain, holding one hand over her mouth.

"*Shhhhhhh!*" was heard coming from just behind the twins.

The pace of the story picked up as the voice found new strength. The arms of the old storyteller danced to the rhythm of his quickening words, "The Good-Minded Twin sought out the Spirit of the Sky, the Spirit of the Water, and the Spirit of the Earth. These spirits helped him make the air, the rivers, and the forests as well as all the animals that live in them. In the same way, the Spirit World helped him create other human beings. He taught the people how to plant corn, beans, and squash. Sapling taught them how to build houses and canoes from trees. The Evil-Minded Twin, who was disrespectful of the spirits, ignored their teaching.

Laughing Rain reached out and squeezed the hand of her sister.

"Yet, all the benefits that the Good-Minded Twin brought forth were countered by the Evil-Minded Twin. Every time that Sapling made a stream, Flint let a tree fall across it so that the stream had to twist around the tree. The twin with the good mind showed the bees how to make honey to make food tasty, but the one with the evil mind gave them stingers. Sapling showed people how to plant corn. Flint, on the other hand, gave every kernel a tough coat, so that hard work was needed—first, to dry the corn and then, to grind it into meal. While the Good-Minded brother created deer, fish, and strawberries, the Evil-Minded brother wove his mischief by making poison ivy, mosquitoes, skunks, and snakes."

As the telling went on, the grasp of the look-the-same girls tightened and loosened. They knew the story well, but they felt anxious with every turn of its unfolding.

"The unbroken fighting finally led the twins to a cosmic struggle. In it, Flint suffered a mortal wound. Triumphant Sapling, however, could not repair all the harm that his brother had caused. From that time on, humans had to take care to keep the spirit of the Evil-Minded twin at a safe distance. The Good-Minded twin taught them to respect the spirit world and to offer them thanksgivings through ceremonies. Today, more than ever, we must live by these teachings."

There was not a sound to be heard. Coughing, sneezing, and stirring stopped. Even the fire, by now glowing ashes, no longer sputtered. No one moved.

The last words of Little Moose Running were directed to the youngest of the listeners, "Children, every day you must remember the great lessons of our ancestors. The story you have heard tonight will help keep you on the Good Path. It tells us that even when evil waits to wreck every good deed, you must always try your best. Now, go to your beds and sleep well. But do not forget the story of Sapling and Flint."

Awakens Corn gave her sister one last mighty squeeze.

From a distance, people returning to the longhouses heard a soft voice: *"Ooo Ooo."*

It was the Spirit of the Night speaking. The great horned owl was there to protect them from evil.

As the twins passed along the pathway hand-in-hand, Laughing Rain asked, "Do you think we are like the twins in the story?"

"No, of course not, you silly girl!" Awakens Corn answered with a hint of doubt, "Well, probably not."

"Do you think anyone else thinks we are?

"No, there is no one."

"We will never do anything to hurt the other, is that true?"

"Oh yes, we will never."

"Then," said Laughing Rain with a cheerful lilt in her voice, "There will be no more talk about taking long journeys."

With these words, Laughing Rain felt her sister's fingers slide away from hers. Awakens Corn left the pathway and disappeared into the night. Each of the girls walked toward their longhouse alone in the darkness, absorbed in her own thoughts and each afraid of what she did not understand about the other.

CHAPTER 3

The Good Luck Cloud

THE WORKERS IN the fields were blessed with sunshine as they started to prepare the gardens and plant the seeds. Awakens Corn and Laughing Rain worked together, as they always did in the field.

The twins began their first day of planting at the stream where fishing weirs stretched across. From the nets they scooped out pickerel, sunfish, and perch and filled their basket. While the fish were still wiggling and flopping in the basket, they said a prayer of thanks. It was spoken by the sisters together in a manner as solemn as any speech given by a great chief.

"Oh, Creatures of the Water, you now become Creatures of the Earth. Your bodies will nourish the seeds of the Three Sisters that we place over you. From your strength, the Three Sisters will become healthy plants that will nourish our people. With you, The Cycle of Life continues on as the Maker of All Living Things meant it to be."

Once afield, one sister dug a deep hole. She wielded a hoe made from a flat bone bound to a wooden handle.[15] The other sister dragged along the basket of fish. On the bottom of each hole, she gently laid out one of the fish. Together, the girls gave thanks to each fish with a short prayer, "To the earth, we give you. May your spirit return from the earth to the water through the nourishment of our life-giving food."

These words spoken, the twin with the hoe scooped the soil over the fish. She built the soil into a small mound and tamped it snuggly underfoot.

The twin with the basket then pressed the seeds a thumb's length into each hill: four seeds of corn, three of beans, and three of squash, taking care that none of the seeds touched each other. Next, she sprinkled soil into the tiny pits and patted it down. As she did, she whispered a short prayer to the seeds. "Seeds, you have been given wondrous power by the Great Spirit. Use well this power as you begin your new life. Grow to strong plants that give us the food for life. For this gift, we give our thanks."

The twins quickly moved onto the next hill, keeping up with all the other planters, but never hurrying their solemn prayer to the fish at each mound. They basked in the warmth of a full sun and breathed air free of the smoke of a crowded longhouse. But other workers in the field noticed that the girls did not chatter continually as they had always done before. Indeed, there was not a word spoken between the twins through the long day.

The wall that had risen between the girls only a few days before did not go away. It was not a wall that they could see. They could not touch it. Still, it was there and neither of them knew how to breach it. Near the end of the day, Laughing Rain tried.

With nearly the last of the Three Sisters firmly underground, Laughing Rain, trying to speak in a lighthearted voice, asked her sister, "Do you remember when we were small children? Only then, our work in the fields was meant to scare away the birds."

Awakens Corn thought about this for a long while. She did not look at her sister but kept her eyes on the forming hills of soil.

"I remember it well. Those were my happiest times." There was another long silence before she finished her thought, "You could always shout louder, and I could always make more noise banging sticks together."

"Oh, I think it was the other way around," replied Laughing Rain. "Anyway, not many birds ate our seeds. We were quite pleased with ourselves."

The planting went on, but no further words were exchanged. Suddenly, an idea popped into the mind of Laughing Rain. She decided to wait before its telling.

When the day of planting was finished, the workers scrambled down to the lake. Splashing, laughing, singing, and joking, they washed away the dust of the fields and refreshed their tired bodies.

That night when all seemed content with the success of their long day's planting and when there was a hot stew waiting to refresh those with weary backs and legs, Laughing Rain drew her mother away from the cookfire. "Mother," she asked, "Tonight, will you tell us an old story, one you have told us many times?" Awakens Corn was within earshot and the corners of her eyes wrinkled up with amusement.

"And what story is that?" answered Morning Blossom.

"The story about when we were born?"

"Again?" Morning Blossom said. "You want to hear that story again?"

"Oh, Yes! Yes! I want to hear it, too," nodded Awakens Corn. "You have not told us about it for a long, long time."

It was late that night before Morning Blossom got around to storytelling. She sat between the girls on her lower sleeping berth. With an arm around each one, she started.

"Well, having two babies at one time is a long story. It happened during the hottest days of the Time-For-Growing that

I felt myself becoming heavier with child. The plantings had all sprouted on newly cleared land, and a full harvest seemed certain. A new baby coming brought joy to everyone. Tail Feather was always at my side. He helped me pick up wood and carry water. He was a happy little boy. He asked many questions that seemed well beyond his age, and he always tried to do things that grown people do. I remember how he practiced over and over with the toy bow and arrow that your grandfather had made."

Awakens Corn interrupted, "But, you were going to tell about us?"

"Ah ha. I was about to come to your part of the story. I wanted to have another child, but this time a girl. I felt strong and ready. And so, I waited with an easy feeling for the baby to come. But things did not go well for the garden at that time. When the corn was waist-high, and the tassels first appeared, the sun rose and set in an unbroken cycle over many, many days without a drop of rain. The ground slowly dried up. In time, great cracks stretched across the fields. Even the mountain streams stopped running. Of course, the plants began to lose their strength for lack of rain. As the drought become more worrisome, all the villagers took their share of water from the lake. It was a long carry from the River and up a steep hill with a heavy pot or leather pouch. The parched earth of the garden drank the water as quickly as it was poured. It was never enough to keep the plants from wilting. Only tobacco appeared healthy. The tobacco plants, as you know, are sacred, and so they enjoyed a good dousing every day."

Laughing Rain interrupted, "Mother, will you wait until I get some water to drink?"

"Of course. Bring us all some."

Laughing Rain was soon back from the water-filled bucket that sat just outside the longhouse. Morning Blossom continued to tell her story. "The endless treks down to the lake to fetch the water fell mostly on the women. The trip back up the long hill was doubly tiring, as their backs strained under the weight of the water containers. Many of the men of the village were away hunting, while others had not yet returned from the journey to Water-With-No-End. The elderly members did what they could, but many were too old to help much. All the children carried what they could, and there was not a complainer among them. Even little Tail Feather tagged along with a pouch slung over one shoulder, hardly spilling a drop.

"The passing days seemed to be hotter than anyone could remember, and the struggle to carry water became ever more tiring. No one said so, but we knew that we were losing the struggle to keep the Three Sisters alive. Without a drenching rain soon, many believed that the crop was beyond hope. You can understand how despair hung heavily over the village. Some had given up altogether, saying that they could survive through the winter only if the men returned from the hunt heavy with meat."

"What if the men did not have a good hunt?" asked Laughing Rain.

"Then," her mother explained, "everyone would have to leave the village. We would live an uncertain, wandering life following the footprints of rabbits and deer. Everyone shuddered at this possibility."

Awakens Corn asked, "What would the coming winter be like, then?"

"Probably many would die from cold and hunger."

"But, Mother," broke in Laughing Rain. "You were going to tell about when we were born."

"We are coming to that now. It was during the most scorching heat of the long dry spell. My body told me that I was soon to have child. I could no longer carry water. The time had come to go to the birthing house. Everyone wished me well."

"You were all by yourself in the birthing house?"

"Yes, mostly. That is always the way."

"Why do you have to be alone?"

"It is a custom that goes back to the beginning. Giving birth is the greatest gift of Creation. It is a matter between the mother and the Creator of Life. Others would only interfere with the sacred event. All women go into the birthing house as they are nearing the time for childbirth. They go alone. In this way, the bond between mother and Creator is strong the moment a child is born. The child, too, will be stronger for it. Of course, all women care about newborn babies, but they leave their birth to their mothers alone."

"But it cannot be easy," commented one of the girls.

"The hardest part for me was leaving Tail Feather. He tried to join me. When his aunt Meadow Bird Singing held him back, he broke into flowing tears. So ample were the tears shed, my sister said that they might be enough to water the plants.

"The birthing house sat in deep shade beneath the great maple tree. A hole at the top of the roof was meant to keep the house cool. Even so, it was steaming hot inside. The women looked after me every day, leaving food and some of their meager supply of water at the tiny opening.

"At last, my baby arrived. It was a girl. She cried out with a strong voice. I cried for joy. Outside, I heard the excited laughter of children. They had been pressing their ears again the wall of the birthing house, wanting to be the first to hear the beautiful sound of a new baby and the first to rush out to spread the joyful news. I remember as a child doing just that with every new baby. They say that news of my baby did bring a smile of relief to the faces of sunbaked, exhausted, and discouraged workers."

Morning Blossom took a long drink of water before continuing. "You could never imagine my surprise when a second baby appeared. Another girl and another strong voice."

"Which one of us was first?"

"I cannot tell. Both babies had full faces and bright eyes. Your cries were full and breathing was easy. But my mind was heavy with the thought of what could happen to them. I tried to keep the babies from crying. But keeping two newborn babies quiet was not possible, and, in time, I knew they would be doomed, anyway."[16]

"Why? Why are twins so bad?" asked Laughing Rain.

"I think you know," her mother replied. "The custom goes back to the Story of Creation. Some people believe that one of the twins will bring bad luck to the clan. But, how does one pick out which is the good twin, and which is the bad? My worry with two babies born at one time was too much to bear. Perhaps, I thought for a time, I could keep one of the twins hidden."

"I would not like that," Laughing Rain said with a smile.

Awakens Corn asked, "Was Father here to see his new babies?"

"No. He was away. The hunters thought that only plentiful game would save the village from a hungry winter. Later," Morning Blossom continued, "I learned that Sparkling Brook lingered behind to listen at the birthing house a bit longer than the other little girls. Then her ears seemed to play tricks. She heard two babies crying! Her head reeled with the startling sounds. She listened many times. There was no doubt. There were two babies! Once she was certain that her ears were telling the truth, Sparkling Brook raced off to tell what she thought was joyful news."

The twins knew that their mother was coming to the painful part. Although they had heard the story many times, it made them both shudder with the retelling. The news of two babies born at one time was not joyful for the weary water carriers. They warned that a double birth was an omen of some kind, and it was not a good one.

The mother's voice picked up as she went on, "Just as the news was spreading throughout the village, a dark cloud passed before the sun. The wind, not felt for a very long time, began to whip up the grass and leaves. A few drops of rain fell onto the shriveled earth, and each one caused a little puff of dust to rise. Then more drops came. And more. More clouds gathered behind the one overhead. Soon, a drenching downpour was on us. The joy within the hearts of the water carriers reached their feet, causing them to dance with much spirit. They twirled themselves between the stands of the Three Sisters, hugging each other and giving thanks to the Spirit of Rain."

The girls exchanged broad smiles, thinking that they had brought such happiness at a time of much trouble.

"Breathless and wet to the skin, the women hurried together to the birthing house to see what they could do for me. I saw them coming through the sheets of rain and greeted them with two healthy babies. Yet, I could make out a change from joy to despair in their faces.

"Steady rain went on without let up for three full days. The ground became thoroughly soaked. The once dusty soil turned soft and thick like wet clay, making deep footprints wherever people danced. The mountain streams began to sing again. Drooping leaves on the corn stalks lifted and lost their withered look. Within days, the corn grew taller, carrying along the entwined beanstalks, now with fattened pods. Wrinkles on the squash leaves disappeared, and tiny yellow knobs covered the vines. The women and children went to the fields each day just to celebrate the renewed life of our Three Sisters. They all gave thanks to the

Spirit of the Plants in their separate ways. And now you know how you got your names.[17]

"I nourished my babies with the same spirit that the rain nourished our fields. I gave attention to the smallest detail and caressed them as the most precious things in the world. Soon the hunters would return. When they did, the fate of my double birth daughters would be decided. Until then, no one dared to visit the new babies. For me, the long days and nights were filled with waves of happiness and waves of worry."

Morning Blossom could hear the deeper, faster breath of the girls, as if they had never heard the outcome of the story.

"The men arrived at the village with much gleeful shouting and laden with game. Their mood quickly turned serious, though, when they were told about the twin babies. They held a council meeting that night and the men talked until dawn, exchanging puffs of sacred tobacco on the long pipe. The oldest of the elders remembered that twin births happened once before in his clan. They were quick to point out that the clan did not keep twins.

"Through the long night of talking and decision making, my heart was torn apart. I tried to hide my tears from Tail Feather, but he was old enough to see my deep worry.

"After sun-up, Chief Red Sun came to my longhouse. His face was without sign of joy or of sadness, as was his way. He spoke slowly, as he always did. 'You know how the Story of Creation speaks of two births at one time.'"

Morning Blossom said, "With these words, I felt my heart pulsing out of my chest. I let out a mournful cry. His next words came as a surprise. 'We have been told how our gardens were near death from lack of rain. We could not understand why the Great Spirit could punish us in this way. We believe that the Great Spirit finally sent a message through your babies that we have suffered enough. The drought has ended, and you will keep your babies.'

"I cried again, this time in silence with long-rolling sweet tears."

"I will never complain about rain again," said Awakens Corn.

Laughing Rain joined in, "Nor will I."

"Everyone wanted to see the new babies," their mother went on. "You looked exactly alike. You had much hair and bright eyes. No one had seen twins before, and every day the curiosity of the other children and of the adults brought a longhouse full of visitors."

Awakens Corn wanted to know, "What did Father say when he found out about two babies at one time?"

"Your father did not return from hunting for many days after you were born. He could hardly speak at first. You know that your father almost never shows his deepest feelings. When he saw two lookalike babies smiling at him, I saw the moisture come up in his eyes. That night, he held our babies for a long, long time."

In the dim light of the longhouse, Morning Blossom thought that she saw in the faces of her daughters an eagerness for more about their first days of life.

"Yes," said Laughing Rain, "but how did you know who was who?"

"I can only say that a mother knows. But I am not sure how. There was always something a little different between you, but I cannot tell you what."

"What did other people think about us?"

"Over the years, the people of the village overcame their worry about you as twins. They always treated you as ordinary children. As you learned to walk and talk, it was not long before you were helping with chores, just as all the other children did. The only difference was that no one could tell you apart. Sometimes, your father and brother made mistakes."

"That part was always fun for us," Awakens Corn said.

"Yes, I know. You always stayed close together through the time of your growing up. Nothing could separate you. You babbled between yourselves all the time, it seems, ever since the day you were born."

"Who babbled more, Mother?" Laughing Rain asked, laughing.

"Oh, that has an casy answer. Awakens Corn. She never stopped from morning to night. You mostly listened." Morning Blossom heard a little giggle. "As I watched you grow up, I think you two even made up your own language."

"Oh, that we did. It was good," said Awakens Corn, "saying things that only we understood."

"We liked to turn things around with words," Laughing Rain added. "Remember how we would say 'We like to go out in the rain'? We really meant 'We hate to stay inside when the sun is shining.' Saying a 'good night's sleep' for us meant having 'a terrible nightmare.'"

"We made up words, too," added her sister. "They were our special words. 'Masup' was maple syrup and 'busk' was buckskin. We called a boiling pot 'boot' and a cold pot 'coot.'"

"So many silly words," Laughing Rain replied. We even had names for ourselves, mixing us up. Do you remember 'Awarain' for you and 'Laffacorn' for me?"

"Of course," answered Awakens Corn. "Only you were Awarain and I was Laffacorn."

"Oh, you two liked to confuse people," Morning Blossom allowed. "Imagine, on a long day of rain in the longhouse, hearing nonsense talk all day long. Sometimes it made me crazy but in a fun sort of way."

Laughing Rain remembered, "We played our favorite game when someone new came to the village."

Her sister explained, "That was the time when one of us went into one side of our longhouse carrying a big pot or a colorful doll, making sure that the visitor saw you or me. An instant later, the other, waiting inside, would pop out of the long house at the far end carrying a likeness of the pot or doll. The prank always surprised visitors."

"Snow soup!" their mother chuckled. "I remember that. You were trick-playing children, but I secretly laughed at the puzzled faces that came after. I think everyone enjoyed your tricks, even if they were played on them. Now you have heard the whole story of two babies at one time. It is time for sleeping. So, up you go."

That night on the upper platform berth that was their bed, Laughing Rain whispered to her sister, "We are here because of a good-luck cloud. Mother told us again tonight. We need each other. Our lives are as close as the bean vines and the cornstalks that they climb up on."

"Yes, I know," her sister replied.

"No matter what happens," said Laughing Rain with a strong voice, "we will always be together."

Awakens Corn echoed, "No matter what happens, we will always be together."

CHAPTER 4

The Rattle

AFTER THE STORY-TELLING the good feeling between the twins came back. The field workers were relieved to see them in spirited talk once again during the planting of seeds. Although they did not know what the twins were planning, they were glad to see their smiles and hear their laughter once more.

Laughing Rain dared her sister to ask permission from their mother to do something special. They had talked about doing it for a long time. With every day warming the earth a little more, with early flowers peeping out everywhere and with animal tracks, even baby ones, often seen, the time had come.

The dare was too tempting for Awakens Corn to resist. That night she found the right moment to speak with her mother as she watched her hands fly over a nearly finished basket. "Mother, Laughing Rain and I have something to ask you. We hope you will let us do it."

"Oh, you know I will if it is reasonable. I am curious. What do you wish to do so much?"

"We want to walk all the way around the lake by ourselves. We have wanted to do this since we were little children."

Laughing Rain joined in, "Tail Feather spoke about wondrous sights along the far shore. He has seen them many times."

Morning Blossom laughed at the idea of such a bold adventure for her growing-up girls. "It is a long walk. Still, I see no harm in our losing two good field workers for a day." She warned, however, "Keep along the shore. Do not wander into the forest." With a hand on a shoulder of each girl, she had just one more thought. "You must start out early in the morning. Take some journey bread and be sure to come back before dark."

Sleep was fitful that night with excitement for both girls. The cornhusks that made their mattress crinkled all through the night. Awakens Corn whispered, "Shall we try to get KyKoo to go with us?"

"Oh, yes," replied Laughing Rain. "She would like that. She went around the lake many times with Tail Feather. Yes, KyKoo knows the way."

"What if she will not go? Ever since Tail Feather went away, KyKoo only stays by BaBa's side. And she always looks so sad."

"We can try to call her away, first thing in the morning."

At dawn, the girls tiptoed to the longhouse of their grandfather. There, KyKoo lay curled up inside a heap of branches. Only her eyes moved as the twins approached. They did their best to get KyKoo to follow them. In their most pleasing voices they told about their walk around the lake, and about the fun they would have jumping across the many streams. But no amount of coaxing, pulling, or pushing would get the wolf to go along. KyKoo crouched down even more in his bed of leaves and branches. Awakens Corn ran back to their longhouse to fetch a strip of meat. Even that brought no reaction from the animal.

"That is all we can do," Laughing Rain sighed. "She will be moody until Tail Feather returns." Awakens Corn left the meat for KyKoo to enjoy alone.

The eager twins scampered across the ledges and through the forest pathway and were soon at the lake near Big Turtle Rock. Across the expanse of water, tiny ripples sparkled from one end of the lake to the other. The girls barely felt the light breeze against their cheeks.

As they walked along the shore, they were startled by a sudden movement in the underbrush. It was caused by a black bird with a white necklace and white spots on its back. The bird waddled comically away. It plunged into the lake and vanished underwater. A long moment later and a long stone's throw away, the twins saw a great splash as it burst from the water. The white-spotted, black bird began to skip along the water, running and flapping at the same time. When it was but a dot in the distance, it became airborne. Flying fast, it quickly disappeared among the mountain ridges.[18]

The two girls looked at each other, smiled, and continued to wander along the shoreline. They ran their fingers through the fuzzy moss that clothed the trunks of fallen trees in greenery. They drank from a brook as it poured out into the lake. Around a bend, they saw a family of porcupines nibbling away at blossoms in the tall grass. The girls held back for fear. Mother porcupine saw them and, in less time than it takes for a hiccough, all scurried away.[19]

Awakens Corn asked, "What do you like best about the Time of Earth Thaw?" Before her sister could answer, she offered her own favorites. "I like the sounds that the warm days bring. The cooing of the dove is my favorite. The voices of the night forest are reasons enough to stay awake: to hear the song of a whip-poor-will or the hoot of an owl. Sometimes there is a chorus of wolves howling far, far away. Rainy nights are the most fun; I can listen to the *thrum, thrum* on the roof the whole night.

Did you know that some nights I leave you sleeping just to go outside and listen to the sounds of the night?"

Laughing Rain was amazed to learn this about her sister. They were both delighted to find something to talk about that they had never talked about before.

The voice of Awakens Corn picked up its fervor. "Earth Thaw happens when the brooks are fullest and their splashing songs the most agreeable. I try to find the places where the different sounds of rushing water come from... maybe against a rock or fallen branch. I listen to every tiny waterfall separately. Did you hear the peepers last night?[20] They are a sure sign of Earth Thaw, but no one can tell us what makes that sound. Some people say it is the leaves talking. Do you believe that? Earth Thaw is a time when the chirping of the red-breasted winged one is the happiest. Do you hear that the wind sounds different in the trees when the leaves have just started to come out?"

Laughing Rain had her own thoughts about Time of Earth Thaw. "You want to know what I like?" Before going on, the girls had to bend beneath a giant branch that leaned across their pathway. "What pleases me most," she continued," are the smells. The woodlands have a special smell in spring. But the smell is always there. What it comes from I know not. The pine needles, the floor of winter-leaves, the moss? Also, Earth Thaw is when the scent of a sassafras twig is strongest, when it makes the best tea. I like, too, that of black birch. It is sweet in smell but bitter in taste. I even like the smell of skunk cabbage. Well, you know that skunk cabbage is the first plant brave enough to push up through the snow. Did you know that there is a little scent even in a fern? I know not another like it. Try this one," she added, as she picked the tip of a leaf and held it before her sister.[21]

Awakens Corn sniffed. "I smell nothing."

"Try again. First, I will crush it between my fingers. Then you must put it against your nose and breath in slowly with your eyes closed," said Laughing Rain.

"Well, ... maybe. But it is faint if there is any..."

As Awakens Corn sniffed, Laughing Rain noticed some movement nearby. She poked her sister who turned to look. There, not twenty steps away, was a great bear. It looked at the frozen girls, then stood straight up, bared some teeth, made a quick nod of its head with a sniff, came down, and slowly ambled off.[22]

It was a long time before Laughing Rain and Awakens Corn continued. Their walk brought them farther along the sandy shore. At times, they had to jump across a mountain brook, often going way upstream to find good footing. They climbed over one fallen tree after another, most of them bleached white by weather.

"Are you tired?" asked one.

"Not at all. This is the most exciting thing I have ever done," said the other. "Imagine, we are far from the village and here all alone."

By the time the sun was at its highest place in the sky, the sisters had reached the far end of the lake. Here, they had to pass up behind some huge boulders that jutted out into the water. As they clambered up around the boulders, Awakens Corn suddenly stopped and placed a finger over her mouth. "*Shhhh!* Do you hear something, something strange?"

They paused along the way and listened intently. All was silent save for a distant caw and a light breeze that passed through the trees. Just as they started out again, a hollow, clicking sound came again for an instant. "I heard it that time," said Laughing Rain. The girls stayed put and crouched along the boulders to hear more.

"What is it?" one asked in a whisper.

"It sounds something like a rattle."

"A rattle? I have never heard a rattle like that. It is the sound of two sticks hitting."

The fleeting noise did come again. And again. It seemed to come from above high boulders where a stream cascaded down between them.

"The sound is not natural," said Laughing Rain. "It frightens me. We must go on."

"But we have to find out what is making it. I am sure the answer is simple," replied her sister. "Come, it will be fun to see what it is."

"No, Awakens Corn. Mother does not want us to leave the edge of the lake."

"But then we will never know what causes such a strange noise. I think it is coming from just above that rocky hill. We can quickly climb up and look."

Laughing Rain spoke with an unusual intensity, "That goes against a trust Mother has in us. No, I will not go with you. I beg you not to go either."

The girls stood facing each other and heard the rattling sound come now and then. Awakens Corn said, "My dear sister, we are growing up, yet we are growing apart. You will not share what I want most. You think a long journey is silly for a woman. You are not curious enough to climb a few boulders with me to learn what is causing a little rattling. I feel I am losing you as a friend."

Laughing Rain stood in stunned silence. She wanted to say, "Journeys of women just for adventure are against our people's tradition. Disobeying Mother is bad enough." Her voice, however, did not speak as she tried to hold back tears. She knew that it was the worst moment in her life. She also knew that she had to give in somehow to hold together their life-long bond. But how?

By the time Laughing Rain found her voice, she had already decided, "Awakens Corn, I will climb with you." Her words steadied, became purposeful. "Of course, I am as curious as you are. Somehow finding out what causes the rattling noise is not as important as holding a trust. Yet, I will go but only to please you."

Each girl felt the twinge of fear, one that of the unknown coming from the top of the hill, the other of knowing that they were disobeying their mother. Bracing themselves, the twins followed the cascading stream upward among the steep rocks. It led to the remains of an old beaver dam. The rattling now was closer than ever, and it came from just behind the dam. Sometimes between rattles, they heard a deep-throated snort. It was spooky moment for both girls. They clutched each other's hand for support. Yet, they were too taken in with the mystery by now to turn back. They struggled to find toeholds in the dam and cautiously crawled up it. As their heads popped above the dam, there appeared a sight so astonishing that neither could believe what lay before them.

Along the edge of a pond, two elk faced each other. One kneeled, its hind end down. The other stood but on shaky legs. There was a bloody gash along one shoulder. Their gigantic antlers were hopelessly entangled. Both animals appeared gaunt and exhausted. The ground around them was pounded down with hoof marks, and the brush was thoroughly trampled over a wide swath. Now and then, the standing elk raised his head with a shake and caused a hollow sounding clatter.[23]

The twins watched the struggle with stunned horror. It was Awakens Corn who was the first to speak. She spoke in hushed tones. "They have been like this for a long time. One seems almost dead already."

"Both these great animals will die from the tangle of their antlers," added Laughing Rain. "Why do they fight?"

"Who could know?" said Awakens Corn. "Remember, our warriors fight people from other tribes for reasons that we cannot understand. I think it is the same thing." She was certain that Laughing Rain would not agree.

The growing fear of disobeying their mother obliged Laughing Rain to say, "Sister, you have had your way. We found what made the strange sound. Now we must go."

"Wait," her sister announced sharply. "I think we could pull them apart."

"No, Awakens Corn. It is too dangerous. The elk will not know we mean to help. They will kick us with sharp hooves and stab us with their antlers."

"But they are too weak to resist. Untwisting their antlers free will be easy."

"No, Awakens Corn. I came up here with you against Mother's wishes only to please you. Now you must listen to what I say. We cannot save these elk. It is too late."

"We could ask some of the older boys for help. I know they would like that."

"I cannot agree," said Laughing Rain. "Like boys, they will come running for the excitement, but they may be hurt terribly. We should not tell them."

"Once again, Laughing Rain," returned Awakens Corn, "we quarrel. Why suddenly are we so far apart?"

"Awakens Corn," said Laughing Rain, "You speak of a powerful idea calling you on a long journey. I speak now with a weak voice but with the power of all my inner strength. We cannot help these elk. We must go now."

The girls watched the elk for a while longer, all the time Laughing Rain tugging at the smock of her sister. The elk struggled on and seemed to weaken before their eyes. Awakens Corn knew her sister was right about the struggle of great animals. Together, in a mood of despair, they descended back to the lakeshore, leaving the two giant, doomed animals to themselves.

The twins began the long walk home, taking the far side of the lake. Here the footing proved more difficult. The shoreline was not sandy but rather was filled with boulders and rocky overhangs that stretched way out above the water. Countless fast-flowing streams, downed trees, and sharp rising cliffs meant a roundabout trek. The twins worked their way over, under and around one obstacle after another.

There was another obstacle, too, besides the ones along the shoreline. The rift between the twins was heavy on the mind of each of them. Their different thoughts about a long journey were like the antlers of the elk: the sisters were now entangled in mortal combat. Neither of the girls could think of a way around this obstacle. Since neither was moved to talk, they walked the whole way back with not a word spoken between them, seeing nothing of the wonderful sights on that far side of the lake.

The sun had long settled behind the mountains and dusk was fast approaching when Laughing Rain and Awakens Corn first smelled the cook-smoke that announced their village. The promise of a thick, steaming stew revived their spirits. The adventure for the day was behind them.

"Now, what do you think about the lake?" their mother queried.

"It is big," answered Laughing Rain.

"And what did you see?"

Said Awakens Corn, "we saw a loon."

"A loon? Are you sure?"

"Yes." Laughing Rain said, "We are sure."

CHAPTER 5

Sky Flower

THE DAYS OF the Time-For-Growing passed quickly in the little mountainside village of Tahawus. The fields were almost always awash in sunshine. Rain fell in short spells but often, and the plants did not suffer from lack of water. Each day the stalks of corn seemed to stand a little taller. The vines of the beans climbed up them a little higher. Many white blossoms appeared on the squash plants that hugged the ground with their broad leaves. It was the miracle of tiny seeds coming to life.

There was another miracle of growing, too, that the look-the-same girls followed with keen interest. They saw it in their baby sister. Good health beamed from her rounded cheeks and her strong cry. She always slept peacefully. In between naps and nursing, she murmured those things that only babies in a cradleboard seemed to understand.

For a good part of every day, the twins made time between chores to hold and to rock Sky Flower. They toted her everywhere in a cradleboard. They talked to her constantly, speaking as if she could understand every word. They played clapping hands. They moved around her and watched those bright eyes follow their every movement. They could always bring out a laugh by making chirping noises and silly faces. If ever a baby were spoiled with attention it was surely Sky Flower. And it was the miracle of Sky Flower herself that brought the two girls close together again.

"Do you remember the day when Sky Flower was born?" Awakens Corn asked her sister.

"Of course," was the answer. "Do you remember how we gave Sky Flower her name?"

"Oh, yes. That was the best part. I remember as if it were only a day ago. Mother went to the birthing house. Suddenly, there was a great rain. We were afraid that the downpour meant another set of twins. I did not want to think about the trouble more twins would cause."

"Nor did I. But the rain stopped just as quickly as it came. Almost at the same time, the sun broke out from behind a huge cloud. At that very time we went to listen for sounds of new life at the birthing house. And it was there that a sky flower appeared in the sky. A sight more wonderful, I had never seen."[24]

"Neither had I. I can never forget it. The sky flower arched over the peak of Cloud-Splitter and seemed to stretch from one end of the world to the other end. Then we heard a baby's cry. Our ears strained for a long time to make sure that there was only one baby crying. We were too excited to do anything but dance around the birthing house."

"Soon, everyone crowded around to peek in at the new baby. Most of all, they wanted to know if it was a boy or a girl."

"I remember how eager we were to tell Mother about the sky flower. That was a good sign," Awakens Corn said. "You asked Mother if Sky Flower would be a good name for the baby."

"No, it was you who asked Mother."

"Me? Anyway, I remember Mother said, 'Sky Flower?' She was a little surprised. 'Well, then, Sky Flower it will be. I think your father will like the name, too.'"

Laughing Rain's voice recalled their joy, "We could hardly believe our good fortune. Now, we had a baby sister. And to top it all, we had the honor of choosing her name."

Awakens Corn asked her sister, "Are you glad that Sky Flower is a girl?"

"What a question! Another of your funny remarks. Of course. Why ask?"

"Well, she could have been a boy. Would that make a difference to you?"

"*Hmmmm,*" answered Laughing Rain, "I think not. What about you?"

"It is good to have a baby sister. Boys are not so much fun to talk to. They are always doing something. Girls are better at telling what they think. But still, I feel a little sad."

"Sad?... Why sad?"

"Why? Because all she can expect is a life spent in one place and filled with endless chores."

"Awakens Corn!" her sister cried out.

"It is true!" returned Awakens Corn, handing Sky Flower back to Laughing Rain. "Like us, she will work all the time at common labor. She will always stay in the village, never seeing the world much beyond our wall of tree stakes."

"You are wrong, Awakens Corn! No one thinks of our chores as bad or unimportant. We do it for the whole village. Sky Flower as she grows up will have a good life, too."

"It is not the work that bothers me. It is that women are kept in one place. What I mean is, if we were boys, there would be chance to see new things far away. Look at us, we can never go anywhere."

"You should not talk that way," answered Laughing Rain. "It will only cause trouble."

"I talk to you, Laughing Rain, because you are the only one person I can tell my feelings to. I trust you."

"I know you trust me, Awakens Corn. But there are some things we cannot talk or even think about. We have said enough. Now, no more words about going away—ever."

"We shall see," replied her sister.

A heavy silence now fell upon the look-the-same girls. Sky Flower, held in the arms of Laughing Rain, began to coo. Tiny bubbles formed around her soft lips. The twins both smiled at the playful sight, but they were smiles without joy. Sleep that night was greatly troubled, soothed only by the distant howling of many wolf voices.

CHAPTER 6

Voice of the Wilderness

AT DAYBREAK THE following morning, the grandfather of Laughing Rain and Awakens Corn came to the longhouse. He roused the family from sleep. "Has anyone seen KyKoo?" The twins jumped down from their berth, tossed robes over their shoulders, and went out on a frantic search for their wolf friend.

"We will find her," the twins said in a single voice. The search led around every longhouse. It went to the meeting circle where KyKoo often slept after everyone else had left for the night. The twins looked through the midden where KyKoo sometimes found a leftover chunk of meat.[25] The last place they looked was the opening in the wall of high stakes that enclosed the village. There in the brush and a tangle of briars that were stuffed into the opening was a slit just wide enough for a full-grown wolf to squeeze through. The twins looked at each other with growing despair.

"KyKoo has run away," Laughing Rain admitted.

"How could she leave us?" asked her sister. "We are her family."

It was with heavy hearts that the look-the-same girls walked back to their longhouse. Along the way, Laughing Rain confided.

"It is our fault. We did not do as we said. We promised to take care of KyKoo while Tail Feather was on his long journey. Instead, we gave Sky Flower all of our attention."

"You are right, Laughing Rain. We can blame ourselves. But KyKoo changed, too. Lately, KyKoo sulked away from people. Sometimes she snarled when we came close. Every night, we heard her join in with the howling that comes from the hills. Grandfather said she would not eat."

"We could go out into the forest and look for her."

"How can we do that?"

"We will just keep walking until we find her. If we call out her name together, it will be louder. She must hear us. We can take along some deer bones that she likes to chew on."

"No, mother would never let us go by ourselves. I think we should just wait. In a few days, KyKoo will be back. She went away one time before, leaving Tail Feather in sorrow. She does not know how to take care of herself in the forest."

On returning to their home fire, they found their mother with a nearly finished basket. She glanced up at the twins as she pulled taut a long strand of marsh grass. She listened to the sad news without saying a word.

"We were wrong, both of us," Laughing Rain admitted.

Her sister expanded, "We did not look after KyKoo. She was always so sad. She needed more of our attention. Tail Feather will never forgive us."

Morning Blossom did not look up as she threaded and tightened more reeds around the basket frame. The twins waited anxiously to hear their mother's scolding. She spoke at last in a soft voice. "Sometimes bad things happen. So, KyKoo has run away. We may not understand why. Such things, we cannot change. And so, we must accept with courage what we cannot change. It can make us stronger, too. Nature had a reason for KyKoo. If KyKoo does not come back, Tail Feather will have to accept change, as well. This is the way of life."

"Mother, do you think KyKoo will be able to take care of herself in the forest?"

"Of course, she is a wolf. KyKoo will know what to do."[26]

"But she has never hunted without Tail Feather. KyKoo never had a wolf friend. Maybe she will starve or be lonely."

"What does your grandfather think about your worries?"

"We did not tell him yet that we could not find KyKoo."

"Then go now to BaBa. Your grandfather knows much about wolves."

It was not long before the twins were at the longhouse of Guiding Star. "BaBa, BaBa," they called. Upon hearing the voices of his granddaughters, Guiding Star emerged from behind the hide flap at the entryway. "Ooooh! You two look sad."

"BaBa, KyKoo has run away," Awakens Corn confessed. "We did not do what we promised."

"Hah! You should not be surprised. KyKoo was not happy here."

"Will you help us look for her, BaBa?" added Laughing Rain.

"Young ones: hear my words! KyKoo is not a creature of a village. She belongs to the forest. Ever since she was a tiny pup, she has been with us. She knows only the world with Tail Feather alongside. Now Tail Feather is gone. Deep inside, KyKoo hears a cry from the woodlands that calls. Every day, her eyes told me that the call was getting stronger. She had need to go back to her own kind."

Guiding Star was mindful of how sorrowful his granddaughters were. He beckoned them inside his longhouse where they all sat comfortably on layers of furs that covered a toboggan. The girls settled among the clutter of carvings and tools that their grandfather was always making: duck decoys, snow snakes, bows, fishing nets, and masks of wood or cornhusks.

"You ask me to help find KyKoo. Keep in mind, KyKoo's world without your brother is different now. We tried to keep her close to us until your brother returns. But she heard the Voice of the Wilderness. It comes by the howling at night. The pull of the forest drew KyKoo away. There is nothing either of you could do about it. Do not think that you were wrong."

With these words, the look-the-same girls felt better. They took turns asking questions. "Do you think KyKoo will know what to do—how to hunt, how to find water, how to keep warm at night?"

"Yes, all those things will be easy for KyKoo."

"Will she be lonely?"

"Yes, I think so. She will find other wolves. One wolf family may not accept her. It will drive her off. She will then go to another and another."

"But BaBa, everyone likes KyKoo. Why would not other wolves?"

"It is the way of a pack. Packs do not often take in strangers. KyKoo does not know other wolves. She does not know how to be one of them. If she cannot find a pack to accept her, she will stay alone. Then she must live on small animals: rabbits, squirrels and fox, not big-antlered animals with sharp hooves that take a whole pack to bring down."

Guiding Star reminded them, "A long time ago, even before she was fully grown, KyKoo went away for many days. Your brother was frantic without his friend nearby. Tail Feather used those days to scour the forest searching for KyKoo, but with no success. He told me that the howling wolves in the distance kept him awake every night."

"That was a bad time for KyKoo, too." added Awakens Corn. "She came home starved and scratched all over and had even lost an ear. BaBa, can we do anything to get her back? Can we look for her?"

"No. Only wait. She may come home again by herself."

"I hope she does before Tail Feather comes back. I do not know what we should tell him if she is still missing when he returns," Laughing Rain fretted.

Guiding Star gave what comfort he could, "For now, children, you must just go about your chores. Your little sister needs your touch. Whatever happens, nature will work out its way. Do you remember the story of Sapling and Flint?"

"Of course," was the quick reply.

"Then, what was the great lesson we take from them?"

Laughing Rain began, "Always do your best."

Awakens Corn finished, "Even when bad things happen."

With these words, the spirits of the twins lifted. They returned to their longhouse and helped themselves to big servings of freshly made porridge.

CHAPTER 7

The Flaming Head

DURING THE TIME-FOR-GROWING, the crops thrived. Rain was plentiful but not too much. The high, thickly tasseled corn stalks threw out their graceful leaves. Bean veins that had wrapped themselves around the stalks reached upward as the corn gained height. Where each of the blossoms on the squash plants withered, there appeared a tiny yellow knob. Day by day the field workers eagerly followed the growing progress. Before starting their work each morning, they reflected on the wonders of Nature and gave thanks for the blessing of a bountiful harvest.

The first of the plants to ripen were the beans. Picking beans from dawn to sundown can be dull work. The baskets fill slowly. In time the hands tire, and the body wearies. Yet, it was work that Awakens Corn and Laughing Rain liked to do together. The task brought them away from the bustle of the longhouse and into the quiet soot-free air of the fields. With joy they returned to the village at dusk with baskets full of the harvest from everyone's hard labor. Also, bean picking was a time for the twins to talk without anyone overhearing. They reflected on the wonder of the Good Luck Cloud and gave thanks for the blessing of their friendship.

The twins always brought a water-filled pot to the fields. To keep the water cool on a hot day, they buried the pot neck-deep in the ground. They also took along a good supply of flat bread baked with many tasty berries. Hoods woven from marsh grass shielded them against the glaring sun.

The days of bean picking started among the plants still sprinkled with morning dew. Each girl picked up her basket, placed the straps around her forehead, and then rested it on one hip. Soon, a layer of plump, green pods covered the bottoms of the baskets.

Even in their contentment, something bothered Laughing Rain. "Do you remember," she asked, "when the beans ripened in the last Time-For-Growing? We could barely see over the top of the cornstalks? Now, the tassels just tickle my chin. Do they not grow strong? Did we plant them wrong?"

"Of course not. The corn grows as fine as ever. You forget, we are growing too."

"Ah hah! You may be right. I sometimes forget how fast we are changing."

"To be honest, Laughing Rain, I think you are getting prettier every day."

"Fox feathers! You know you are just teasing me. Everyone says we look just the same."

"Of course, they all say that," Awakens Corn agreed. "But I know that you are getting prettier. I am just staying plain. Have you noticed how Noisy Goose looks at you? All through the Story of Creation, his eyes never wandered away."

"Noisy Goose?"

"Oh, yes. Noisy Goose."

"But he is such a clumsy boy, and much too proud of himself."

"Perhaps. But he passes by our longhouse every time he returns from the forest, and his longhouse is on the other side of the village."

"We should talk about other things. Boys cause problems. They do not talk much. Boys only think about hunting and running games. They do not make friends with girls."

"Even Tail Feather?"

"No, not Tail Feather. Of course, he is different. He tells us everything. He never acts self-important."

"You are right. We have been blessed with a good brother."

To ease their work, the sisters played little games. Counting aloud, who could pick one hundred beans faster? First with one hand, then the other hand? Who could pick one hundred beans faster using both hands? Who could pick more beans with her eyes closed while counting to twenty? The winner kept changing, but it was fun for both.

There were word games, too. Who could say the longer word and say it the same three times? They made up rhyming songs. Who made the truer bird sounds: the owl, the crow, the duck and, hardest of all, the robin? Whose cry of the loon sounded real? Who could sound more like a fox's bark or a squirrel's chatter? Who was better at wolf howling? They took turns at this last imitation, then, laughing, joined together. Their lively chorus of howling amused them until they had hardly any voices left to howl.

Then Laughing Rain broke in hoarsely, "Were you telling the truth?"

"The truth?"

"Yes. About Noisy Goose."

"Oh, him. Yes, he gives you much attention."

"Are you sure?"

"Yes. I am surprised you have not noticed."

"How does he tell us apart?"

"I cannot say. He just does. He is Tail Feather's best friend, after KyKoo, of course, and he often comes to our longhouse. He must find something different in us, something that he likes better in you."

"Now you are silly, Awakens Corn. Mother told me that our warriors brought him here when he was a small child. Tail Feather told us that Noisy Goose cannot even remember the village where he was born."

"Oh, ...and I wonder if he knows how he got his name," her sister mused.

By late afternoon, there was a lull in the talking and singing and imitations. The only sounds were the snapping of pods as they broke away from their stems. After a while, Awakens Corn could endure the silence no longer. She asked half in jest, "What are you thinking about, Laughing Rain?"

"Oh,... nothing."

"Nothing? Really, tell me. Who can think of nothing?" Awakens Corn said in a playful mood. "We think all the time, even when we pick beans. Even when we sleep."

"I was ... just thinking about little things, nothing important," said Laughing Rain.

"Such as?"

"Oh, something that would be fun to do. Perhaps make a pot. I was thinking about making a pot with a special design."

"A special design?"

"Uh Huh. To use my name to decorate a handsome pot."

"Oh, you must do that. Everyone will know who made it."

"I was thinking, too, of the day when Tail Feather returns. How glad he would be. And how hungry. I tried to imagine what we could cook special to welcome him home. Yet, he will be sad to learn about KyKoo. Will he be angry with us?"

"No." Awakens Corn shook her head slowly, thoughtfully. "No, he will not be angry, but he will go into the forest to look for her."

"You are right. He will face that danger." Laughing Rain wiped a drop of sweat off the inner edge of one eyebrow with the back of her hand. "Now, I have told you. What have you been thinking about?" she asked in good humor.

"Oh," came the high-spirited reply. "I was thinking about just about how good it would be to feel free, to go somewhere."

"Stop!" Laughing Rain blurted out before her sister could finish the thought. "I cannot listen again about something so impossible, so against our ways. I beg of you, talk about something else."

"But you asked me what I was thinking, so I shall tell you," shot back Awakens Corn. Her sister braced herself for what was painful to her ears.

"Sometime while I am still a young woman," Awakens Corn went on, "I will go where there is water as far as you can see. To where wind blows from far across the water and leaves a cool tingle on the cheeks." Awakens Corn looked directly at her sister to give her words more meaning. "I was thinking about Water-With-No-End. I only want you to know that."

Just at that moment, Awakens Corn saw the face of her sister suddenly freeze. Laughing Rain's eyes stared wildly, her mouth wide-opened. The cheeks turned taut and ghostly pale.

A rustling '*whisssh*' came through the stalks of corn behind Awakens Corn. She spun around. There, floating over the field of tassels was a head. The head was on fire! No, not fire! It was hair bright red on top and all around the face. Looking out were deep-set, piercing blue eyes. The flaming head floated straight toward the girls. A step or two away, it stopped. In another instant, a hand stretched high up above the tassels. In it, an object sparkled brightly in the sun. Then, the raised hand with the shiny thing in it made a strange crossing motion.

Out of this creature came a raspy voice, speaking familiar words but ones that sounded strange to their ears. The voice said, "Have no fear. I mean you no harm." The sisters turned into stone. The head came a little closer. "I come to bring a wonderful message to your people." Then, two hands parted the stalks of corn to give the sisters a full view of the talking alien.

The girls-turned-to-stone saw that the hairy red head sat atop a long black robe. This body covering started at the neck and drooped to the ground. The alien underneath was as slender as a sapling birch. In one of his hands was a black and round object. A small pouch hung from one shoulder.

As if the red-on-black creature had dropped from the sky, Laughing Rain and Awakens Corn glanced at each other with bewilderment, then looked back at what was surely a being from another world. They tried to speak to it, but neither could make her tongue form words. Although they dropped their baskets with the thought of running, they could not make their feet move.

"I come in peace." He did not say the words in the true Mohawk way, but his listeners understood. He repeated, "You must believe, I come in peace." The voice was high-pitched and quivering; it was not the voice of an ordinary man. "I ask you to take me to your village. I bring a message of great joy to your people. But first, I must take food and rest from my long journey."

With these words, the stranger stood unmoving before them, with one arm raised above his head. The look-the-same girls simply stared, death-like still and silent. A long moment went by before he lowered his arm and held the shiny thing across his chest. Then, he raised his other arm and placed the round, black thing on the head with red hair. The face became even more eerie in the shadow of its broad rim. The stranger, standing just a step or two away from the frozen girls, waited for a response.

In what seemed like a whole day, Awakens Corn found enough voice to whisper to her sister, “What do we do?”

A whisper came back, “Run.”

Awakens Corn, gaining strength in her voice, said, “He comes in peace.”

Laughing Rain thought differently, “How do we know?”

With this exchange, the twins, without thinking, lapsed into their, childhood language of turned-around ideas and made-up words.

“See his borro and wab.” [He has no bow and arrow and no war club.]

“Did basprit fall from the air?” [Is he a bad spirit from beneath the earth?]

“Look! He eats too much.” [He appears starving.]

“No. As he sleeps.” [Yes. He looks exhausted.]

“And he warspeaks.” [His words are friendly.]

“No matter, I am brave.” [Still, he frightens me.]

“Cantrus. Vilgo.” [We can trust him. We must go to the village.]

A look of confusion came upon the face with red hair.

Slowly, the twins became aware of life coming back into their feet. Doubt gave way to the natural desire to help a stranger in need. Talking in code ended.

“He is too hungry and too weak to cause harm,” said Laughing Rain, whispering with one hand hiding her mouth from the stranger.

Her sister replied, "Yes, he looks as sad as the elk with tangled antlers."

"We agree, then," she returned.

"Yes, we agree." Awakens Corn spoke up boldly to the gaunt man in red and black, "We will take you to our village."

Not long after the girls and their strange companion had started the journey back, Laughing Rain nudged her sister exclaiming, "The baskets! We forgot our baskets!" They stared at each other for a few seconds in disbelief, and then suddenly twirled around, running back to pick up their almost forgotten harvest of beans. While waiting patiently until they returned, the flaming head thought about the happiness he was going to bring to the people of this unknown tribe.

CHAPTER 8

The Message of Joy

AWAKENS CORN WAS the first to enter the village from the passageway through the staked wall. A step behind came Laughing Rain. Their baskets were filled with enough freshly picked beans to please everyone. But no one noticed the beans. The eyes of the people standing nearby were fixed on the gaunt figure with the flaming red hair that followed. A blinding bolt of lightning from a clear blue sky striking the meeting post could not have caused a bigger stir. The people standing nearby gasped. Word of the stranger spread rapidly. Soon the entire village gathered to stare at the awesome sight.

By custom, the villagers quickly formed two lines through which a visitor was expected to pass. The red and black alien walked slowly and solemnly through the pathway, bowing with every few steps. Everyone viewed him with amazement. The long cardinal-red hair that covered his head and chin was tangled and covered with pine needles and dirt. His face was sunken; there were many scratches on his forehead and hollowed cheeks. The black garment that hung from narrow shoulders was soiled and shredded. Poking out from the bottom were mud-caked, wooden sandals and in them, bloodied feet.

The formal arrival ended at the meeting circle. There, Chief Red Sun appeared, hastily adjusting his headdress of antlers and donning his heavy robe of turkey feathers that were his badges of office. People crammed forward, trying to get a better view. The Chief stood stiff with his arms folded before him and raised to shoulder height. The stranger, in turn, bent down on one knee and bowed his head. Standing once again, he faced the tribal leader and made the crossing sign with the shiny thing that the twins, standing by his side, had seen before.

Chief Red Sun was the first to speak. "Enter our village with good in your heart and you are welcome among us. Tell us what brings you here?"

The stranger replied, each word measured and spoken in the way of the Wyandots (Hurons), an Iroquois nation to the North. "My name is Brother André. Because we are all brothers, I have traveled from far away to bring you a message of great joy."[27]

The Chief answered with the grace born of age-old tradition. "Honored traveler, you are tired from a long journey. You are in need of food. Come rest and share what we have to eat. Later, we will hear what words you have to bear."

People, seeing after all that he was only a man, though a strange one for certain, led him to the council longhouse where a bed of furs was quickly prepared. The curious streamed in. Someone in the crowd handed the visitor a cup of steaming tea smelling of sassafras. Next, the stranger received a wooden bowl of porridge. Roasted venison appeared on a turtle shell plate. Corncakes cooked in bear fat came last.

The black-robed man sat quietly, legs folded beneath him, and savored each item with much satisfaction. Through it all, his deep eyes rove round and round at the throng standing before him.

In turn, not a pair of eyes strayed from the visitor, not even for a moment. The watchful gazes continued through the long sleep that followed.

After nightfall, everyone in the village assembled around the meeting post. Their rested visitor stood before the open fire. The dancing flames gave him a demon-like appearance, exaggerating his slender frame, big-brimmed and flat headdress, long red beard and loosely hanging robe. Everyone waited eagerly to hear what message could be so important. The look-the-same girls, with a sense of finder's pride, crouched at front. Laughing Rain held her baby sister, Sky Flower.

It was Chief Red Sun who spoke the first words. "We gather to listen to the great words that this good man has come to tell us. Let him have his say."

Brother André bowed to the Chief. He then stood erect and looked straight back at the onlookers. His voice, however shrill and halting it was, gave notice of his unwavering belief in his words. "I come to your land from a place far away." He paused to gaze from one end of the crowd to the other. "My journey took me across a great space of water in a great canoe driven by the wind. Landing at your shore, I have come on foot to your village. You can see that I bring nothing but words. Here is all I have," he said, letting one hand flow from head to foot. "Yet, kind people, my message is simple. It is a message that can bring to you hope for all time to come."

Awakens Corn whispered to her sister through a cupped hand, "This is exciting! What do you think he is going to say?" A sharp tap on her shoulder from behind ended further inquiry.

"If you believe in this message," the traveling man went on, "you will be blessed by everlasting life. When you leave this world of strife, you will enter a new world. It is a world where peace never ends. It is a place called Heaven."

The speaker then turned silent. Nor was there a stir among the crowd. Chief Red Sun rose to say, "Tell us of this wonderful place. You have our ears."

Brother André bowed again, then slowly, with carefully chosen words went on, "I am but a humble servant of our Creator. Even so, I will tell the story as best as I can. To begin, there is but one Supreme Spirit. There is no other."

The idea brought the entire crowd to inhale as one.

The words of Brother André quickened, "We call this Great Spirit by the name God. God loves all the people of the Earth. If you live according to God's will, you will enjoy all the blessings of his Kingdom. When we cross over into that world beyond life as we know it, believers in my God will rest forever in Heaven. Those that do not accept the word of God will spend everlasting time in a dark and dismal place."

Children began to stir restlessly. The elders became perplexed. There was some aimless milling around among those standing.

The red hairy-faced man had more to say, "We are all creatures in the same world. Even though I look different from all of you, we can all join together on our final journey toward Heaven. I ask you to accept my word and to believe in God the Supreme Being and no other spirits before it is too late."[28]

Brother André spoke with all the conviction that his soul possessed. Yet, he was answered in chilling silence. Despite careful attention to his words, none of the listeners found any joyful ideas in his message. It went against everything that their ancestors taught. They knew that spirits were everywhere: in the sky, the streams, the trees, and the animals. The Creator from the Sky World had made it so. Why does this stranger come to them with such an empty message?

Laughing Rain and Awakens Corn remained speechless, as did everyone else. The twins looked at each other as much astonished as when they first saw the stranger among the tassels of corn.

Brother André waited a long time for some response. None came forth. He then invited questions. "Who among you wishes to know more about God? You may ask."

There followed questions. Questions came so fast that Brother André could barely talk. Someone asked, "If there is one Great Spirit, what about the Spirit of the Tree that you stand under?"

"And the Spirit of the Sky?" said another.

"And the Bear?" someone else added.

"What about the Spirits of the Three Sisters and the Mountain and the Moon?" asked a voice in the back.

An elder asked, "Where did you learn about this God?"

"God spoke to the people of the world through his only son, Jesus."

"God had a son?" someone dared to ask.

"Yes, a holy son. Jesus came to teach us the word of God. He gave his life to save us from everlasting darkness."

Another wanted to know, "Where is this place called Heaven?"

"It is the place where those who have lived a just and holy life spend eternity after this life."

More questions from excited voices rang out.

"Where do you come from?"

"Tell us about your great canoe that goes by the wind!"

"Why do you call yourself 'Brother'?"

"Do other people in your village have red hairy faces?"

Brother André did his best answers to answer all the questions. He was keenly aware, however, that his listeners were not satisfied. He tried another approach, "Who will be the first to accept the blessings of Almighty God?"

No one moved.

"Who cares to change his life by accepting the greatest gift of all? You may step forward now."

There was not a flicker among the entire ring of onlookers.

Yet, Brother André was not to be denied. He said firmly, "In time, you will all know the blessings of God, the one and only Great Spirit. But for now, only one person of your village will be blessed to receive this precious gift. I will choose among you the youngest."

The slender man in the long black robe approached the twins and reached out for baby Sky Flower. Laughing Rain hesitated at first, but Awakens Corn nudged her forward. After glancing around at those nearby, Laughing Rain saw the approving faces of curious people. Chief Red Sun nodded. Sky Flower was soon in the arms of the black-robed stranger.

Brother André brought the baby up to one shoulder. He reached down into a log trough of water nearby and scooped up a palm full of water. Waving the hand over the infant's head and chanting words that no one understood, he sprinkled some drops on the baby's head. The eyes of startled Sky Flower popped open.

"With this sacred water, I baptize you." Turning to Laughing Rain, he asked, "What is her name?"

Her big sister whispered, "Sky Flower."

"Sky Flower, then, I baptize you in the name of His Holiness, our God. May this infant forever enjoy the blessings of all Believers in the Lord our God. You are the first of your people to rejoice in the divine sacrament." Having spoken these words, he handed the baby back to her sister and made the sign of a cross on the body of Sky Flower.[29]

The crowd watched carefully, taking in each detail of this odd performance. Curious eyes then gazed down as Brother André knelt on one knee and raised his head and arms toward the sky. He spoke words that no one understood. In conclusion to this part of the ceremony, he bent his head forward and brought his hands together for a silent moment. All eyes then looked up as a smiling Brother André raised his body to an upright position and made a sign of a cross at the people. At this gesture, the crowd suddenly stiffened — as if a magical potion had been spread over them. Whether the spell was for good or evil, no one knew.

And so, the people of the village heard the joy message that the black-robed visitor brought from far away. One by one, they went back to their longhouses to think about its meaning. The meeting circle was soon empty of people. The council fire slowly died out.

By High Sun on the following day, Brother André had packed some dried meat and journey cakes into his shoulder pouch. He wore a bearskin cape and new moccasins. At the opening in the wall of trees, he stood before Chief Red Sun, saying, "You have nourished me. You have filled my pouch with many things to eat and provided me with clothes for my long journey home. I will return. I trust that all your people will receive the Blessed Sacrament in the Name of God." Having spoken these words, Brother André turned toward the many onlookers and made a crossing motion with his shining crosspiece. In another moment he was gone.

Everyone shared a version of the visitor's message. Most were amused; after all, new faces seldom came to their village, and this one was truly unlike any seen before. Others felt let down with the lack of any real news. Some were simply baffled to think that anyone could believe that there were spiritual ways other than those taught by their ancestors. Some were uneasy because he used the kind of language spoken by their hostile neighbors. There were even a few, especially the elders, who were so offended by the words of the black robe that they refused to talk about them.

Laughing Rain and Awakens Corn, to be sure, had much to say to each other about the encounter. After all, it was they who brought the stranger to their village. And it was they who let him bless their sister.

"I am afraid for Sky Flower," confided Laughing Rain. "Do you think he sprinkled a spell on her?"

"No. It was just water."

"But perhaps there was magic in it."

"I think not. Sky Flower does not seem changed. Besides, it was interesting to hear about his One God."

"Awakens Corn! No! This idea is against everything we have learned."

"You are right, Laughing Rain. But some day other strangers will come in black robes to Tahawus. We will hear more about their Great Spirit and his son, Jesus."

"It may happen," nodded her sister. "I must tell you that I have heard too much about this story already.

CHAPTER 9

The Letter

Monseigneur Ricardot, Evêque d'Arras
Par la grâce de Dieu maintenant je peux vous fournir un compte rendu de mes nombreux mois passés dans les régions sauvages de la Nouvelle France. Si cette lettre vous parvienne, ce serait dû aux bonnes grâces de Jésus-Christ, notre Sauveur...

My esteemed Bishop,
By the grace of God, I am able now to send you an account of my many months spent in the wilderness of New France. Should this letter reach you, it would be by the good graces of Jesus Christ, our Savior.

Little was I prepared for the rigors of this journey or for the trials of bringing the Gospel Word of God to an uncultured people. Yet, I exerted every fiber of my body and soul to this virtuous task. If my services have made even the smallest benefit to Our Savior, then I believe my suffering is my sacred privilege.

After no fewer than five months in the wilderness without hearing a single civilized voice, I returned to our encampment. I am now honored to write you of this long hardship. My letter I will entrust to our brave seamen sailing under the devout Christian master pilot, Samuel de Champlain. I will pray that they have a safe homeward voyage.

My journey: On 6 June of this year, I left the pleasures of our cozy fishing settlement in Port Royal, and traveled by open boat up the Canada River. Where the river narrows suddenly, there is a cluster of dreary huts at the base of high, gray cliffs on the northern bank. It is a place that the Wyandot Indians call Quebec.

From there, native people became my guides, as they paddled me in a tiny flimsy boat covered with the bark of a white tree. On the long journey westward, I busied myself learning the language of my untamed companions. Along the way, we encountered people in small villages. I brought them the holy Message of God and baptized many of them.

Cascades ahead made further travel by boat no longer possible. My guides stopped by an oak grove at the foot of a tall hill. An aged, wrinkled member of the local village came forth. He told us that as a young boy, he had seen a great canoe with white wings that ventured this far in the river. I learned with much pride that it was the ship of Jacques Cartier, a God-fearing master pilot of our mother country. Trappers say that Master Cartier named the tall hill at this place of rapids Mount Réal to honor the King of France.

And thus, my journey by boat ended. The guides would not continue, even overland, because they feared the hostile tribes beyond the rapids. Rather than return with them, I chose, against their advice, to wander south into the forest, there to spread the Word of God throughout the wilderness.

And so, it was on 27 June that I departed their company, carrying with me only my cross, my Bible, my beads, a small diary, and my zeal to do good work. By exchanging the relative comfort of a boat for the hardship of a forest trek, I could experience the Glory of God's earth first-hand. The vastness of the trees and lakes is beyond imagination!

For many weeks I encountered not a soul. Always on the verge of starvation, I resorted to eating berries most bitter, even frogs and insects, and to chewing the bark of trees. I had to wade through frigid streams and endured unmercifully cold nights. My feet, shod only in wooden sandals, blistered so that with every step I stumbled forward in agony. I was tormented night and day by biting flies and other buzzing insects that made me itch terribly.

My trust in the beneficence of God saved me from a fate of starvation and fatigue. As it was, the Will of God came to me through the voices of wild animals. On approaching a field of shoulder-high plants--my diary states that the day was the eighteenth of August—I heard the sounds of birds and four-legged creatures. A chorus of eerie howling seemed to beckon me. I approached them without fear. To my utter astonishment, the beastly voices brought me to two girls who were working in the fields, girls in straw hoods, girls who looked exactly alike.

The twins, fearing not, led me to their village. The people greeted me with kindness and refreshment. They gathered round to listen to my Message of Joy. I told them of the Glory of our Lord and of the rewards of Heaven. They offered one infant named Sky Flower. She is now baptized into the Kingdom of God. Thus, I left these godless people with a sense of great hope for their salvation in the eyes of our Maker.

Before retracing my steps to our encampment, my benefactors provided me with meat and hard bread of grounded meal. They gave me a thick fur for cover against the night chill and spare leather slippers for the long walk. Most important of all, they showed me how to find food in the forest, how to fish and how to make a fire. And so, these uncivilized people of the forest saved me from starvation and from exposure. To express my gratitude, I promised to return one day and tell them more about the Word of God. With this offer, the people were most gracious.

Thus, my account of God's Word in la Nouvelle France! It was only with the generosity of The Order of Jesuits and of the Goodness of the Holy Spirit that I was blessed to serve in this humble way.

May God bless you in the abundance of safety and comfort that our beloved France has to offer,

Recevez, Excellence, l'expression de mes meilleurs sentiments.
Votre très obéissant serviteur,
Fra. André Benoît.

CHAPTER 10

The Arrow

MORNING BROKE WHEN a child pointed to an arrow buried into the meeting post. By tradition, the arrow in the post was a sign that someone had something of importance to announce. That someone, everyone knew, would speak at the Time of High Sun. The child ran through the village crying out her find for all to hear.

The Time of High Sun always came when the shadow of the meeting post fell on the hollowed-out place in the center of a great boulder. The hollow formed a bowl on the boulder's flat top. It was a bowl worn down by ages of women who pounded maize into meal. In a world of changes, one never-changing event was the crossing of the shadow over the bowl at The Time of High Sun, no matter how short or how long the days. It was altogether fitting to have the maize be at the center of it all.[30]

As the post's shadow moved toward the bowl on this day, people began to gather to hear the news. At the very moment it crossed, a young warrior burst forward in feathered headdress, a red mask painted across his face and black stripes along his naked upper body. It was Gray Tail Flying, known to all for his long scalp lock. He whooped and pranced and stomped before the crowd. Gray Tail Flying then leaped onto a log that lay in front of the meeting circle fire. His bare scalp shone in the full sunlight. He lifted his arms, one bearing a war club, to full height and bellowed, "Tomorrow I will hunt for big game. There will be moose and elk and bear."

Those standing around the meeting post were baffled. Hunters went out all the time without making a big show of it. Hunting was an ordinary part of village life.

Gray Tail Flying shouted, "People from other nations come into our land to hunt. Now we must show our strength by hunting deep within their land." He stomped from one end of the log to the other. "With my arrow deep into the meeting post, I dare all to hunt with me in the land of our enemies. Those of you with strong hearts and body, let yourself be known."

The crowd drew back. Gray Tail Flying was known to be restless and quick to anger. He was also shrewd. He spoke of hunting, knowing that the clan mothers would never approve of his leading others just to fight. Everyone knew that he would lose face if no one joined him on such a reckless venture into the land of enemies. No one stepped forward.

Gray Tail Flying leaped down from the log, at the same time letting out a taunting yell. He began to dance around the meeting circle, head bobbing, knee lifting, heel stomping, knee bending, waist twisting and high jumping. All the while he held his war club high, as great warriors do, and kept up a wild chant.

Some of the other young men were caught up in the display of growing manhood. One by one, with bow and arrow in hand, they entered the circle of dance. Each boy-almost-man raised the bow and let fly his best copper-headed arrow. One by one, the arrow struck the meeting post, sending splinters in all directions. Each arrow was a pledge to go with Gray Tail Flying into forbidden land.

The last and youngest of those to join the circle of dance was Noisy Goose. He appeared hesitant at first but soon gained the courage to raise his bow. He pulled back the bowstring and held it taut so that all could see his newfound manhood. His arrow glanced off the post with a thud. It wobbled through the air and buried itself into the ground beyond the meeting circle. It was not a proud moment for Noisy Goose. He did his best to walk in a stately way to retrieve his arrow. His second try proved successful.

Altogether, there were twelve prancing young men. Their yelps and shrieks seemed to bounce off the mountains, as their steps became more frenzied. It was a splendid show of power and endurance. The war dance lasted long beyond the time that the shadow played on the pounding rock. It ended when Gray Tail Flying drew his arrow from the post and held it overhead. The others in turn followed. Then, together in a final gesture of bravado, they gave a terrifying whoop and quickly dispersed.

Later that evening, the twins lay restless on their upper berth, going over the ceremony in their minds. Awakens Corn asked in a whisper, "Now, what do you think of Noisy Goose?"

"He shows he is brave. Still, he is too young for such danger."

"I agree," said Awakens Corn. "Of course," she added, "there may be fighting. What is the need? There are enough animals to hunt here in Mohawk valleys. Why do they do this?"

"It is their nature," answered her sister. "They must show that our people are strong, that others cannot come into our land and take our game. They accept these risks for us. You heard what Gray Tail Flying said. I believe he is right."[29]

"Laughing Rain! It is useless. The fighting never ends. The hunters in other lands will only bring trouble. Our people came to the mountains to leave behind constant raids and retaliations. Gray Tail Flying is not a good person."

"Again, I listen to you, Awakens Corn. But I cannot agree. Gray Tail Flying may give his life to make our clan stronger."

Her sister then said something that had been on her mind for a long time. "Laughing Rain, my dearest friend ever and always, sometimes lately, from what you say, you do not know me at all."

"You may speak true. Sometimes, I think that you are no longer a Mohawk."

The comment drew a long silence, in the way sudden, stunned quietness follows an unexpected clap of thunder.

Awakens Corn broke the tormenting stillness saying, "From your soft voice, Laughing Rain, arrows fly that strike deep into the flesh. They are little arrows, but they are the most painful of all. Did you know that?"

"I speak only of how good, how brave these young men are. You know that our village will perish if it cannot defend itself. How else do our warriors learn the skills of war without fighting? These are proud young men, ready for battle. They are the ones who will protect us. One day, likely, we will marry one of them."

"Perhaps, if they live. Still, to tempt a fight is wrong. Why cause grief just to prove oneself worthy? Worthy of what? It means nothing."

"Awakens Corn, my loved sister, I am getting so that I cannot to talk to you anymore."

"Oh, I am sorry, dear sister, that I do not say my thoughts in a way that you can find agreeable. If you could only know how strongly I feel about useless fighting. Our ancestors made peace among the Five Nations of our Iroquois family. We honor that pact. Our grandfather came to these mountains to be away from the conflicts among all people. Now, our young men travel far away to hunt in the land of others. Why? Simply for the excitement of battle."

"Let us not talk in this way. It frightens me."

"Yes, it frightens me, too. I need to feel the night air on my face."

With this need, Laughing Rain climbed down from the high platform bed, tiptoed to the end of the longhouse, and pulled aside the hides that draped over the opening. She stepped out into the cool darkness. What caught her eye was a face seen in the dying firelight of the meeting circle. It was the face of Noisy Goose. On sight of her, he pulled back and in an instant was one with the darkness.

Laughing Rain returned to bed and, although troubled, once again felt the comfort of warmth from her sister sleeping beside her. It was the same body warmth that she had felt every night of her life. But her sister was changing, and she sensed that the life-long warmth of their friendship was chilling.

CHAPTER 11

The Agony of Victory

The hot days of the Time-For-Growing passed slowly. There was much work in the fields for the women and children. Children were kept busy in the garden pulling weeds and picking insects off the Three Sisters. The youngest of them took turns in the serious work of shooing away crows. As always, time was meant for weaving and stitching smocks and moccasins of softened deerskin. And, of course, the cookfires with their pots of stew needed attention.

Over time, large, plump ears soon appeared on the stalks of maize. The ears had to be husked, and the kernels stripped and boiled. Then came the arm-aching work of pounding the kernels into a fine meal for making bread. Need it be said that the whole village busied itself with harvesting and preparing the maize.

One day at the pounding rock, a raucous yelling was heard beyond the wall of tree trunks. "The hunters!" someone shouted. A cautious chorus of joy went up. Everyone had been counting the days until their return: "Eighteen!" A crowd gathered anxiously at the entrance of the village to learn their story. First among them to enter through the narrow passageway was Gray Tail Flying. Last to enter was Noisy Goose. The hunters shouted and raised their arms in heroic gestures of victory. They pranced around the meeting post, sending shrills of defiance against their enemies, and displaying their valiant spirit. There was much rejoicing, too, among the village because all twelve hunters had returned.

There was another concern. None of the hunters carried game, big or small. Bruises and cuts of all kinds were seen on nearly all of them. Some walked with a limp. The bow arm of Gray Tail Flying was wrapped in a sheet of bark. One side of the face of Noisy Goose was dark and swollen. The eye on that side was bright red. His nose was bent toward the other side.

The traditional Dance of Victory was brief and half-hearted. Each warrior quickly retreated to his own longhouse, there to recover from his wounds. The healers of the clan scrambled to fetch enough salves and potions to treat all of them.

Meanwhile, the simmering squabble between the sisters had come to a boil. Awakens Corn stood directly in front of Laughing Rain, her fists pressing against each hip. "You see now! What have they proven? Nothing! What do they have to show for it? Broken bodies! Who knows what happened on the other side. How many were hurt? Were some killed? And still, for all their trouble, they bring no hides for clothing or meat to smoke for winter."

Laughing Rain gulped. She drew herself up tall to deflect the hail of words, saying, "My dear sister, I cannot explain why bad things happen. Only that we must accept them. Our mother and father do. Our grandmothers and grandfathers did, just as our ancestors did. Nothing has changed. This is the way of people. We should give thanks to these wounded men. All we can do is try our best to make things better."

"How can we make life better when fighting for nothing can be so wrong?" Awakens Corn pleaded.

"You ask too much, Awakens Corn. Life is made up of good and bad. For me, I will go to Noisy Goose. Perhaps I can help cheer him."

"He will like that, Laughing Rain. For me, I will look for a place where I can know peace. Perhaps there is a place for me far away, a place where there is only water. There I will learn why we have such different thoughts."

Laughing Rain found her sister's remark disturbing. She would ask about her meaning as soon as she returned from Noisy Goose. When she returned to her longhouse, however, Awakens Corn was asleep. "So," Laughing Rain murmured to herself, "I can wait until morning." With these thoughts, she raised herself onto the berth and crawled beneath the warm covers next to her sister.

CHAPTER 12

Laughing Rain

LONG BEFORE DAWN, Laughing Rain became dimly aware that the warmth that she always felt next to her was gone. She thought that maybe she dreamed of cool wind that had blown through the longhouse. As the first rays of sun broke through the smoke hole, Laughing Rain awoke. Awakens Corn was not there.

Laughing Rain jumped out of the berth. She ran frantically among the longhouses, calling her sister's name. All the while she suspected that Awakens Corn was nowhere to answer. From longhouse to longhouse, many of the children joined Laughing Rain on the search. At last, panting and hoarse, Laughing Rain stopped at the open passageway through the wall of wooden stakes and stared out at the forest beyond. It was with fainting spirit that she admitted to herself, "Awakens Corn has left me alone."

Her mother and her mother's sister, Meadow Bird Singing, came to stand by her side. Each put an arm around the wobbly-kneed girl and tried to calm her.

"What has been troubling Awakens Corn?" asked Morning Blossom.

Laughing Rain tried to find the right answer. "I cannot say. We often speak of growing up and how the days ahead will be.

Sadly, we have quarreled much. About what? It is our secret."

"We have all seen something come between you and Awakens Corn. Whatever caused it will clear in time," her mother said. "Growing up is not easy. Every girl must discover how to grow up in her own way. You two are no different from all the others."

Meadow Bird Singing offered her thoughts. "Laughing Rain, you and your sister have come to an age when life brings doubt about many things. I believe that Awakens Corn will soon get over her childish notions and will grow into a good woman in our village. She will come back to us soon."

These were comforting words for Laughing Rain. The three walked slowly back together to the longhouse. Yet, Laughing Rain, walking between her mother and her aunt, felt cruel loneliness for the first time in her life.

Morning Blossom appealed to Chief Red Sun. "Our hunters could quickly find Awakens Corn. Then we can learn what causes her to run away."

Red Sun thought about her request for a long time. His face did not show his feelings, and the fretful mother waited breathlessly for his reply. At last, he said, "A bad spirit has seized Awakens Corn. It is now inside of her. I believe she must face this bad spirit by herself. The forest is where the best visions take place. It will tell her what this spirit is. Then and only then, will the shaman help her chase it away. We must wait until Awakens Corn returns to our village."

That was the final word. The men of the village would not bring Awakens Corn back.

Each day in the absence of Awakens Corn, Laughing Rain became more withdrawn. She stayed inside the darkened longhouse. She seldom came from beneath her bearskin. She ate barely enough for one sparrow. She could not sleep. She barely spoke.

Morning Blossom could do no more. One not-quite-grown daughter had disappeared into the forest, leaving behind a mute and grief-stricken sister. Her husband and son were far away on a dangerous journey. The Black Robe may have sprinkled bad magic on her baby. Yet, she must hide her worries from Laughing Rain. She must try to comfort her. She must smile. She must cheer others. These are the sacred duties of a mother.

One day followed another without any sign of Awakens Corn. Throughout this terrible time, the mind behind the downcast sister churned continuously. "What should I do? I cannot go on this way or a bad spirit will take over my body." As these thoughts raced around her head, Laughing Rain noticed her mother sitting on the other side of the glowing fire. A basket in her hands was slowly taking shape.[31]

Notice of her mother's work suddenly became a defining moment for Laughing Rain. "I am like a basket. If all the reeds are drawn tightly together, the basket will remain strong despite the heaviest load. The only answer to mend a fragile life is perfect discipline." She made her decision. "I must weave for myself a tightly woven basket. It will be my strength."

With this pledge to herself, she changed abruptly, throwing herself into work. No one had seen a busier person. She harvested corn, husked the ears, and ground the kernels into a fine pulp. She scraped deer hides until they were free of fat and then softened them in steaming water. She made long strings of dried sinew and with them sewed together leather for moccasins and shirts. She gave no attention to aching arms and sore fingers. All this, long into the night.

Laughing Rain liked to work close to other women, and she heard all the gossip. She listened carefully for something said about

Awakens Corn, although no one ever spoke of her. Laughing Rain did not join in on the conversations, but rather kept her thoughts to herself.

Life without her twin sister was almost unbearable. Laughing Rain tried to find strength through hard, ceaseless work. But strength was slow to come. Suddenly, one day, an idea popped into her head. "I will make something for Awakens Corn. What if I make a clay pot, a big one, all by myself. I have seen others do it many times. I think I can remember all the steps. Besides, I can think of a new reason to have a big pot—to count the days that pass until she returns."

First, Laughing Rain made her way up a mountain stream, well beyond where the clan went for the clay. It was a place where she and Awakens Corn were delighted to find a niche of fine, colorful clay for making toy bowls and dolls. The clay under shallow water lay just beneath an overhanging flat-topped rock. But without her sister there beside her, their secret place was haunting. Then, to her horror, she saw fresh markings of fingertips dug into the pink clay. Someone else had been there! Who? Was it Awakens Corn? Had she come this way?

Laughing Rain quickly plunged her fingers through the chilling water, dug into the clay and placed a few handfuls in a pouch. She did not linger at the stream where once she and her sister had enjoyed the magic of discovery.

Returning to the village, she rekindled a nearly burned out fire by adding many branches from a good supply of hardwood. While the fire was taking hold, she kneaded the large blob of clay into a tight ball. Then, she forced one fist into it, creating a central hole. As she turned the clay, the hole became bigger, and then she thinned the walls with a smooth, wooden hand paddle. The glob of clay slowly took on the shape of a pot.

Molding the pot into a perfect shape was the most exacting task, and this one, she was determined, would be a proper Mohawk pot. She kept turning and smoothing the pot until its rounded bottom could sit in a small depression on the ground. She narrowed the neck so that it could be hung with a cord. The rim took the most expert crafting. The rim had to be squared off to make for easier pouring. To finish the design, Laughing Rain molded the rim. She drew on it the pattern that only potters of the Mohawk Nation made. After all, every nation took pride in its own design.[32]

While the clay was still soft, Laughing Rain had a whimsical thought. She would add her own markings to the pot. Tradition was against personal designs on timeless earthenware. Yet, what trouble could come from a little decoration? Of course, she would smooth it out before firing the pot.

Using the fine point of a porcupine quill, Laughing Rain carefully drew slanted lines all around the pot. At the bottom of the pot, she bent the lines back into a graceful curve. She knew that anyone would know instantly that these were streaks of rain that turned into a smile. The design told who made the pot. Oh, how Awakens Corn would be proud of her handiwork! They had even talked about it.

Then, she had second thoughts about smoothing out her creation. "Would Awakens Corn leave them as they are? Yes, I think so. No, I cannot go against tradition. Yes, no one would care. No, the elders will punish me for it."

It was during this period of indecision that the fire was ready to receive the pot. Once heated, its shape and decorations would be fixed forever. She took one more look at the smiling raindrops. She was about to decide when she became aware of a figure standing behind her.

"You are always sad these days. Here, I brought you something." It was Noisy Goose. Draped around his shoulder was a full-grown turkey. The big bird slid off lifeless and plopped at the girl's feet.

Finding her voice, she praised, "You are good with bow and arrow."

"No, not so. Turkeys are not easy to hunt with arrows. I chased it until it was too tired to run."

"Why didn't it fly away? Turkeys are good flyers."

"When you find them in the forest, there is not enough room for them to spread their wings. They try to run away. They are good runners, too, but they do not run as long as a strong runner can."

"Oh. Then you are a strong runner," Laughing Rain said, turning to take a good look at the speaker.

"Ah, ha! As good as your brother." The words of Noisy Goose were spoken with an awkward pride. "Are you making a pot?" he asked.

"Yes. See? It is ready to harden by the fire."

"What are the marks on the side?"

"Can you guess?"

"No."

"Look. These are the lines of rain. They turn up at the bottom in a happy way. Now, can you guess what they mean?"

"No." Noisy Goose waited for an answer.

"Oh, they are pretty," was his only answer.

She asked, "How is your wound? It seems more swollen and darker all around the eye and nose."

"Tuuh! Every day it gets better. I can breathe through one side of my nose now."

"Good. Did your breath get short while running after the turkey?"

"A little. But it was a good chase."

With this exchange, the visitor smiled and left Laughing Rain to her pot making.

She took another look at the dead turkey. "How beautiful it must have been in flight," she mused, "with those shiny feathers." She squirmed at the thought of the awful task of pulling them off, then taking out the insides before cooking. She knew that her own insides would go upside down. Awakens Corn, she admitted, was much better at turkey cleaning than she was, even though she, too, hated the task.

Laughing Rain then turned her attention to firing the pot. It was the most demanding part of the making. The pot will crack if placed too close to the fire. It will not harden if placed too far away. The pot must heat evenly, so constant turning was necessary. For turning, she used a fork made from the antlers of a deer. The steam from wet moss stuffed in the pot helped heat the inside.

When the slowly turned pot was hard enough, Laughing Rain filled it with water. She picked up white-hot rocks out of the fire with a pair of antlers and carefully lowered them into the water. She watched the water come to a boil. Keeping the fire going, refilling the pot with water, and adding more hot rocks was a long task. At last the pot was ready to leave overnight to cool.

In the morning Laughing Rain took her finished work to her mother. Morning Blossom was astonished at the sight. "You are a good pot-maker, Laughing Rain."

"You think so?"

"Yes. It is a beautiful pot. I have never seen a pink one before. What are those lines on the side?"

"Those? They are my special sign, just for fun."

"Oh, yes. Now I see, Laughing Rain. Clever. How happy Awakens Corn will be to see your creation."

"Do you think so?"

"Of course. She will ask you to help her make one."

Laughing Rain's voice tightened, "Will she come back?"

"Yes. But it may take a long time. When she returns, she may seem like a different person."

"I do not care, Mother. But I want her to come back soon."

Morning Blossom answered in a bracing voice, "Sooner or later, she will come back. You must believe that as I believe."

"I will, mother. With my whole heart."

CHAPTER 13

Awakens Corn

AWAKENS CORN HAD been awake that night when her sister returned from her visit with Noisy Goose. She had pretended to be asleep until she was sure that Laughing Rain was sleeping. Then she tip-toed out of the longhouse and into the moonless, starless night. Once at her village's hidden entryway, she began the awkward and painful task of crawling through the thick tangle of brush and thorns. Scratched and sore, she finally reached the opening in the wall of wooden stakes and stepped into total darkness. Fingertips now became her guide as she felt her way across the clearing to the edge of the forest. At a familiar brook her ears took over as guide. *Splash!* It was easy to follow the gurgling sounds. She remembered every turn and rise of the brook.

By the glimmer of early dawn, the climber had reached a flat rock that hung partway over the brook. Beneath the rock, shallow, clear water ran over a bed of clay. This was exactly the spot where the sisters had often come to gather clay for making dolls and pots. It had the best clay of all—soft and pink. The location? Of course, they kept it a secret. Of course, everyone asked where they had found it. One twin would always answer that only her sister knew, and the other said the same thing. And so, no one ever found the place of the pink clay!

On an impulse Awakens Corn scratched across the layer of clay with her fingertips, feeling the cold water rush across her hands and feeling the smooth, soft clay beneath. It was a moment of magic that recalled many happy times.

But now, there was no more time for memories. Awakens Corn needed to be far away before anyone found her missing. She left the path she knew so well and struck out into the unknown of the dense woodland, being careful not to break branches or walk through wet lowlands where she might leave footprints. The deerskin smock hanging to the ankles and knee-high boots helped her glide through the thicket. Footsteps felt softer, too, for she had laid an extra layer of doeskin in her moccasins.

It was High Sun before the run-away climber stopped to rest. By then, she had come to a broad clearing of tall grass that bordered a lake. Along the lake's edge were reflections of mountaintops that rose on all sides. Although walking was easier here, Awakens Corn realized that the meadow did not give good cover from those who might follow. Turning away from the shore, she made her way back to the forest.

Each step through the heavy growth of evergreens took her farther from her village. Each one brought her closer to that place in her mind where she would find peace and freedom. She did not know where that place was, but it was surely up ahead somewhere.

With the joy of solitude, her pace slowed. She began to smell the fragrance of the pines and to hear the faint cooing of doves. She admired how the roots of some trees grasped great boulders much in the way the talons of an osprey grasp a fish. Between the talon-roots grew thick clumps of moss and ferns. Her spirits lifted to a height she had never known before. "Is this," she wondered, "the heaven that the Black Robe told us about?"

As the sun began its descent toward the horizon, Awakens Corn came upon a little pond shaded by long limbs of white pines. A giant, round-topped boulder lay at the edge and partly in the water. She climbed onto its smooth gray surface to rest, no longer fearing discovery. A tiny bug with ungainly long twigs for legs caught her eye. It stood in the water, making little dimples on the surface at each point of contact. Awakens Corn counted six dimples. Suddenly, the bug scurried across the pond, leaving a path of tiny ripples. How wonderful, she thought—the notion turning into a smile—it would be if we could walk on water![33]

The rock held the contour of her reclining body, and its hardness against her back gave a feeling of security. She followed clouds as they moved slowly across peepholes among the overhead branches, slowly changing shape. She heard in the distance the thumping of a woodpecker. Just overhead, she spotted a brown spider. It dangled from a delicate strand that swayed slowly in long arcs.

The workings of the world around her absorbed her attention. She found her thoughts no longer jumbled and tearing at each other. Her new world had become serene and in the dappled sunlight she basked in its glory. She was with all the other creatures of the forest, each performing its role as the Great Creator had intended. It was in this state of peaceful happiness that she dozed.

The sun was low among the trees when Awakens Corn rose from her nap. By then, the spider just above her had already woven a pattern of threads. They reached out from one bough to another and sparkled where sunrays crossed them.

The girl on the rock stretched and glanced down into the pond. There was not a breath of wind. The black water was as still as the stone on which she was lying. Reflections on it appeared with stunning clarity. She knelt for a closer look. Below her was the same cloud that she had been watching above her. It floated slowly past the tips of the evergreen branches.

Bending forward, with her face almost at water level, she looked at her own reflection. She was first amused, and then surprised. Never had she seen her own face so clearly. After all, the only image of her face she had seen before was at the lake near the village. There were always some ripples in the lake that played games with how one looked. Besides, she and her sister had been told ever since she could remember that they looked the same. There was little reason to doubt what they said.[34]

But now look! “My eyes have a different shape from those of Laughing Rain. My nose is not so narrow. Her lips are more delicate than mine. Her eyes and mouth are separated by fine cheekbones.” Awakens Corn smiled broadly, “See, there is no dimple on one cheek like the one Laughing Rain makes when she smiles.” She frowned; she puckered up; she beamed as if surprised, remembering all the expressions that she knew so well in her sister. “But we have such different faces! I know Laughing Rain would agree. How could all the other people be so wrong?”

And so, Awakens Corn contemplated her face. She played tricks with how she looked by making ripples in the still water. Oddly, when one eye closed, it was the eye on the other side that closed. When she held one hand up, it was the other hand that came up in the water. As she did, a rustling sound in the distance suddenly interrupted her musing. With her head spun around toward the sound, she saw a doe run close by. Just behind the doe was a spotted fawn and just behind the fawn were many yelping wolves in close pursuit.

The doe cut its direction sharply. It headed toward a nearby ledge. Only the most fleet-footed could climb its steep and narrow rise to the ledge. In three or four bounds, the deer was on top. Her fawn followed, scaling the rise in quick, hopping steps.

On the last step before the ledge, one leg of the fawn slipped back. At that instant, the jaw of a wolf was on it. With a strong twist of its neck, the wolf flung the fawn back onto the ground. At once, five growling wolves covered their catch in a frenzy of motion. Not a moment later, the wolves ran off with furry, red pieces between their teeth. In another instant, the woodland was quiet again. The doe, standing at thc rim of the ledge, back arched, and stomping her forefeet, saw it all. Awakens Corn had to turn her head away.

She looked back into the water. Now she found a different face, one with fear, anger, and sadness. Tears ran down her cheeks and mingled with the black water of the pond. "There is where I want to be... deep in the pond... peace at last... watching forever a cloud passing overhead." Only the chill of nightfall brought her out of the trance-like brooding.

Next to the rock Awakens Corn made a bed of needles and covered them with evergreen boughs. Between these, she spent the night. She tried to sleep but could not. Thoughts of the fawn came back to her over and over as she unwillingly re-lived every detail of the sight. A chorus of wolves heard in the distance gave no comfort. Her visit into the forest to find peace had only brought her more anguish. She cried until there were no tears left.

Morning came with a hint of sunshine splashing through the trees. It fell upon an unhappy girl, struggling to find some reason for the ways of nature. Warmth from the speckled light raised her. With stretched arms, she timidly greeted the new day.

The cobweb above her was still there. Now, circles of threads pulled all the dangling threads together. And at its center, was a large fly. The fly turned this way and that. With each turn, it seemed to become more tangled. Soon the wings no longer moved and only thrashing legs told of any sign of life.[35]

Awakens Corn saw her way to performing one meaningful act. "The fly struggles to live. I can set it free." As she reached up and passed her hand through one side of the cobweb, the web fell toward the other side. She immediately withdrew her hand. "No. This fly will be a nice meal for a hungry spider. It is not for me to change fate. The spider has made a clever trap. A fly is a good flyer. Was it not clever enough to fly around the cobweb? Luck just ran out for the fly. No, I will not help. It is the way that a web-maker has to feed her babies."

Awakens Corn's thoughts drifted to the wolves. "Wolves have cubs to feed. Their only way of staying alive is to find meat. Deer are quick and clever. They depend on speed to escape animals that take them for food. It is the weakest deer that are caught, and their babies are the easiest prey. It is the way of nature. The turtle has its hard shell, the skunk, its dreadful smell, and the porcupine, its sharp points all over." This she said aloud, "Every animal has a way of protecting itself, but sometimes it is not enough."

She stood up and brushed the pine needles from her smock. Then she ran her fingers through her hair and twisted it into a single braid. "Bad luck for some animals is good luck for others. I always knew this much about life. Yet, it took a fly in a cobweb to make me see more clearly how nature is meant to be. I can accept what a spider must do. The Great Spirit intended it to be so."

Her thoughts carried Awakens Corn back to her people. She spoke aloud, "Surely, our hunters must kill animals. Furs make blankets and clothes for winter. Meat is needed when there is not enough corn and squash. Bones make tools and sinew make thongs. Our hunters always thank the spirit of the animal who gives its life for our good. It is the struggle between people that I cannot understand. It makes no sense. Laughing Rain thinks it is necessary because it has always been that way. No, I cannot agree with the need for people to fight. Like the elk, fighting for no reason brings needless hurt."[36]

Awakens Corn had to leave her sad place. She wandered farther into the world of trees. Her mood brightened with the spotting of a family of beavers hard at work along a stream.[37] Farther on up, where the shallow stream widened, she found so many speckled trout that the water seemed to boil. It was the kind of fishing place that Tail Feather dreamed about. Her footsteps aroused a black snake. It slithered into the water and soon drew up on the other bank. Awakens Corn found great clumps of jewelweed with full pods and amused herself by popping out the seeds.[38] She stopped from time to time to sip from the little streams that rushed through the forest. There was a moment when she sat on a ledge just above one of the streams to enjoy the one corn cake that she had tucked into her smock the night before leaving longhouse. The sound of the stream and the song of an unseen bird brought a newfound sense of the harmony of all things.

The sun rose and set many times as Awakens Corn continued her quest for that happy place just beyond. And every day grew hotter. Sweat trickled into her eyes. The long doeskin smock was soaked through. On the fourth day (or was it the fifth) she came upon a tumbling waterfall that poured over a ledge into a deep pool of quiet water. The pool narrowed at its rocky outlet where the water gushed into a crashing cascade. It was the perfect place to cool off. Her soaked smock and moccasins would dry atop a big boulder that lay at the edge of the stream.

At first, the coldness of the water was painful on her feet, but the pang quickly went away. She waded out to shoulder depth and let the passing water stream through her hair. The warming sun on her face and, at the same time, the chilly water flowing across her body were refreshing.

What caused a greater chill, though, was catching sight of a huge black bear with cubs strolling along the shore.[39] One cub would follow closely behind while the other would dawdle here and there, and then run to catch up. Mother bear approached the big rock where Awakens Corn had draped her clothes. She did not know of any black bear attacking people, but a mother bear with cubs, she had been told, is a different matter. Awakens Corn hunkered down so that just her eyes were above water, coming up now and then catch a breath through her nose.

The big bear took a whiff of the smock. She tossed it onto the ground and began to rip it apart with her long claws. One of the cubs tried to get in on the fun, chasing the flying smock until she caught one end in her teeth. The other cub, coming up from behind, found a moccasin and shook it playfully.

As the bear family frolicked with her clothes, Awakens Corn felt the numbing cold of the water. It was a cold that quickly drained away her strength. She knew that she had to do something, and soon. A glance at the shore on the other side of the pool showed a rocky overhang that was not possible to scale. Downstream, the water crashed over boulders, not a place where she could escape or hide. Awakens Corn realized that her fate depended on how quickly the bears would get bored playing with her clothing. She was, for the moment, a fly caught in a spider's web.

As Awakens Corn felt her teeth chatter and her arms and legs stiffen from cold, mother bear raised up on her hind legs, and gave a leisurely look all around. Nose up, she sniffed in every direction. Awakens Corn took a deep breath and slowly pulled her head underwater. When she came up for a breath, she saw the mother bear amble away with one of her cubs at her side. The other lingered awhile, then ran off. It was the last to disappear up behind the waterfall. And with the cub went one of her moccasins.

Struggling to half-swim and half-walk, she made it at last to the shore. There she pulled herself onto the grassy rise as her body shivered all over.[40] Her legs by now were useless. Her only thought was to crawl to the rocky ledge, hoping that the sun had warmed it. Her last measure of strength was needed to move at all. She slowly slithered along snake-like, pulling herself on knobs of grass. At the ledge, she gathered together what was left of the tattered smock, tucked it underneath her and tried to soak up what little warmth the ledge had to offer.

Her thoughts were slow in coming. "Would the bears come back?... Is there a fire in the longhouse?... Where is Laughing Rain?... Mother, I need you... The cold... The cold." Then, her thoughts stopped, and her eyes closed. Awakens Corn sprawled by the big rock, her strength fully sapped.

The sun had fallen behind the tree line by the time that Awakens Corn opened her eyes. She lifted her head. She found herself still shivering and her fingers as dark as blueberries. But life seemed to be coming back into her arms and legs. She stood unsteadily and looked around for bears. All was quiet. She turned her mangled smock over and over trying to work out how to put on what was left of it. There was only one moccasin. But first, she must rest and re-warm her body. In the morning, she would find the strength to continue.

Around her were hardwoods: chestnuts, maples, and elm. Awakens Corn scooped their wrinkled, dropped leaves together into a waist-high pile. She then climbed inside. Her cocoon was surprisingly warm. Sleep came quickly.

Morning light found Awakens Corn ready to travel. She headed downstream but walking in the forest on one bare foot quickly proved painful. When she began to limp, she tried putting the moccasin on the other foot. Soon, she had two sore feet. Another idea came to her. She tore off a length of her smock and wrapped it carefully around one foot, the one with the fewer cuts and blisters. The invention worked, if not perfectly, and at least it helped.

A day on tender feet brought her no closer to that imagined place where she longed to be. Dusk seemed to come on quickly. With it, the now weary and despairing girl came to admit that she had no notion of where she was. She had no place to go. She had not thought through any of the ways to live in the wilderness. Hunger was slowly setting in. All she could do now was to make another bed of pine needles and boughs in a well-protected place. Sleep that night was welcome. Surely, by morning a plan would come to mind.

Sometime during the night, a drop of water fell on her forehead. She stirred but slept on. Soon she became aware of drops falling all over her. She awoke to face a new, wet dawn. The sky was overcast, and a fine drizzle covered the landscape. Life in the wilderness had changed.

The raindrops throughout the day became steadier, pelting her hard as if they were falling acorns. Her smock, soaking wet, became a heavy weight. She stayed with the stream. In time, it led to a large rocky outcrop on a hillside. Beneath an overhang was a shallow blind cave. There was enough space to squat out of the rain. The bottom was sandy and dry. It would do for the time.

Awakens Corn, wet, cold, and discouraged, hunkered inside the cave and listened to the water pour off the edge. She wrung out what was left of her doeskin smock until her wrists ached. The smell of animals was thick in the air. The uneasy thought kept coming back that the cave belonged to the bears.

Night finally came. There was not a thing to do except listen to the continuous *thrum* of the rain. It gave Awakens Corn time to think about home, the warmth of the longhouse, and her mother's quiet voice. Mostly, she thought about her sisters. She could barely wait to tell Laughing Rain about the reflection, about the spider web, and about the family of bears. She wanted so badly to hold Sky Flower in a tight hug and watch her eyes sparkle in the firelight. The time had come, she knew, to return to her village.

She thought, too, about being punished for running off. Was her mother worried? Would anyone understand why she needed to find her own place, even for a few days? Did anyone care? "Tomorrow, I will find my way back to the village. But how?" It was a question she did not want to think about. She had not learned the secret of what made her different from her sister, but she did have a better idea of herself and her own place in nature. Laughing Rain would surely agree with her need to seek the answer in the forest even if the others did not.

"In the morning when the rain stops," she promised herself, "I will climb a tree on top of a hill. From there, it will be easy to see the smoke from the longhouses. But the rain did not stop. It went on for another day and a day after that. At times, a sheet of water spilling off the edge of the outcrop was as thick as the hides that covered the entryway of a longhouse.

It was a time of much despair. Solitude is what Awakens Corn had sought. Now, the quest had brought her deep into the forest. Up until now, she had never known a moment of loneliness in her life. Solitude was not what she had envisioned in her mind's eye. One chilly and boring day now followed another. She was lonely beyond anything she could ever imagine, trapped in this house of rock and sand on all sides and a slant of rock overhead with an endless wall of water in front.

It was on the third night hunkered in the cave that Awakens Corn heard a faint rustle in the leaves beside her. She was not alone. In darkness, she fretted—sleepless—until first light of day. What she saw was a huge snake with a distended belly. As she pulled back in fright, the snake raised its tail and shook it with a terrifying rattle. Awakens Corn felt a new shiver rising in her arms and down her neck and back. This creature was not the companion that she would have chosen to ward off loneliness. Even so, they spent the day and the following night together out of the rain, giving each other plenty of breathing space in the cave.[41]

On the morning of the fourth day in her rocky shelter, she awoke to find her long companion still there, half buried in the sand. Although thick clouds covered the sky, the rain had stopped. Awakens Corn decided that she must be on her way but not before saying 'goodbye' to her friend with the rattles and the large belly.

Now, determined to find home again, she started out into the forest, only to realize that she was faced with a new problem. She knew not where she was. Which way should she go? Awakens Corn hesitated, unable to decide, for a long time on which direction to take, growing evermore fretful. Then, the sun broke through the clouds. Steam now arose eerily from the flooded flat land. She would walk toward the sun.[42]

Puddles everywhere meant slogging through deep mud. Her makeshift moccasin needed to be fastened again and again. Sometimes, it came off underwater, and she had to reach shoulder deep to feel for it. As if these problems were not enough, the steaming air was abuzz with mosquitoes and stinging flies.

It was still morning when Awakens Corn came to a rise of land, and there she headed upward. Panting for breath near the top, she found a tall cedar tree. She climbed branch by branch almost to the top. Up there, she had a view of unending blank space. There were no villages, no smoke trails, and no signs of life. In the far distance, the sight of Cloud-Splitter's peak brought thankful joy. But it was a view of the mountain that she had never seen before. She could not tell which side of Cloud-Splitter she had come to.

Elsewhere, one tree-rimmed ridge joined with another ridge as far as she could see. Snowy white mist settled in hollows between. There was, too, an awful silence she had never known before. There was not a breeze. There was no chickadee chirping among the branches. There was not a rustle of a chipmunk scurrying among the forest floor. She listened for the caw of a crow and the hum of a rushing stream. Nothing. Only when she breathed did her ears catch anything at all. With a sinking feeling she climbed down from the tree.

The voice of Awakens Corn broke the silence, pleading with her legs, "Legs, do what you can. Keep walking. Take me to Cloud-Splitter. It is far away. I think our village is on the other side. With luck, you can find the village from there." And so, speaking to her legs, she became aware of two companions, her legs, and these had always been faithful, save for the time when they had become so cold. Talking to them eased her bleak loneliness.

On reaching level ground, she found that the peak of Cloud Splitter disappeared among the trees. Once again, she felt hopelessly lost. Tail Feather would know how to find the way home. BaBa had taught him these things beginning when he was a small child. Girls did not learn about them because there was no need. No need, that is, for her, until now.

Awakens Corn tried to gain her bearings. She remembered that the sun was at her back on the morning when she entered the forest. After that, she did not pay attention to direction as the sun moved around. Now she had to start toward the sun and try to keep in mind its changing position. But she soon realized that she was walking aimlessly in the forest. Aloud, she forced herself to say, "Legs, we are lost." The universe consisted now only of her, the trees, and the sky.

There was one bright point in a day of wandering. Near a swampy clearing where beavers had left many standing tree stumps, she found a sprawling patch of brambles. The stalks were heavy with blackberries. Her eyes could hardly believe such a lucky find. The first one tasted more delicious than anything Awakens Corn had ever eaten in her whole life. She was soon pulling them off by the handfuls. She was too hungry to be mindful of the thorns that scratched her arms and face. "Bear Meal," she said with amusement. "That is what the hunters call it. Eat as much as you can while you have it, so they say."[43]

A time soon came when stuffing her mouth with blackberries slowed down. Not long after, her insides told that she had eaten too many, far too many.

As dusk fell, Awakens Corn made a thick bed of needles and tried her best to rest for another day. But she knew that she was no closer to home. Every bone and every muscle ached. Her feet were skinned raw. There was also a sickening taste of blackberries and queasiness in the belly. The nauseous feelings came over her like rippling waves that washed over her and slowly receded. With great discomfort and misery, the down-spirited girl spent a long, sleepless night.

The new day began just as the last one did and as the days ahead would: endless plodding to nowhere in particular. Awakens Corn discovered that her own voice gave some comfort from the awful silence. She sang repeatedly the songs that she learned from childhood. She recited every poem that she could remember. She made up parts that she could not remember.

One song had always been a favorite. It was a game song that she and Laughing Rain had played as little girls.

Dance, dance away — dance, dance all day.
Step your feet faster — faster and faster.
Lift your knees higher — higher and higher.
Swing your legs wider — wider and wider.
Circle round tighter — tighter and tighter.
Dance, dance away — dance, dance all day.

What fun to remember how a circle of laughing children grew tighter with each round of the song until the ring collapsed in on itself! The rhythm was too much a part of her ever to forget. It kept her moving along through the forest on legs too weary to stand.

When Awakens Corn grew tired of things remembered, she spoke aloud to her devoted legs. "Go this way around this tree; go that way around the boulder; walk up this small rise; lift over the log; step on that rock; be careful of the toes."

It was not long before the voice and the legs seemed to separate from each other. The pace quickened. Legs went faster and faster. A voice cried out, "Hold back." Awakens Corn, knowing better, found herself running. The feeling of flight took over in a screaming panic. She plunged headlong through the underbrush, broke branches, slipped on muddy ruts, stumbled over exposed roots, and leaped over fallen trees. Pine branches slapped against her face. The runaway legs brought her, exhausted and gasping for air, to a huge, moss-covered log. One foot landed on top, but the slippery bark caused it to slide to the other side. Awakens Corn came crashing down.

The stunned girl found herself stretched out against a rock with her face pressed into the scuffed ground. She tried to catch her breath, but breathing was too painful. The shoulder on the arrow-arm side hurt, too, and she could not move the arm. A trickle of blood came from above one eyebrow. She felt a cold moisture over her face and her muddied hand had become white. As these troubles were not enough, there came a strong urge to throw up.

Tasting dirt, the unhappy girl tried to lie still. "What if I were to die here, alone among the silent trees? Am I ready? I will never see Laughing Rain again in this lifetime. Will Mother forgive me? Would Sky Flower remember me when she is grown up? What happens to a dead child in the afterlife when her people cannot give a proper burial?"

These thoughts forced Awakens Corn to try to go on. And go on she did. She pushed and pulled herself onto her feet and stumbled forward. Walking, now, was slow and tortured. Legs, shoulder, head: all hurt with every step. Even worse, each breath gave a sharp pain on the arrow-arm side. Her makeshift moccasin unraveled quickly. She tried to tie it again but the pain in her side was too sharp for bending.

But if things could get any worse, Awakens Corn was soon to find out. Approaching nightfall, she came to a thick bedding of pine needles. It was surely an inviting find for a worn-out footslogger. Then, to her horror, she realized that the pile of needles was one she had made the night before. "Legs," she confessed, the voice weakened, "We have walked in a circle. I am sorry." And with these words, the will to keep on was snuffed out the way a pot of water dowses a cookfire, but this time it made only a feeble hiss and gave out no steam at all.

She sobbed quietly with her face buried in the bed of needles. She forced herself to think of three wishes before she crossed over to the other world. "I wish that Mother overcomes her constant grief. Before I take my last breath, I want to tell Laughing Rain that I am sorry; after all, I am the "Flint," the trouble-making twin. Then I wish that the Black Robe could sprinkle me with his magic water before my journey into the afterlife." In her mind she went over these wishes many times. Yet, she knew that not one of them was going to be fulfilled. After a time, the racking pain on turning and on breathing brought a fourth wish. "I hope that dying comes soon."

Sometime during the fitful night, Awakens Corn became aware of the crackle of leaves nearby. There was, too, the sound of deep, quiet breathing, interrupted now and then by what sounded like a full tongue-slapping yawn. What if it were a bear or people-eating monster waiting until daylight for an easy meal? What did it matter? She had no fear. After all, what could anyone who is dying be afraid of?"

With the earliest glint of dawn, she saw a pair of eyes looking down on her not more than an arm's reach away.

"Is this a dream?" She stared at the eyes. "Is this the afterlife?" She blinked hard. "Am I already dead?"

It was sometime before there was enough light to make out what the eyes were connected to. It was an animal, a big animal. Slowly, in the gathering light, she saw a long snout. It was a wolf. The wolf sat back on its haunches and stared at Laughing Rain. It yawned some more. Then, she noticed something even more startling: the wolf had one missing ear.

"KyKoo! Oh, KyKoo," she cried out. "No, you are not a dream. I am not dead." Awakens Corn started to reach out to touch the wolf but shrieked with side pain. The wolf pulled back with a yelp. It hunkered down again but a few steps away. Soon, there was enough light for Awakens Corn to see the coloring of its fur and the shape of its tail. The wolf was thin. The fur was matted with patches missing. Yet, she was sure now. It was KyKoo!

"KyKoo, come here. You remember me? Awakens Corn. I won't hurt you. I am your friend." She spoke quietly for a long time. Slowly, she crawled toward the wolf. This time, the wolf did not pull back.

With one arm around the neck of the wolf, the girl found a new energy in her voice. "KyKoo, you have not been eating the way you should. You have many scratches and you have lost much fur. Have you been fighting?" She crept closer. "You have suffered, too." She laughed quietly, "We are now the same pitiful creatures."

Awakens Corn tried to brush out some of the tangled fur. "We are together now, KyKoo. We can go home. Help me find the way."

The worn-out girl followed KyKoo as she walked through the forest. Although she did not know where KyKoo led, she knew that the wolf was her only chance of finding her way. They walked for a full day, always KyKoo keeping well ahead, then stopping, sitting, and looking back to wait for the plodding girl to catch up. Where were they going? To her village? To a wolf pack? To a den even deeper into the forest? To anywhere?

Awakens Corn was too tired to walk far without stopping often to rest. If she walked too fast, breathing caused her to double over in pain. "KyKoo," she pleaded, "do not leave me here alone." But KyKoo always turned back until his companion caught up. At night, Awakens Corn could lie next to her friend and was happy for the heat that came from her body.

All sense of time and days was lost. Her only thought was to limp along behind KyKoo until her strength gave out completely. She tottered near that point when they came to a small brook that meandered down a gradual slope. She stepped across onto a flat rock. The rock looked familiar. It was the rock that hung over the secret pit of pink clay.

Awakens Corn pushed on toward the wall that circled her village.

CHAPTER 14

The Healer

A CHILD CALLED out, "Awakens Corn! Awakens Corn!" Other children joined in chorus, "Awakens Corn! Awakens Corn!" The name soon echoed through the village. On first hearing, the head of Laughing Rain jerked up sharply from the deer hide that she had been scraping. She quickly wiped her grease-covered hands on the grass and dashed toward the opening in the village wall. There, standing in the distance she saw her sister. KyKoo stood quietly by her side.

Laughing Rain ran to her sister, then stopped short a few steps away. She recoiled in horror. Awakens Corn was covered from head to foot with scratches and swollen, red blotches. Her pinched face told of her starving. Her hair hung in matted tangles. The mud-spattered smock was in shreds. One arm was outstretched. The other was held awkwardly in front with a big unnatural bulge at the shoulder. Her bare feet were painful to look at.

Laughing Rain, speaking to herself, said, "I must do something. Awakens Corn needs help before it is too late." Laughing Rain spun around and raced off to fetch what her sister needed most: food and new clothes.

The spirit of Awakens Corn soared with joy to see her sister running toward her. It then plunged into a bottomless gorge as she saw Laughing Rain then turn away, running at full speed. Speaking to herself, she said, "Laughing Rain runs from me, just when I need her the most. Now I know the truth. She hates me. Better I should have died among the trees."

Morning Blossom was soon by her daughter's side. She concealed her shock at first sight. She did not conceal the happiness felt within. Yet, her hug caused Awakens Corn to flinch back in pain. Smiling broadly, she stroked her daughter's cheeks gently with the backs of her hands. "My dream has come true," she said, trying to hold back tears. "You have come back to us."

"Yes, Mother. But now I am more a burden than ever."

"You have suffered much in the forest," her mother allowed. "Do not look so sad. The shaman will look at you. Soon, you will have your good spirit again."

Laughing Rain did return to her stricken sister, this time carrying a basket and some clothes. She broke through the wall of curious greeters with many questions. She led Awakens Corn to the big trough of water at the meeting circle. There, they found themselves alone—well, almost alone—not counting every child in the village.

First Laughing Rain handed Awakens Corn a still warm bowl of pudding made of black raspberries. The sight instantly caused hungry Awakens Corn into spasms of gagging. She raised a hand in refusal.

Laughing Rain thought, "My sister starves. Still, she refuses to take my food." Tormented from misunderstanding Awakens Corn's rebuff of blackberry pudding, she did not pause in her purpose. Without a word, she began to scrub off the dirt, beginning with one hand and moving from place to place over the rest. Slowly, the mud yielded to splashes of water mixed with ashes. Scrubbing over each washed part with a corncob came next. Throughout it all, Awakens Corn remained voiceless and limp as a doll. She resisted the washing of her arrow-arm arm, however, protecting it close across her chest. The round bulge in front of the shoulder told Laughing Rain that something was terribly wrong with the arm. "Why will she not tell me about it?"

Laughing Rain followed the scrubbing with care to her sister's many sore places. She spread a balm of dandelion roots in beeswax on the worst of the insect bites. She washed the tangled hair over and over and between rinses carefully brushed it to its former luster with a comb made from a flat bone. Lastly, Laughing Rain rubbed a sweet-smelling salve of bayberry all over and gave her a new set of clothing, including a fresh tunic and one of her own pairs of moccasins. Through it all, she could not find the words that she most wanted to say, "My life can start over again now that you have returned."

Even the painstaking grooming did not rouse Awakens Corn from her silence. Head down, eyes staring at the ground, she wanted to shout, "None of this washing and combing matters. Stop! Look at me, Laughing Rain! Talk to me! You should know that it was thoughts of seeing you again that brought me from the forest. You were the strength that made me go on. Now, all you want to do is make me look clean and smell good. All this could wait." But she was unable to open the thick, prickly wall that had grown between them.

Laughing Rain tried again to think of ways to tell of her feelings, but her voice could not find them. "Why do you not talk to me? Why did you leave me? Do you know how terrible it was? Did you think of how I suffered those many days? Do you hate me so?" As she finished washing, scrubbing, rinsing, and rubbing, an idea suddenly sprang into her. "I have something to show you," she said with a newfound voice. "Just wait here." Laughing Rain skipped to the longhouse and was soon back with her new work of clay.

"A pot!" Awakens Corn uttered with a puzzled tone in her voice.

"I made it."

"You did?" Awakens Corn held it, cradling the round bottom in her lap as if it were a newborn baby. She gently ran her fingers across the squared off rim with her good arm. "It is perfect," she gasped. "Perfect in every way. And there are beautiful lines all around."

"I made it for you."

"You even made it with our secret clay. And there are pebbles inside."

"Oh, those. I keep some of the prettier ones found here and there, many from our secret place of clay."

"What are these lines on the side?"

"Look where they curve up at the bottom. They make a smile, my sign."

"Hah! You are becoming daring, Laughing Rain."

"Mother liked it. Others look a little surprised but do not complain."

"But things about oneself never go on a Mohawk pot. People always say that is our tradition."

"Oh, I know, Awakens Corn. But it was fun to do something in a new way. I began to see why you like to be daring."

"But are you becoming too daring, Laughing Rain?"

"Perhaps. But not like you. Sometimes you can be too daring for..."

"For my own good?" interrupted the sister.

"I think so."

Once word came that the shaman wanted to see the injured run-away, both girls immediately obeyed the summons. Upon entering the dark, empty council house they sensed a strange presence. Chief Red Sun was not there. Instead, they found a bent-over figure, his long hair turned all white. Coming from the far end, he walked stiffly, his steps short. The shaman motioned for Laughing Rain to stand in the shadows. He brought Awakens Corn nearer to the glowing fire and stood before her.[44]

The shaman gently held the injured arm at the wrist, supporting the elbow with his other hand. He slowly drew the arm toward him. Awakens Corn winced but did not speak. Gradually, the arm loosened. Pushing here and pulling there with merciful gentleness, he tested the limits of motion.

"Child," the shaman said gravely, "your arm is not broken. Tell your mother it is out of place at the shoulder. It needs putting back, but not now. You must first have something to lessen pain. Your mother will give you a strong tea just at sundown." Turning to Laughing Rain, who was still standing in the shadows, he said "The tea will have the bark of meadowsweet, leaves from the elm, and fresh stalks of yarrow. Can you remember that?"[45]

"Yes. I can remember."

"Good. When the moon begins its rise, you must come here again."

"And me?" inquired Laughing Rain.

"Yes, come with your sister. You will help me?" he asked.

"Yes. Yes, I will."

All the shaman's instructions were followed. As twilight fell, the narrow slit of moon was seen just above the mountaintops. The twins walked timidly toward the council house. There was dread of the unknown by both girls. Awakens Corn was fearful of what might be done to her. Laughing Rain was fearful of not knowing how to help.

This time, the shaman did not speak. He wore a mask. It was the kind made from cornhusks and used only for healing. A string of bear teeth dangled around his neck. He walked slowly around and around the badly weathered girl, head bowed, then head up. In a single tone he chanted the traditional words of healing, all the while shaking a turtle shell rattle and blowing ashes all over her the awestruck girl. With one last walk around her, chanting and rattling, the shaman came to the next part of the healing ritual.

Beginning with his hands, palms down, circling over her head, the shaman slowly moved them down on one side, all the way to her feet. His hands came back up on the other side. They stopped at the arrow-arm arm. The buckskin shirt was pulled aside for a look at the shoulder.

Now the shaman beckoned Laughing Rain to stand by the side of her sister. He showed her how to place one arm beneath the patient's shoulder on the arrow-side, and the other beneath the shoulder on the bow-side. Then, he had her grasp Awakens Corn's hands together in a strong grip. This Laughing Rain did, feeling not only a part of the healing but once again the joy of holding her sister in a strong embrace.

Now, the shaman stood flat-footed on the arrow-arm side of Awakens Corn, facing her. He nodded as if to say, "Are you ready?" Awakens Corn nodded, even more fearful for what might be ahead, but mindful of the comfort of her sister's embrace.

With both hands, the shaman held her wrist and slowly bent the arm at the elbow to about halfway. He then brought the elbow up to shoulder height. With the motion came spasms of much pain. Awakens Corn grimaced but made no sound. "Steady now," he said, not letting off a bit.

"Shout, scream, cry" pleaded Laughing Rain in her mind. "It will be easier." But Awakens Corn, though trembling in agony, remained silent. Beads of sweat poured into both of their eyebrows!

Slowly, the spasm in the arm receded. When Awakens Corn had recovered from the worst pain, he brought the flexed elbow toward the back a little at a time. Suddenly, there was a faint pop. With it, the pain went away. The round bump in the front of the shoulder disappeared. The patient wiggled her fingers, then moved the arm up, down, across, and around with ease. The twins, amazed, turned to give thanks to the shaman. He had already disappeared.

The girls strolled slowly, hand-in-hand, toward their longhouse. Their steps bounced with happiness over their renewed friendship. The voice of Laughing Rain rose with a fresh energy, "I know you will recover quickly. Mother will make all the corn porridge you can eat. The bites will clear soon with salve. Even the blisters on your feet will heal in time. What was so terrible was thinking that you could not use your arm again. Now, it is as if new."

"You know much about these things, Laughing Rain. I worried, too, about my arm. What if I could not help you with all the chores? Now, all I can think about is eating bowls and bowls of Mother's porridge. You must promise me that there are no blackberries in the porridge."

"Promise? Why make such a promise?"

"It is a happy-sad story, one I will tell later," said Awakens Corn.

"Then, I promise. But you must promise to tell me the story."

All agreed. Laughing Rain turned to face her sister directly and said, "We are back together as real sisters. That is what makes me the happiest."

"So, too, am I," returned Awakens Corn, "and we will be real sisters for as long as we live."

"I am glad that you said that," said her sister. "Now, you have had your dream of traveling far away."

"It is true," answered the other girl, "I have gone far away, but not in the way that I dream about."

"No?"

"It is true. You must know that I still want to paddle to "Water-With-No-End."

The answer was not what Laughing Rain wanted to hear. She let go of her sister's hand and pulled back.

Both girls had the same thought at the same time, "After all this trouble, we have not come one step closer to understanding each other."

CHAPTER 15

Morning Blossom

The wall between Laughing Rain and Awakens Corn was once more so high and so thick that no words could describe the awful ache in each girl's heart. The look-the-same sisters pulled away from each other. They did all their chores apart. People gossiped, but no one could learn the reason why.

On a day that was too hot for fieldwork, Awakens Corn sat alone against a lightning-twisted elm at the far end of the village. Her hands, with fingers entwined, were folded in her lap. Her chin rested uneasily on her chest.

A long shadow approaching broke up the spotted sunlight. Awakens Corn glanced up and saw her mother. At first, they did not speak. A gesture invited her mother to sit down beside her.

There, Morning Blossom stared into space. She crumbled a dried leaf into a fine powder and began to sift it from one hand to another, spilling a little each time, until there was not even powder left. Without looking at her daughter, she said, "You have been looking sad these many days. Will you tell me what troubles you?"

Awakens Corn, startled at first by the question, turned away with a shrug. Her mother placed one hand on her daughter's clasped hands.

"I know something eats away at your insides." She turned her head toward Awakens Corn and their eyes met. "There is no need to tell me. But if you want to, perhaps you will feel better for telling."

"But I do want to tell you. Only," she admitted, "it is hard to find the words."

"Then, try. My ears are still good."

"I have been wrong, Mother, to go on my own journey," Awakens Corn began. "Yet, there is something about me that needs to fly away. Laughing Rain cannot understand me. I do not understand myself." Her voice rose in pitch. "Still, that is how I feel."

"And so, you torment yourself because you are different?"

"I think so. Laughing Rain is happy with everything she does. She accepts her place. She does not want anything to change. I cannot find the same joy when one day is the same as another, with no change ever to hope for. In a way, I feel more like my brother than my twin sister."

"Do you talk about your differences with Laughing Rain?"

"We did before I left the village. She does not like my ideas. Now, we hardly talk about anything."

"Did you think that going into the forest would make things better?"

"That I did. At first, I was happy there by myself. But it was not long before I learned my mistake."

"You caused us much worry."

"I am sorry. Did anyone come to look for me?"

"No. Chief Red Sun thought you and you alone must find the bad spirit that got inside of you. You had to free yourself of it by yourself. But all through those many days, I could think of nothing else, day and night. I tried to weave and cook and sew, but nothing could take my mind off you. Many times, every day, I walked to the lake and looked over the great space and into the mountains beyond, wondering where you were, and what had become of you. Every speck in the distance, I thought, could be you returning to our village."

"What do you think happened to me?"

"Oh, in my mind, everything horrible." Morning Blossom gazed toward the peak of Cloud-Splitter and spoke in a far-away voice. "You fell and were lying helpless in a ravine, animals nibbling at you. Hunters found you and took you far away forever. Listening to the steady rain day and night, I dreamed that you were drowning as you tried to cross a flooded stream. Then, the mosquitoes were so terrible after the heavy rains that I knew they must have been eating you alive. Even so, I never gave up hope of seeing you again. With your father and your brother away for so long, the thought of losing you became even harder to bear."

"I see that I have caused you much grief, Mother. But now you know who I am."

"What do you mean? Who are you?"

"About Sapling and Flint. I am the evil twin. I am the one who causes mischief."

"No," Morning Blossom said with a hollow chuckle. "No," she repeated louder, more seriously. "There is no evil twin. There is no good twin. You are different from your sister in some ways, nothing more."

Awakens Corn shifted her eyes onto her mother. She heard, "When you were just babies, I could see a difference in the way you moved, in the way you slept and in the way you cried. You crawled and walked before your sister did. You were the first to use words. Laughing Rain was always more careful about what she did and what she said. No one else saw these differences, but as small children they were clear to me."

"Even then?"

"Oh, yes, even then. As a child, you sometimes wandered alone through the village. You liked to climb trees and jump from high places. Your sister liked to stay near our longhouse and play with dolls and toys that she made from cornhusks and clay. You reminded me of when I was a girl. I had the same spirit."

The last remark startled Awakens Corn. "Like me?"

"Oh yes, much like you."

"Did you cause trouble, too?"

"At times, but for different reasons."

"Will you tell me?" asked Awakens Corn.

"If you wish. Our mother long suffered from pain. Her swollen hands and knees kept her from an active life. Your aunt, Meadow Bird Singing, was much older than I was, and had to care for me since I was very young."

"But the healers have strong medicine."

"That is true. For a while, a tea made from sweet fern helped. Later, she took a tonic of boiled wintergreen leaves and the bark of the birch. But in time, her painful swelling worsened. All day, we found her rubbing a lotion of witch hazel over the sore joints. There was little more that the healers could do for her."

"Did my grandmother know about us, two-babies-born-at-one time?"

"Oh no, she crossed into the other world long before you were born. Even I was a little girl at the time. Your aunt, Meadow Bird Singing, my sister, took our mother's place to care for me. She was strict. She found fault with everything I did. I tried and tried to clean hides and weave as well as all the other children did, but she could always find something wrong with my work. There was a weak stitch in a moccasin, or a scale left on a fish. There was never enough firewood for cooking. My hair was not braided tightly enough. In time, I felt the terrible burden of failing in everything."

Hearing about these experiences, Awakens Corn was aghast. "But, Mother, you do everything right. Everything."

"No. It may only seem so. I will tell you about when I began to rebel against my sister. It was when I was moving from childhood to womanhood. At first, there were seldom cross words between my sister and me. After a while I began to do things in my own way, even to speak out for my ways. At times, Meadow Bird Singing became angry with me. She once told me that she only wanted me to grow up in the right way, wanting me to become a good Mohawk woman and a good wife. The right way, of course, was always her way."

"But Mother, Meadow Bird Singing never married!" Awakens Corn said with some surprise."

"What you say is true. I believe she was so strict with me because she never had a husband. To change the way of my behavior, she sought the help of the shaman. It was during this time of the strife between us that your grandmother died. In her last breath, she brought my sister and me to her side. She told us she was sorry that she could not help me more. She asked Meadow Bird Singing to be patient with me. I know that our mother knew how harsh my sister had been with me."

Awakens Corn knew none of this story. She only wished that Laughing Rain were there to hear it all, too. "Was Aunt Meadow Bird Singing kinder to you after that?"

"No, not at all. She meant to do what was right, but she could not change her ways. She always believed that her demands were best for me. Still, I cursed my life under her endless fault-finding."

"Mother, you are good friends now. I know that."

"You are right, Awakens Corn. But our good feelings did not come easily. One day, I returned from the field and found that a basket I had been weaving for many days by the night fire had been pulled apart. I knew that Meadow Bird Singing had found something wrong with it. But I had worked on it for a long time, longer than on any other basket. It had a special shape, like the opening bud of a yellow poplar. That was my own design. It was a shape that I liked."

"A special work, like the smiling lines on Laughing Rain's pot?"

"Yes. Like that. I also found reeds of many colors to make a pretty pattern. Later I found out that it was the shape that offended her. It was not a Mohawk basket. On the day that I found my basket lying on my bed in a shredded pile, I became furious. I did not know what to do with my anger, and so, I ran sobbing into the forest."

Up until now, Awakens Corn could easily fit the story into the early life of her mother. But her running away—that was too much to even imagine. She asked, "The way I ran away?"

"The same. I hid not far away. There was a small cave that everyone knew about. We played there as children. It is a place where an angry runaway child might hide. There I waited for someone to come and get me, to say that my anger had good reason. I listened sharply to every sound, hoping to hear in the distance the calling of my name. What finally crushed my spirit was to realize slowly that no one was coming to look for me. I had to work out my wretched feelings by myself. Being alone in the forest was a terrible experience for me. I even began to miss my sister."

"How long were you there?"

"I spent two tearful nights in that awful cave. Then I went back to the village, feeling shaken and ashamed of running away from my problems."

"What happened to you after that?"

"Meadow Bird Singing said that she worried about me all the time. But instead of seeming happy to see me again, which I know she was, she scolded me."

"Were you punished?"

"No, not punished. But my sister became ever more demanding, and life for me became even more unpleasant."

"Your life could not stay like that."

"No, something happened. I married."

"Did Father change the ways of Aunt Meadow Bird Singing?"

"First of all, Awakens Corn, you should know something about that time. It was not your father I married."[46]

Awakens Corn blinked, then shook her head in disbelief. She heard the words repeatedly in her head, but she could not set them right in her mind. She gulped, "You were married to someone else?"

"Yes. I agreed to marry when I was too young. My husband was kind to me. He helped to keep my sister away from me."

Nearly swallowing her words Awakens Corn just managed to ask, "After that was life better for you?"

"Much better. But I found myself still trying to do everything in the perfect way that my sister expected. It was as if she were always looking over my shoulder."

"Did your husband like the perfect things that you made?"

"It may seem strange to you, Awakens Corn, but my husband, who was always kind, did not even notice. It was not his way."

Dumbstruck, Awakens Corn was barely able to get out her next question. "What was his name?"

"We called him Wolf-With-Night-Eyes."

"Was he our real father?"

"No. Kicking Elk is the father of all my children."

"What happened to Wolf-With-Night-Eyes?"

"Once, during the Time-Of-The-Strong-Cold our village became short of food. Hunger showed on the face of everyone. Wolf-With-Night-Eyes went out to hunt deer with three other men. While they were gone, heavy snow and fierce wind came and lasted for three days. We never saw any of the hunters again."

"What happened to them?"

"People said that the cold was too severe. Your grandfather thinks that the men knew how to get through the worst blizzard safely. He blamed other hunters for their death. We will never know what happened."

A long, long thoughtful pause followed. Finally, Awakens Corn found her voice. "Will you tell me about father?"

"Yes, if you would like. Your father came to our village in the following Time-For-Growing. He was just a boy, then. And, of course, I was just a girl."

"Father always speaks of the good things that you make. He likes the way you add a pretty design to a smock or a basket."

"Yes, your father makes me happy. I have tried hard to please him. Now, the everyday choices that I once hated are easier. Now, making something special is fun for me."

"Mother, did you ever think of going on a long journey?"

"How do you mean?"

"About going to a place far away just to see new things and to visit other villages."

"Yes, sometimes when I was a child."

"And now?"

"You ask so many questions. No, not now. My life is here with our people. There is no need to go other places. We know peace here in the mountains. Travelers who return from far-away places tell of many strange people coming to our land, people who are always fighting. No, the telling stories are enough for me to learn about the world."

Her daughter squirmed impatiently.

"What is wrong," Morning Blossom asked.

"Mother, will I be punished for doing what I did?"

"Punished is a strong word, Awakens Corn. The elders will decide what to do. I know that they have been talking about you. Still, I cannot tell you what they will decide."

The words sent chills shooting up and down the neck of Awakens Corn. She tried to say what was on her mind, but could only come up with the words, "I will be ready for what comes to me, no matter how terrible." Looking away, she added softly to herself, not knowing if her mother heard, "I do not think I can change my way."

Her mother did hear. "Perhaps you do not need to make a big change," she said. "Only enough change for others to accept."

While this response was some comfort to Awakens Corn, she was not satisfied, saying, "But, Mother, there are some things in my life that I do not like. How can I change them?"

Morning Blossom rose and held both of her daughter's hands, saying, "You should not expect to change the world. At the same time, hold on to your dream. The most we can hope for in a lifetime is to make some little changes for the better."

Awakens Corn thought about this idea, then asked, "What should I do?"

"For now, you must go to Laughing Rain," answered her mother. "She needs you... just as you need her."

"But how do we become friends again? You told me that you were like me. How did you come together with your sister?"

"Ah, ha. Meadow Bird Singing grieved along with me when we gave up hope of seeing my first husband again. We thought it would be good to make a string of seashells.[47] We would make a design on it with seashells in his memory. Over the time that we worked together on making holes in the shells and rubbing them down to round pieces—sometimes into the late night—we came to realize how important we were to each other."

"Do you still have the string?"

"Oh yes. I keep it in a safe place."

"Will you show it to me?"

"I would like to. One day, both you and Laughing Rain will see it. First, you must become friends again."

"Do you think we can?"

"Of course."

"Tell me how?"

"So, you say you cannot change your way to her liking," Awakens Corn's mother responded. "Then, try what made Meadow Bird Singing and me come together. Ask your sister to help you make something. You once told me that you wanted to make a gift for your grandfather. Laughing Rain is good at pottery. She will help you. I learned that working together is the best way to mend a broken friendship."

"You speak wisely, Mother. I will try."

CHAPTER 16

Noisy Goose

AWAKENS CORN WAS too caught up with her mother's advice to sleep. She spent the whole night going over in her mind the story of her life as a child and about her mother's first marriage. But mostly, she thought about how to kindle the warmth between herself and Laughing Rain.

With her sister's first stirring in the morning, Awakens Corn whispered, "Laughing Rain, Laughing Rain." There followed a deep yawn.

"What is it?" came a puzzled, sleepy reply.

"I ask a favor of you."

"A favor?"

"Yes. Will you show me how to make something?"

"Make something?" a thickened voice of early morning answered.

"Yes. Something of pottery."

"Make what?" The voice's pitch rose with newly awakened curiosity.

"Make a bowl for BaBa. A long, shallow bowl to hold his little wooden animals."

The idea stirred Laughing Rain. She bolted upright, sitting with her arms stretched behind, her hair falling loosely across her face. "Oh, I like that! He has carved every animal in the forest ... and even some fish. Now they need a place to be together. One long bowl with many small animals. Of course, I will be happy if we could make one."

There followed a flurry of activity: a jaunt upstream to their secret place for pink clay, gathering firewood and building a fire, collecting a basketful of thick moss, and filling a standing pot with water. The twins then kneaded out the clay into thin rolls on the smooth boulder at the meeting post. Few words were spoken between them. Yet passersby noted the twins in a joyful mood, something they had not seen for a long time.

With a sharpened twig, Awakens Corn drew the outline of a bowl on the hard-packed dirt. Her hands formed the shape. It was a long, flat-bottom bowl that came up in a gradual slope. At the top edge, it turned in slightly. The ends were tapered to a point so that the bowl resembled a canoe.

As the girls began to work the clay, one wound the narrow rolls of clay starting at the bottom; the other smoothed them out as the sides were formed. They dunked their hands in water from time to time to keep the clay from sticking. As they wound and smoothed, Awakens Corn asked, "Laughing Rain, do you think we look the same?"

Laughing Rain pulled back in surprise. "Of course! Another of your silly questions! Everyone says we do. We look exactly the same."

"But are you sure?"

"You ask me with something in mind. Let me hear it."

"I saw something in the forest that made me question what everyone says about us."

"And what was that?"

"A quiet pool. A pool without a breath of wind, not a ripple. Against the black bottom, there came a reflection that was as clear as my hand before me. I looked at my face for a long time. It was as if I were looking at another person. The truth is that you look completely different than I do. For one thing, you are much more beautiful."

"Now, you are just making fun."

"No, no. I mean it".

As they talked in amused disagreement, they became aware of a figure standing behind them.

"Are you making another pot?" It was the voice of Noisy Goose. He came in for a closer look.

"No," Laughing Rain replied without turning back. "Awakens Corn wants to make a long bowl for our grandfather."

"Yes. It will have my special design," added Awakens Corn.

"He will like that. How long will it take?"

"After we finish shaping the bowl and Awakens Corn draws her design, we must fire it until it becomes hard. The bowl needs to be turned over and over close to the fire, but not too close. It will not crack if we do it right. Then it must set over night. In the morning, we will have a fine bowl."

"What will your grandfather use it for?" he wanted to know.

"For his animals," answered Awakens Corn. Over her shoulder, she could see a disbelieving look. She explained, "He takes much pleasure in taking little pieces of wood and making them into small animals. They look as if they were alive. Soon BaBa will have a place to keep all of them."

A bit distracted by all the questions the twins tried to make themselves look busier than ever. Maybe their curious visitor would get the hint that this was not the right time to talk idly. And so, the girls kept on winding the rolls of clay and shaping them. Nevertheless, despite their deliberate burst of speed, more questions came.

"What kind of animals?"

It became clear to the bowl-makers that Noisy Goose was not going to go away soon.

"All kinds: a deer, a turtle... a raccoon, a skunk, a turkey, some beavers, even a brook trout," answered one.

"You forgot about the rabbit," added the other. "That is my favorite."

As the last layer of the coil found its place at the top edge of the newly-formed bowl and the ends came to canoe-like points, the twins turned to look up at their inquisitive visitor. Laughing Rain noticed, "Your wounds are healing. Your nose is almost straight."

Noisy Goose walked to the other side of the handiwork. He stood boldly in front of the girls, his arms folded in front, his feet planted a little apart. The fur of a mountain lion hung over one shoulder. He seemed much taller and broader than they remembered. His arms and chest appeared brawnier. They realized that Noisy Goose had passed from boy to man. There was now a new Noisy Goose: powerful and bold. They were not surprised to see that he wore a streak of hair along the middle of his head in the way of others who had proven themselves as warriors.

Having come to a place in bowl-shaping when they could slow down, the girls came up with their own questions.

"What happened on your hunting trip?"

"Then tell me what you want to know."

"Were you frightened?"

"Jumping Turtle! Of course not!"

"Well, what was it like?"

"I will tell you then. Twelve of us left Tahawus in high spirits. We walked for four days, stopping to rest only at night. All the time, Gray Tail Flying kept in single file. Each person stepped in the footprint of the one in front. There were many deer and some bear. Once we saw a small herd of elk grazing down in a ravine. We could have easily swooped down upon them or waited downwind for them to pass by. Gray Tail Flying wanted to hunt where it was more exciting, so we continued on for two or three more days until we were far into the land of the Lenapes."[48]

"Was it?" asked Awakens Corn.

"Was it what?"

"Was it more exciting in Lenape land?"

"Oh, yes. More exciting than expected. We walked along a stream that ran between high cliffs. The strangest part for me was the feeling of being there before. As we moved along, I saw rocky overhangs, caves and giant boulders. I somehow knew each one as if I had seen them before."

"Had you?"

"No. You know I have never been more than a day's walk from our village before. This was my first long hunt."

Laughing Rain had a question, "Why do you walk in the other footprints?"

"So that no one can tell how many people made them."

"Oh."

Awakens Corn followed with, "How do you explain knowing about the caves and rocks, then?"

"I had no way to know. Yet, I knew where the cliffs would end, that there was a clearing just ahead. As we came to the end, we were startled to see a young hunter standing alone on the path. His arms beckoned us to come forward. A bow was slung over one shoulder. Two feathers stood in his headband and a huge shell hung from his neck. As we came closer, I heard someone whisper from behind that there were many other braves hiding on top of both sides of the cliff."

"You were afraid then, at least a little bit."

"I did not think about that, but only about how brave I would be if we had to fight."

"Is that when the fight happened," Laughing Rain asked.

"No. Gray Tail Flying stopped us there. He walked alone toward the man standing before us. From the distance, we watched him exchange greetings with talking hands. Then, Gray Tail Flying signaled us to join him. He told us that we were welcomed in the land of the Lenapes. Other hunters came down from the cliff tops. One by one, each in turn greeted Gray Tail Flying with deep bows. We counted fifteen hunters altogether."

Awakens Corn broke in, "And you were only twelve."

"It is true, but the Lenapes seemed friendly enough. They beckoned us to follow, which we did. We were more curious than worried. Their many arrows, spears, and clubs gave us little concern."

"What were you thinking? There could have been much trouble ahead," Laughing Rain worried aloud.

"Gray Tail Flying did not think so. We trusted his good sense."

"Then what happened?" Awakens Corn asked. "Gray Tail Flying is known for his reckless ideas." Her sister, thinking the comment in poor taste, gave a gentle poke in the ribs. Awakens Corn jumped with a sharp yelp; the jab happened to be exactly in the place where she hurt herself in that terrible fall. The sudden jump made one side of the bowl bulge out of shape.

Noisy Goose did not seem to notice, but went on with his story, "The Lenapes led us to a clearing just beyond the cliffs, just as I had imagined. There, they had venison and turkey roasting on spits. They also had a good supply of cornbread. We all sat around the fire, most of the Lenapes on one side toward the cliffs and Mohawks on the clearing side. A few of their braves sat behind us. We were relieved with such good luck, and we enjoyed our first proper meal in many days."

Four dripping hands now smoothed out the bowl one last time. The twins were nearly finished with its shaping.

Noise Goose was not distracted. "We could see that the Lenapes were in a happy mood, laughing, chatting, and singing. What seemed odd was that I knew some of their songs. Suddenly, the hunters put on a spirited show of dancing. They pressed food on us until we could not take another bite. So much food, that we all felt sleepy and too stuffed to move. In some ways it was fun; in another, it seemed strange to be greeted by our enemies in such a way."

Laughing Rain asked, "Do you like it this way?"

"Well, at first..." Noisy Goose replied.

"I was talking to Awakens Corn," said Laughing Rain.

"Yes. It is beautiful," her sister answered. "I am going to make a little rim at the edge where it curves in. Like this. What do you think?"

"Even better," answered Laughing Rain. "It is almost ready for the fire." She turned to check. The fire needed to be stoked. For this, a forked antler came in handy. Soon, flames leaped out. The twins stuffed wetted moss into their bowl, being careful to keep the shape.

"Do you want to hear about the Lenapes?" interrupted Noisy Goose, with a trace of impatience in his voice.

"Of course, we want to hear. We were just in a delicate place for a pot-maker. We can listen now." Laughing Rain dipped her hands in the water once again and continued for one last smoothing of the clay.

Noisy Goose kept on with his story, "While we all rested from our heavy meal, I realized something odd. The Lenapes talked among themselves. I was surprised that some of their words were as clear to me as if they were spoken in Mohawk."

"Words like what."

"Words like 'many' or 'warriors,' 'morning,' 'surprise,' and 'captives.'"

"What do you think they were saying?"

"I had no way of knowing. I told Gray Tail Flying. At first, he scoffed at me for making up a story. As the Lenapes talked on, I could show him that I really did know some of their words."

"Did you speak with the Lenapes?"

"I wanted to, but Gray Tail Flying told me to listen carefully. He would not let me say a word to them, not even a friendly greeting. One word that I heard was 'fish trap' –of that I was sure!"

"Fish trap? That is strange! What did Gray Tail Flying think they were saying?"

"He told us, 'Now, I see their plan. They have sent someone back to their village to bring many more warriors. Their friendly manner is meant to keep us here in the morning. By then, when the others arrive, we will be caught in their net between the cliffs. Many braves will come down on us the way a pack of wolves pounces on a nest of rabbits."

"Gray Tail Flying knew that we had to act, and surprise was our best weapon. He tried to act natural. He smiled, ate more venison sprinkled with cornmeal, and spoke softly to the others, one by one. I heard of his plan from Turtle Nose. It would start at the first light of daybreak. Until then, we were to entertain the Lenapes with songs and dance, then pretend to sleep and wait for the signal."

Laughing Rain interrupted, "How could you dance, stuffed full of venison and turkey?"

"Not well, but our lives depended on making a good show of it."

"Are you a good dancer?" asked Awakens Corn.

"I am trying to tell my story," Noisy Goose shot back.

"Then, go on. I will not interrupt again."

Noisy Goose was only too eager to go on, "It was quiet as dawn came. We made as if we were sleeping. In faint light, Gray Tail Flying suddenly sprang up from make-believe dozing and gave out an ear-splitting whoop. We all followed him as he raced back along the stream through the long stretch between high cliffs. The Lenapes were startled. Those that blocked our way rose quickly with swinging clubs. We broke our way through them, and then I just remember more clubs swinging and blood-curdling howls. We suffered many blows but kept running."

"Is that when you were hurt?"

"It was then. I remember feeling sudden pain in my face. All the Lenapes were soon at our heels. We raced all day but kept well ahead of them. Spears fell at our feet. Arrows came whizzing by. They struck no one. By the time of afternoon shadows, the enemy was far behind us. For a short time, we rested in a dark ravine. But to be cautious we separated under cover of darkness. At first light, we gathered together and started on the long walk home."

"How did you find each other?" came a quick question.

"Gray Tail Flying makes a true turkey sound: three gobbles, then two gobbles after a long breath. That was the calling signal. We walked in the direction of gobbles."

Laughing Rain spoke with admiration, "So, you saved everybody from capture."

"Do you think that?" Noisy Goose, standing higher, responded with a voice of mock modesty.

"Yes. How did you know some of their words?" inquired Awakens Corn.

"After we returned, an elder told Gray Tail Flying that the river Mohawks had captured many people, including me, from a village in that territory. I was a little boy then. They took me along to our village."

"What do you remember of your Lenape village?"

"I can only bring to mind a few things about my mother and an older brother."

The twins had one more question for Noisy Goose. "How can you tell us apart?"

Noisy Goose was startled by the question. His cheeks became red with blushing. His bravery was tested again, this time in a different way. He had to tell the truth, "I have been watching you at work. Sometimes, I can watch up close for a long time," he admitted. "I thought no one ever noticed me."

"Well, how can you tell us apart?" insisted Awakens Corn.

"When Laughing Rain smiles, she makes a little dimple on one cheek."

CHAPTER 17

Chief Red Sun

DAWN CAME TO Awakens Corn with a gentle squeeze on her big toe. It was her mother whispering, "Wake up. Wake up."

Her daughter popped herself up to sit at the edge of the sleeping platform. She rubbed sand from the corners of her eyes.

"It is important. Chief Red Sun wants to talk with you. He waits for you in the council house." There was a trace of worry in her mother's voice.

Awakens Corn jumped to the floor. The dreaded time had come at last. She knew what was ahead: she would learn about her punishment for running away. Would it be a scolding? Standing at the meeting post to recite all day long how sorry she was to everyone who passed by? Nasty work, such as cleaning fish every day? What she feared most of all was being sent away from the village. "It is true," she told herself repeatedly, "my great wish is for a long journey. But to be sent away, never to come back, no, I would rather die." In short time she was ready for the day. Laughing Rain awakened, too, from sound sleep. In breathless silence, she caught a glimpse of her sister leaving their longhouse.

At the council house, the returned run-away braced herself for the solemn encounter. She timidly pulled aside the hide that draped over the entryway. Like the last time she was here, the dark, empty area seemed immense and a little frightening. Stepping inside she let her eyes adjust to the dim light. She scanned its length. There at the far end facing her sat Chief Red Sun on a bed of furs surrounded by water drums and the ceremonial poles of his office. A robe of feathers draped neatly across a pole nearby. A small fire flickered in front of him, its narrow, spiraling column of smoke finding the way up to a tiny smoke hole. Shadows of hanging masks danced ghost-like across the walls. Animal faces that were carved into the ceremonial poles stared down at the Mohawk girl as she presented herself to her Chief.

The tribal leader gestured for Awakens Corn to come to him. She approached warily, her knees trembling. A strong thumping came from her insides.

"You appear frightened, child."

"I am... a little."

"There is no need. Come, sit here beside me."

Awakens Corn did as she was told.

"Now, tell me why you left our village."

Awakens Corn did not want to give her real reason. Her dry throat only got out a stammering, "I... I had need to be by myself."

"By yourself? But why?"

"Because of my sister," she answered, fidgeting with one of her braids.

"Your sister? Did you quarrel?"

"We do get along. I cannot live without Laughing Rain. She cannot live without me. But she does not understand me. My ways are too different from her ways."

"Then, does she think a spirit entered your body and not hers?"

Awakens Corn struggled for an answer, “She may think so. I cannot say.”

“Some people go by themselves into the deep forest to lose a bad spirit,” Chief Red Sun said, taking on a soothing tone that she had not heard before, far different from his chief voice. “Is that what you did?”

“No, there was no bad spirit. I ...” She hesitated and stammered some more, “I only wanted... I only wanted to be by myself... to find a new happiness.”

“Alone! Alone in the forest? But the forest is filled with life.”

“I learned that,” Awakens Corn replied, now fidgeting with the other braid.

“Then, what did the animals and the trees of the forest teach you?”

“Only that I am small in a big world,” answered Awakens Corn shifting nervously.

“Is that what bothers you?”

“No. I already knew that.”

“Then, tell me what is wrong. Help me understand.”

“I do not know how to explain.” She bit down on her lower lip.

“My child, you fidget like a chipmunk when the shadow of a hawk passes overhead,” Chief Red Sun remarked, half amused. “Would it help if your sister were here, too.”

“Yes, I think so.”

“Go, then. Bring her.”

In a skip, the twins were squatting together on the bearskin mat, both in a state of high tension and looking up at the stern face of their clan’s leader.

“Now, one of you must tell me what happened between you two.” Chief Red Sun fixed his eyes on Laughing Rain and waited for a reply.

"I can say nothing," she struggled to say aloud.

"And why is that?"

"Because I made a promise to Awakens Corn." It was not easy for Laughing Rain to speak so boldly to the clan's chief. She did tell the truth, expecting no less than a harsh scolding or even the same punishment that her sister was certain to get.

"A promise?"

"Yes."

"What kind of a promise would send your sister all by herself into the forest?"

"It was a promise of secrecy," came Laughing Rain's answer.

Chief Red Sun shifted his gaze toward Awakens Corn. "Well?"

Awakens Corn stirred uncomfortably. There was a long pause before she admitted her deepest desire. "Laughing Rain knows that someday I want to follow the River-That-Flows-Two-Ways all the way to Water-With-No-End. Just one time in my life, I want to travel to a far-away place."

"The way your brother is doing?" he asked.

"Yes. Laughing Rain thinks that I am wrong for thinking this way."

Chief Red Sun stood, took some sips of his steaming tea, and slowly walked around the two girls. He then hunkered down before them in thoughtful silence. Both bore the awful suspense without a hint. Yet, Awakens Corn felt a warm flush pass through her body. Laughing Rain, on the other hand, felt a wintry blast.

"So, that is why you quarrel."

"Yes," came two voices at one time. Each waited for the heavy hand of the ages to come down on their heads. Instead, they heard:

"Allow me to tell you a story that was told to me by my grandfather and to him by his grandfather. The story goes back a long, long time." He stirred the dying embers before him until their glow once again lit up the council house. "It was a time when there was much fighting among the Nations of the Iroquois. It was a time of frequent battles that sapped the people of their bravest and strongest men. The nations carried on a never-ending state of war."

The twins beamed well-hidden glances at each other, wondering how their wrongdoing had prompted such a story. Even so, their faces showed a trifle of relief.

"Once, long ago, there was a village of people that we called "Crooked Tongues."[49] This name came about because they spoke in a way that was different from the speech of other Iroquois. A woman of these people had a vision in her dreams that her unborn son would one day do great things for all people. The boy was unusually healthy looking at birth. He grew rapidly and became strong and robust. All remarked on how handsome he was. At an early age, the boy showed a gift for speaking. He always spoke what he believed was right. Most of all, he believed that fighting between people was wrong. He even said that the Great Creator had sent him to earth to spread a message against such a terrible evil. Of course, such a promising boy created much jealousy. Do either of you children know the name of this man?"

"Yes, I do," said Laughing Rain.

Awakens Corn joined in, "I do, too."

"Well, then, what was his name?"

The twins spoke at the same time, "Deganawidah."

"Good. Good. Do either of you know where Deganawidah came from?"

Awakens Corn answered, "From the Long-River-That-Blows-Cold-Wind."[50]

Her sister was quick to add, "He belonged to the Nation of the Wyandots."

"Good," returned Chief Red Sun. "You have learned your lesson well. But your answer is not perfect. The mother of Deganawidah lived in another tribe. She and her son were the only ones who survived a raid on her village. Although she soon attached herself to a Wyandot village, the people there never fully accepted the newcomers as their own. Mother and son stayed in the village, but they were treated badly. Remember this, Deganawidah refused to change his peaceful way.

"Now, when Deganawidah had grown to manhood, a spirit spoke to him. It happened on the night before the warriors of his village planned to attack another village. The ever-changing face of the spirit had neither head nor body. It spoke in an urgent voice, 'Hear my words, Deganawidah. This need for bloodshed' the voice said, 'brings nothing but grief to your people. You, Deganawidah, must appeal to the warriors to live in harmony among all people. They live in constant fear of attack. This mission will be the biggest fight of your life. You will find your courage tested to the breaking point. Now you must act before it is too late.'"

"Who was the spirit with no head or body?" queried Awakens Corn.

"We will never know. Perhaps it was a dream. After hearing the message, Deganawidah was too troubled to sleep. The message he had heard was against all the thinking and training of warriors since the time when they first held a bow and arrow."

Laughing Rain asked, "Why did Deganawidah..."

"Now, children. I will never finish my story with so many questions."

"We will be quiet, then," Laughing Rain offered meekly.

"Yes," said Awakens Corn, prolonging the interruption just a bit more.

Chief Red Sun continued, "In the morning after his vision, Deganawidah told the young warriors about the face that spoke of a Spirit of Peace. He did his best to keep them from taking the path to war. They did not accept his pleading. They called Deganawidah a coward and dared him to change his mind. It was a terrible time for Deganawidah. In the end, many young men went off to raid a distant village. None of them returned. Their defeat only angered their people to seek revenge for their lost men and to prepare for a larger fight. Nothing that Deganawidah said could stop them."

The twins listened with fascination. They had never heard Chief Red Sun say more than a few words at a time and then it was in the ceremonial way of his office. Now, they were beginning to enjoy their festival of talking. It was not what they had expected on entering the Council House.

"With more fighting," the chief went on, "and more fallen men, Deganawidah left his village. He wandered in great anguish, alone, along the river looking for those who would share his vision of eternal peace. Yet, he could find no one who would listen to him. People made jokes about his timid way. He continued to roam from village to village, but in each one he met the same response. Finally, he sought solace in the shadows of the deep forest."

"The way Awakens Corn did?" interrupted Laughing Rain.

"That may be. We will talk about Awakens Corn later, but we speak of Deganawidah now. By the Time-When-Maple-Leaves-Turn-Red, the spirit of this unhappy wanderer was near breaking altogether. Then, he found a weeping man sitting on a rock. The two men both spoke the language of the Iroquois although they came from tribes that were far apart.

Deganawidah learned that the man's name was Hiawatha.[51] He came from the Nation-of-Many-Hills, the Onondagas.[52] He, too, had wandered through the forest far from his homeland that stretched along the River-Through-The-Mountains.[53]

"Hiawatha told Deganawidah he was crazed with grief due to the death of his wife and seven daughters, one by one, from some mysterious cause. Yet, the people of his clan were too troubled with their constant fighting to listen to his sorrowful story."

Awakens Corn broke in, "What were their names?"

"Whose names?" asked Chief Red Sun.

"The names of Hiawatha's wife and his seven daughters?"

"Oh, that, I know not. But, let me go on," the chief chuckled for the intrusion of this sad story. "Hiawatha blamed the deaths of his loved ones on a sorcerer who possessed evil medicines. Do either of you know the sorcerer's name?"

"It was Todadaho," Laughing Rain called out excitedly.

"Good. And do you know what he looked like?"

It was Awakens Corn's turn to answer, "Todadaho had huge fangs for teeth, and his body was distorted with seven crooks in his back."

"Was there anything else?" asked Chief Red Sun.

Laughing Rain added, "They say that living snakes squirmed about in his long hair."

Her sister added, "He liked to eat raw flesh, and no one wanted even to think about where the raw flesh came from. People said that the terrible man lived hidden in a deep ravine."

"You are both right. Perhaps you should be telling the story. Now, where were we? Oh yes, Hiawatha admitted to planning revenge against this monster."

"What did...?" With that said, Awakens Corn felt her sister's elbow jab her in the ribs.

Chief Red Sun persisted in the telling of the story, "Deganawidah told Hiawatha of his fruitless efforts to promote harmony among all people. He explained how he thought of humankind as a great tree of pine. The trunk of the towering pine is the strength of all people; its roots spread to the four directions of the earth. These roots will lead those who wish to follow on the noble path to peace. Can either of you children tell me what this token of everlasting peace, buried deep beneath the tree, was?"

"Yes," Laughing Rain and Awakens Corn said without hesitation and at the same time. "It was a tomahawk."

"Again, you are correct. The branches of the pine tree touched the sky so that living people can communicate with their ancestors. In the shade of this tree, the council elders will form the laws of peace that will be expressed for all time. All who obey the Great Laws may find shelter beneath the Tree of Peace. Now you know why the pine tree is sacred to our people."

By now the twins sat calmly as if happily transported into another world.

"Hiawatha listened to the message of Deganawidah and was impressed by his solemn wisdom. It was the message of hope to end all warfare. 'But how to do this?' Hiawatha asked." Pausing in the story, the chief addressed his attentive listeners. "Now, children, what ideas do you have to change this terrible condition among people?"

"First, we must forgive our enemies," uttered Laughing Rain without a moment's hesitation."

Awakens Corn knew what came next, "We must carry this message of peace to all the people."

"Oh, you children have learned your lessons well. That is exactly how Deganawidah answered Hiawatha's question. A circle of hands held tightly by friends and enemies alike does not break easily. The noble path to peace will come at last to all people. It will lead to happiness for their children and for their grandchildren.

"Still, Hiawatha was doubtful of Deganawidah's strange talk. 'The monster Todadaho has taken away my wife and my children. I will never have grandchildren. How can I think of lasting peace?'

"'My friend,' replied Deganawidah, 'There will always be grandchildren, not yours perhaps. You must be a friend to all children, taking them into your confidence and helping them to believe in your message of peace. The people of the earth will continue to live, but they must choose to live either in conflict or in harmony. It is among the children that the hope of humankind will be entrusted.'

"Do you believe that, children?"

Both girls were a bit startled by the question. Awakens Corn spoke first, "I had never thought in this way before."

"Nor I," replied her sister.

"Then you must listen carefully," continued Chief Red Sun. "The words of Deganawidah swept the anger of Hiawatha away. The two men departed, Deganawidah to return to his home among the river dwelling Wyandots. There, he tried again to convince his people to change their warring ways, but— as before— he had no success."

"Why not?" asked Laughing Rain.

"The people of Deganawidah could not change their aggressive ways, despite his powerful words."

Awakens Corn asked, "What happened to Hiawatha?"

"Well, Hiawatha returned to his lakeside Nation of the Onondagas. He tried his best to instill the ideals for peace in his people. No one listened. They thought he was going mad. He traveled to other nations of the Iroquois world, but in each they did not treat him kindly. At last, he found a shared feeling with one of the Iroquois women of the Nation-of-the-Great-Stone, the Oneidas.[54] She was the first to accept his bold new idea of a Great Peace among all people. She lit a fire and promised to keep it burning as a symbol of this idea. Do you know the name of this great woman?"

Without a moment's hesitation, Laughing Rain asked, "Was her name Jikonhsaseh?"

"Hah. Exactly. So, you children know the story already."

"Only parts of the story," admitted Awakens Corn.

"Well, then, you must know that Hiawatha, with the urging of Jikonhsaseh, who became the Mother of Peace and the Mother of Nations, descended into the deep ravine where Todadaho lived. He offered to comb out the living snakes in his hair. While doing so, he told of meeting Deganawidah, the Prophet of the Wilderness and of his message of peace. He told of the eternal fire that Jikonhsaseh promised to keep. The head of Todadaho cleared as the snakes were driven from his hair. He became intrigued by Hiawatha's words. When freed at last from all the snakes, Todadaho pledged to follow the spirit of this message of peace.

"With this remarkable change of Todadaho from Evil to Good, news spread rapidly throughout the land of the Iroquois nations. In time, five nations of the Iroquois agreed to form a pact. They agreed to live in peace with each other. Can either of you tell me the names of all five nations?"[55]

Laughing Rain was the first to respond, "These were the nations of the Oneida, the Onondaga, the Cayuga, and the Seneca."

"You forgot one," Chief Red Sun commented.

"It was Awakens Corn who spoke up, "The Mohawk Nation, the nation of our people."

"Perfect! And what is the symbol of the pact?"

Both girls answered at the same time, "Five arrows bound together at the center."

"You have been listening carefully to the telling stories. But to go on, all members pledged not to make war on any other member. Jikonhsaseh became the clan mother for all the nations. She appointed Todadaho as keeper of the fire."

"Why did the Wyandots not become an arrow in the League?" Laughing Rain asked. "They speak the language of the Iroquois."

"That is a good question, children, but I have no answer. Deganawidah was not able to persuade his people to join the league. They thought in a different way, that war was necessary to be strong. His heart was broken. As far as we know, Deganawidah spent the rest of his days trying to bring his Tidings of Peace to all people."

"Did you ever know him?" Awakens Corn asked.

"No, no! Deganawidah lived long, long before I was born. Since then many people have been born, grown up and crossed over to the other world. Yet, you have now heard the story of how the League of the Iroquois was formed exactly as I heard it as a boy."

Chief Red Sun shifted his position so that he was kneeling directly in front of the sitting girls. Their eyes were all at the same level. Chief Red Sun then, looking directly at Laughing Rain asked, "And what does that story mean to you?"

"It means that people can live together without fighting if they obey the rules of wise men and women."

"Wonderful. Now, you," nodding to Awakens Corn, "What does the story mean for you and your sister?"

"That demons can be cleared from our thoughts. Then we will understand each other. There would be no more quarrels."

"Good. I am proud of both of you."

Growing bolder, Awakens Corn asked, "What was it like when you were a boy?"

"You two!" he said with a smile that almost seemed too broad for his broad face. "So many questions!"

"We would like to hear about that," Laughing Rain added.

"Well, then... But just a little. When I was a boy, I belonged to the Nation of Mi'kmaq. We lived along the Long-River-That-Blows-Cold-Wind where it enters the Great Water. We spoke the language of the Algonquins."[56]

"What was your name then?" asked one of the twins, feeling much bolder.

"More questions! They called me Little Red Squirrel. The men packed pelts into canoes and took them far away to the ocean, a journey of many days. It is the same river that brought the Black Robe. At the place where the river widened, we had our first view of the strange men with hairy faces; they had come in great canoes that glided in the wind on giant wings. They had come from across the ocean to trade for furs. Our men returned with axes and hoes that cut sharply. They also came with soft warm blankets. Before long, trading was changing the way of our people. But that is a long story."[57]

"What is the ocean?" one of the girls asked.

"Hum, well, an ocean is where there is much water."

"How much water?"

"I thought one of you might ask. Well, 'ocean' means water as far as you can see."

"Did you ever go to the ocean?"

"No, but I tried. I wanted to see these strangers from another world. One time, crazy with curiosity, I hid within a thick pile of furs in one of the canoes. It was the biggest canoe and held the most pelts.[58] I waited until we had traveled a long way before popping my head out, to the paddlers' great surprise."

"Were you punished?" was the question on the tongue of Awakens Corn.

"Only by receiving a terrible scolding. The paddlers called me a foolish boy. They said I would be punished on returning to our village. But they chose not to turn back but to continue the journey. That moment was the happiest of my life. Little did I know what was ahead."

"Did you see the giant canoes with wings?"

"Wait, now. I must tell the story as it happened. We came to the place where there were high cliffs on the bow-arm side of the river.[59] Suddenly, many canoes bearing Mohawks came upon us. They had been waiting for us along the riverbank. Instead of furs, they carried spears and war clubs. Escape was not possible. In the struggle, our canoes were overturned."

The twins were breathless as the story unfolded.

"I hid underneath a canoe. I could hear the fighting. It was terrible. Later, I heard sloshing sounds as the Mohawks picked up the pelts. Some of them came to my upside-down canoe, banging it with their spears. I felt my heart banging in my chest. I could not breathe.

"After all was quiet for a long time, I peeked out from beneath the canoe. The river was empty of people dead or alive. I swam to the nearest shore, the one with the high cliffs. After resting until sunset, I walked along the riverbank under cover of night to our village. There, I found nothing but smoldering ashes. I looked inside our burned-down longhouse but my mother, my two sisters and brother, who was just a baby, were not there. I never saw them again."

There was a gasp among the listeners.

"It was in a confused state of sorrow and anger that I wandered without concern of where to go. In time, some Mohawk hunters found me. They took me to a valley along the-River-that-Flows-Through-the-Mountains. There, they taught me Mohawk ways. I learned well. I tried to forget the terrible fate of my family. Hunting and fishing gave us enough food, enough to last through the Time-Of-The-Strong-Cold. I saw how the nations of the Iroquois League were at peace with each other and only wished that our Wyandot elders had chosen to join them long before.

"After many winters of drudging work around the long-houses, when I became a young man, the women admitted me into the clan. I was happy for this act. From then on, I could hunt with the men."

There was a pressing question on the minds of the twins, "Was it your new clan that burned your village and killed your family?" Yet, it was a question that two speechless girls could not bring themselves to ask.

"What I did not like was the hostility of the Mohawks to those nations that were not members of the League. The warriors often went off to distant lands and returned, whooping and dancing, with captives bound together—men, women and children—and with trophies taken from the dead."

At last, Awakens Corn found her tongue, "Did you have to join the warriors?"

"Oh, yes. A few times. It was expected of me. Yet, I hated this way of life. Many others in the clan did as well. Some of us formed a secret bond. Your grandfather Guiding Star was the first one to speak of leaving the village for a more peaceful life. It was after your grandmother died that he brought those together who were against all hostility. At his urging, we chose to leave the bounty of the river and to live isolated among the mountains. There, we would have no need to fight. Your grandfather, whose name is Guiding Star, but you always call him 'BaBa'..."

Awakens Corn interrupted on an impulse, "My sister and I are making a clay..."

"Not now. As I was saying," Chief Red Sun went on, "Your grandfather led the way into the mountains, even on a painful, bent leg."

Laughing Rain found the courage to explain, "My sister was telling about the little house we are making for Baba."

"Good. But, children, you must let me finish my story. The long path of the peace-seekers took us to a lake that lay snuggled between snow-covered mountains. The peak of the highest mountain seemed to split the clouds."

Laughing Rain found the words to say, "And that is why we are in Tahawus?"

"Yes, and that is why. When all the people, some carrying babies, arrived here late in the day, the low setting sun lay just between two mountain peaks. We decided then that this high plain by a strong stream would become our new home. Even through the worst blizzards and the longest droughts, we have never regretted our choice. Once having decided on a place, the women had to choose a leader. They named Guiding Star. He gave thanks to them but explained that he was unable to lead in a proper way. We all knew that his old leg injury was the reason, but he did not say so. The women then picked me as their chief. And now you know all about me, even how I got my name."

Chief Red Sun noticed the girls beginning to shift uneasily. "You have heard enough stories for one day. You may go now."

"But," Awakens Corn said in a tone of surprise. "Have you decided about me?"

"About you? In what way?"

"How I will be punished."

"Punished? Hah! Why punished? I admit that what you told me was painful for you to say. From the wilderness, you have learned something of your own life. We all do our best in our own way, but remember, everyone is needed in a village. Go back to your duties. Do not think about a woman making a long journey. Times change our ways and perhaps one day your dream of a long journey for women will come to be, if not for you, for your children." He paused before adding, "Or their children."

With their heads filled with stories about Creation and how their village came to be, the sisters sensed that it was time to go. As they rose and bowed politely, Chief Red Sun asked, "Well, are you going to tell me about your house?"

"Our house?" their startled voices sounded together.

"Yes, your house of clay."

"Oh, of course," the sisters said almost in unison. They took turns describing their toy house meant for their grandfather: He could keep all his little carved animals in one place. The house would look like a hollowed-out log and be made of the pinkest pink. The rim would be decorated with imprints of needles and leaves. There would be pictures of trees scratched along the sides. A path would twist all the way around the trees. The animals would feel that they were in the forest. And finally, there would be a five-pointed star near one end of the longhouse.

Chief Red Sun listened attentively, then said, "Your grandfather will like that. You must show it to me as soon as you finish. You must go now. Sleep well."

After this exchange the twins sauntered back toward their longhouse, only too eager to share each other's version of their conversation. Once out of earshot, Laughing Rain asked, "What do you think of Chief Red Sun, now?"

"He is a great man. He cares much for our village," said Awakens Corn.

"I cannot think of him as a little boy," her sister added, "a little boy hiding in a canoe full of pelts." Both laughed quietly at the thought.

Awakens Corn asked, "But why, if he is so much against fighting, did he not stop Gray Tail Flying and the other young warriors from hunting in enemy lands?"

"You know that he was against their actions, as were all of the elders. Do you think anyone could change the spirits of young men too restless for excitement?" Laughing Rain paused for a moment, then confessed, "You should know, my spirit is happy now. There will be no punishment."

"I was surprised, too," Awakens Corn confided. "I expected something harsh. I thought I would spend the rest of my life scraping hides. Chief Red Sun was kind. Still, he did not please me altogether."

Stunned, Laughing Rain managed to ask. "No! How could you say such a thing?"

"Because I cannot forget about going on a journey to a faraway place," answered the firm voice of Awakens Corn.

Her sister pulled back. These last words suddenly plunged the joyful spirit of Laughing Rain into a deep and hollow place.

CHAPTER 18

Kykoo

THE TIME FOR GROWING had been good for the Three Sisters. Long sunny days, never too hot and with just enough rain, made the corn stalks stand tall with ears bursting with fat kernels. The squash plants were plumper that anyone could remember. Bean picking was better than ever.

In the Heavens at night, the Hunter was seen beginning his chase of the Great Bear.[60] The time of the harvest was approaching. The plentiful harvest meant much work for the entire village, but everyone made it cheerful. There were husking bees and singing while scraping the kernels of the corncobs. Pounding the kernels into meal in rhythm helped to forget about aching arms and shoulders. Shelling circles readied beans for drying. Cutting squash in the longest spiral with sharpened copper knives was always a spirited contest. The spirals then hung to dry in the sun.

Fingers tingled from the chores that began early in the morning and went on until after sundown. Yet the long days of making food ready for storage was a happy time. And at the end of the day, everyone enjoyed a cleansing dip in the lake. Splashing, laughing and joking went on until well after dark.

In the bustle of harvesting, the workday was different. All noticed that KyKoo was nowhere to be seen, not sticking her nose in this, knocking over that, playfully wiggling her way between crowds of workers, all for a little attention. No one minded a little wolf-mischief now and then. For her pranks, KyKoo received her share of friendly strokes. Now, of course, everyone asked the twins, "What has happened to KyKoo?"

Although the girls always answered by telling how KyKoo liked to stay near their grandfather, they really did not want people to know the truth. KyKoo had changed and she had changed in a bad way. The sisters blamed themselves. After all, they had promised KyKoo that they would take good care of her while their brother was away on his long journey. In that, they had failed. And so, every explanation of KyKoo's strange behavior came with a heavy sense of guilt.

Here was the problem: KyKoo would not leave the pile of brush into which she had burrowed. Day and night, she hid back in the shadows, snarling whenever anyone approached. Even BaBa could not get close with a handful of fresh meat.

The spirits of the twins lifted when their mother made a special request of them: "BaBa asked if you would like to look after KyKoo. It means feeding her every day and making sure that she always has plenty of water." The girls leaped at the challenge. "We can do that. This time we really will," Awakens Corn said eagerly. Laughing Rain agreed, "Oh, we will. First, we need to know what to do."

"Oh, that will be easy. You must ask around to find a family with leftover meat. Everyone will be happy to give you what scraps they can. BaBa leaves the meat near her pile after the sun goes down. Always make sure that her bowl is filled with fresh water. KyKoo will come out after dark if no one is around. Be careful not to get too close. We are getting afraid of her. Never try to pet her."

Laughing Rain responded eagerly,

"We listen to you, Mother. I think KyKoo will be back to her old self when Tail Feather returns."

Awakens Corn asked, "Is something wrong with BaBa?" The question came with a worried tone.

The answer brought a sudden chill, "Something is wrong. Your grandfather is not as strong as before and he tires easily. He does not eat all the soup that Meadow-Bird-Singing and I cook for him. Also, he has lost the color in his face. From now on the shaman will see him every day. For now, he must stay quiet and rest."

"Can we see him?"

"Yes. But you had better wait until morning. Now, be off with you to find something for KyKoo."

A nagging worry about their grandfather stayed with the girls as they sought some wolf food. People of the clan were generous. Soon, the basket was full of meat. There was even KyKoo's favorite—fresh, raw venison.

The twins waited until dusk had settled in before they softly approached the wolf. They heard the snarling long before they could make out a black snout just visible in the pile of dried brush. The twins pulled back. A bit frightened, they left the meat at a safe distance and came back again, this time with clean water.

As they departed, Awakens Corn came up with an idea. "If we hide and stay really quiet, we may be able to see KyKoo come out to eat."

The suggestion struck a chord with her sister. "Yes, that way we might see what is wrong, why she behaves so strangely."

The twins crouched down behind a bush, keeping well out of sight of KyKoo but with a watchful eye. The time passed slowly as full darkness came on with just enough moonlight to see the small opening in the brush pile. For the expectant observers, the hardest part of waiting was to keep from talking (a skill at which they were never good). In time, however, the girls could wait in silence no longer. "What is happening?" Laughing Rain finally whispered. "Does KyKoo know that we are here?"

"She must be hungry," her sister responded. "I think that the food is too far away. I am going to push it a little closer."

"No, no!" Laughing Rain shot out. "We promised Mother not to get too close."

"Yes, I know, but I will be careful." With these words and against her sister's wishes, Awakens Corn pulled away from her grasp and crept toward KyKoo. She started to shove the plate of meat closer when the wolf again growled in a threatening way. It was a fearsome moment. And then, Awakens Corn thought she heard another sound. It was more of a squeal. She listened intently. It came again and again, clearly heard over KyKoo's growls. The tiny sound was like none that she had ever heard before. As her mind raced for an answer, she heard two squeals at one time.

Dumbstruck, Awakens Corn made her way back to her sister. "I have the answer to KyKoo's strange way. You must hear it," she pleaded. With some persuasion, Laughing Rain agreed to creep near to the nest. There, she, too, was enchanted by the unexpected sounds. The twins listened intently until they were certain that there were two, and only two, little squeal-makers.

Eager to talk about their astonishing discovery, they returned to their hiding place. Laughing Rain was the first to speak, "More twins! What are we going to do with two baby wolves?"[61]

"We can raise them ourselves. Think of the fun we shall have."

"No. You forgot about twins. They are not welcome. The elders will leave them out in the forest. Then KyKoo will go looking for them and never return. Tail Feather will never forgive us."

These thoughts had not come to Awakens Corn. "No, I think everyone will love wolf cubs."

"But," her sister quickly added, "Do you remember how much trouble KyKoo caused when she was small?"

"Of course. Tail Feather never slept, caring for her. Once, when she had grown a bit, she tipped over a pot of maple syrup. Mother was furious after all the hard work of collecting it and boiling it down."

"No, it was honey. Father collected it after suffering many bee bites. Remember how it stuck all over KyKoo and she rolled and rolled in the leaves to get it off?"

"Now, I remember. For a long time, she looked like a walking log. Do you remember when KyKoo burned herself? She ran out of the longhouse. After that, she would never go back in, even in the worst blizzard."

"Yes. Once she chewed one of Mother's new high boots until it was just shreds."

"Oh, the way a bear cub chewed mine!"

"What bear cub?"

"Ah, that is a story for another time. We must sleep. First thing in the morning we will see these pups."

"But before that we must go to see BaBa."

"Yes."

The sisters walked away in silence toward their longhouse, each knowing what the other was thinking and each with the powerful mixture of joy and worry. Could they keep the pups? Was BaBa sick? The questions preyed on their minds, and they feared the answers.

CHAPTER 19

Guiding Star

Sleep was troubled for the look-the-same girls. The first blush of daylight brought them to their feet. They found their mother already at the cookfire.

"Your grandfather needs good food now," said Morning Blossom. "Here is some fresh corn porridge. He likes it sweetened with maple syrup and flavored with nuts and berries. You can help by pounding the hickory nuts and acorns over there into a fine dust. There are some dried blueberries and strawberries in one of the hanging baskets."

Awakens Corn said excitedly, "We can take it to BaBa in the new clay house."

"Good thought!" her sister joined in. "The clay has been cooling overnight. If there are no cracks, it will be just right."

Soon the twins were at the longhouse of their grandfather. They worked their way between the double-stacked platforms on each side. His compartment was at the far end of the longhouse. In most longhouses, things such as corn, reeds, and pottery were stored in this section. Elders, however, often lived in the end compartment as a privilege for their age.

Guiding Star's section was filled with a clutter of bows,

drums, turtle shells, deer hoof rattles, decorated strings of shells, snowshoes, duck decoys, and many sparkling stones.[62] A painted elk hide hung on one wall. In the array of wonderful objects, they quickly became aware of the peculiar and unmistakable odor of illness. The granddaughters stopped short, taken aback even more by their grandfather's appearance. For one thing, the twins had not ever seen him lying down before. More than that, his face had a sickly pallor and his cheeks were drawn in.

Guiding Star beckoned them to come closer. "There is no need to be timid." With a trembling hand, he tapped the hand of one twin, then the hand of the other. He spoke but with a weakened voice. "You are seeing your grandfather not the way he would like."

"But you will be better soon, BaBa," the twins stumbled over each other to say.

"Perhaps. The shaman gives me strong medicines, his most powerful. You know that the shaman has special powers. Many illnesses he has cured."[63]

Laughing Rain said, "I know they will help you."

"Surely," he cautioned them, "you know that even medicines do not always help. There comes a time when a powerful spirit takes over an aging body."

"BaBa," the twins let out as one, "we do not like to hear you speak like that."

"I can tell you," their grandfather went on with a faint chuckle. "The shaman is good at driving out bad spirits. Yet, in the end the spirit of many winters wins out, and we pass on to another world. It is a world where our ancestors walk together for all time. It is called Strawberry Heaven for there are always berries to pick. This place does not have the strong colors, smells, and tastes of our world here, but there is nothing to fear. No one who has led a brave and honest life on earth needs to fret about dying. You must believe that dying is not ending. It is a changing."[64]

The twins tried to take in these overpowering thoughts. A long silence was finally broken by one who said, "But you will be strong as before, BaBa," Awakens Corn insisted.

"You are wise, Baba," added her sister. "We need you for clear thoughts."

"Perhaps. Whatever the days bring, you need not fuss over me. It is truc, my years have seen great changes. But I fear they have not all been for the better. There is too much war. The white people have come in their great ships with their iron things and arrows of spitting fire. They want us to give up the teaching of our ancestors. Yes, we are safe from them here, but I fear that your lifetime will find them breathing down on you."

This talk was too somber for the twins. They tried to change the mood. "We have brought you something." Awakens Corn handed him the clay house. "Laughing Rain showed me how to make it."

Guiding Star picked it up. "A long bowl! And perfect in every way! And so big for a taste of porridge."

"It is a longhouse bowl," said Laughing Rain.

"A longhouse bowl, is it? Open at the top. Ha!"

Awakens Corn explained, "We made it for your tiny, carved animals. They need a place to live."

"Ah, yes." His shaky hands slowly turned it around and around. The still-sparkling eyes examined every detail. "I will always keep your longhouse bowl close to my heart. And what is here along the side? Pine trees, needles, and leaves. And what is this, a pathway through the trees? Here at the end is a star, a beautiful star with seven points."

"It is meant to be your name, grandfather."

"Yes, I can tell. Good food in a handsome longhouse for my little animals! I will use it with you on my mind." With, as always, his easy smile, he added, "I am feeling a bit tired. You may go now."

The twins walked slowly to their longhouse. They reflected in disbelief on the unhappy scene that they had just left.

"What do you think?" Laughing Rain asked.

Her sister replied, "I cannot bear to see BaBa in this way."

"I, too, feel sad. We must make him better."

"Mother will know what we can do."

Morning Blossom heard the story. "For a long time, I have seen him change. Day by day, his voice seemed weaker, his steps not as sure. Do you remember when he made the canoe with Tail Feather? Tail Feather did all the heavy work. That was not like the grandfather that you have always known. Since then, I knew that something was wrong."

Morning Blossom saw the anxiety on the faces of her daughters. "For you, your grandfather has been strong and always cheerful. Now," she admitted, "we have a different BaBa. He will need our help."

"We will do our best, Mother."

"Yes. I know you will."

After a long and worry-filled day the twins returned to their grandfather. With them came their mother carrying their little sister. What they all saw was an even more enfeebled old man. His cheeks were pinched, his breathing uneasy. The food that they had brought in the morning lay untouched by his side.

Guiding Star forced himself to speak, but his once singing voice was barely heard. "Come a bit closer. There is no need for so many frowns. I am happy for many things."

The sick man's bed lay in a slender sunbeam that slanted through the smoke hole. "I hear the birds and thank the Creator for their songs. I smell the pine needles and rejoice for the Creator's care for fragrance. I see the flowers and am grateful that the Creator loves color. The animals of the forest and of the water and the air show the Creator's joy of life. And just as day turns into night, so each life will enter a time of darkness. I am thankful that the Creator has made a pathway of stars into the Sky World."[65]

Guiding Star turned his eyes toward Morning Blossom. "Daughter. Stand by me for a moment. I have watched you grow from a small child, and then have your own children." One hand bent around the elbow of Morning Blossom. There was a breathless manner in his words, but he continued. "Never has a moment passed that I have not been thankful for the care you have given your family and your clan."

"I am grateful, Father, that I have a family and a clan to care for. I only wish that my husband..."

"Yes," interrupted Guiding Star. "Yes, I understand. You worry about our travelers. But you must overcome your fear. Whatever happens, I am certain Kicking Elk, and Tail Feather too, will face their fate bravely and with honor to you and your children." Morning Blossom tried to cover the tear that had already trickled down to a corner of her mouth.

"To you, my daughter," Guiding Star found the strength to say, "I pass on what your mother's hands made before the pain took away her art." The old man reached behind him and pulled forth a folded doeskin. Spread out, it was a cape, brightened with beadwork along its edges. On it was a painting of a single flower of many yellow petals around a purple center. He handed the cape to Morning Blossom. "It has been at my side for many winters."

Morning Blossom let the long cape drape over her free arm. She held it tenderly, close to her body.

The old man paused for a long time, as if to gather his strength. "And now, my look-the-same granddaughters, I have something to say to you."

Guiding Star brought the twins to his side. "You are nearly women, now. On your shoulders will be borne a heavy burden for the good of all. First, you must renew the good feeling between yourselves." A pointing finger stretched upward to full arm's length. "A longhouse cannot stand if the poles that hold the roof do not agree."

Saying only these words seemed to sap his strength further, but he insisted on going on, "I know you have both suffered from some inside wound that no one else understands. You must learn to see each other's way. Only then will you become useful and happy women in whatever the future brings."

"We listen to you, grandfather, and give thanks for your good thoughts," Laughing Rain said.

Awakens Corn added, taking her sister's hand, "And we promise to be good sisters to Tail Feather and Sky Flower."

"Your words please me. For each of you, I have made something of sweet-smelling hickory." Guided Star held out two spoons. On the handle of one was carved the figure of an owl, on the other that of a loon.

The twins beamed in delight. "They are too beautiful to use, BaBa," said one.

"No, they are made to use."

"And who should get which spoon?" asked the other.

"That, you must decide between yourselves."

"And you, little one." Guiding Star turned his head toward Sky Flower who peered out from her mother's arms. "You are the youngest among all of us." He placed his little finger into the palm of the baby's hand, and the hand responded with a strong grip. "My footprints along the path of life are fading as I begin to cross over to the Spirit World; your footprints are yet to start. May you grow in the good graces of your mother and your big sisters on a long and happy journey."

The baby's eyes stayed fixed on her grandfather's slightest movements.

"Here, little one, is something that you may grow up with." With these words, Guiding Star reached to a shelf above his head and brought out a doll. It was a blank faced doll made from a cornhusk. A thin hide dressed the doll in a doeskin smock. The smock was plain aside from frills at the hem. A string of tiny shell beads formed a necklace. The feet were clad in painted moccasins.[66]

The gaze of Sky Flower shifted to the doll. All were certain that a little smile came upon the baby's face.

With these efforts, the strength of Guiding Star seemed to ebb further.

Laughing Rain thought it a good time to announce, "We have good news for you, BaBa." She hoped to hide her sadness with a cheerful sound.

"And what is your good news?"

"It is about KyKoo."

"KyKoo? Good news about KyKoo?"

"Yes. KyKoo had pups. Twin pups."

"Hah!" A smile came over the face of their grandfather. "So, that is why she behaved as she did. Even in my old age, I am still learning." He rose a little on his elbows to ask, "And what will you do with two wolf cubs?"

"We will try to keep them," answered Awakens Corn.

"Good," came a breathy reply.

"The cubs will be like our children," Awakens Corn assured her grandfather.

Her sister added, "We will spoil them with attention."

"I know you will," their grandfather answered in a thinning voice.

That is enough talking for now, Father," Morning Blossom said softly. "You must rest. We will go now. What can we bring you in the morning?"

"I need little. I am content to have walked a long trail with the many joys that you have brought me. At night, I watch the stars pass over this smoke hole. They will be my new home in the sky world."

Away from the longhouse, the twins could not wait to ask, "Why does BaBa talk this way, Mother? Will he get better?" They searched for some comfort in her answer.

"I know not. I worry, though. But sometimes with sickness, we can only wait and hope for a good outcome. The shaman will do all he can. Yet, we know that the oldest people resist remedies for healing the most."

"We can help," Laughing Rain said with an eager voice.

"Then, go find some strawberry leaves. I will boil them into a tea. Your grandmother told me that it was BaBa's favorite tonic. I will add a little honey, just as she always did."

On the edge of the garden where strawberries grew, Laughing Rain asked her sister, "Do you like the doll?"

"Of course. It is a beautiful doll. I know that Sky Flower will keep it close to her for her whole life. Think of the fun she will have decorating it as she grows older." Awakens Corn teased, "If she is like you, her doll will become fancy."

"Do you think so? What face did you imagine the doll has?"

"Oh, I picture a baby's face, one with which Sky Flower would feel kinship."

"I thought the same. In time, the face will grow older in our minds, just as hers will."

"Yes," replied Awakens Corn. "When Sky Flower has grown, it will show the hard lines of endless work with no hope of traveling far away."

"Awakens Corn! Stop! Stop now!" The mouth of Laughing Rain tightened. "I will not listen to that talk."

"Well, that is how I imagine the face will change. I wish BaBa had painted a face. That way, the doll would look the same for all time. She would never show her aging. She would be forever young."

"But you know why dolls have no faces. It is in all the legends."

"No, I cannot remember why. Do you?"

"I think so. Part of it, anyway. Here is what I remember. Once the Creator made a doll-child with a beautiful face. He sent her to earth to teach children the ways of a happy life. Every time the doll-child passed by a puddle or still pond, she stopped to admire her good looks. She became so caught up with her perfect looks that she soon forgot the lessons that she was meant to teach the children. After several warnings, the Creator took her face away. Dolls are always faceless now. That is our tradition. It shows that what is important is how we are inside, not how beautiful we are outside."

"I know you are right, Laughing Rain. It is a good story," Awakens Corn replied. "But you know how I make trouble. It is my way."

"Yes," Laughing Rain chuckled. "We cannot change that."

The sisters talked late into the night. They talked about how they would help their grandfather get better; of how they would take care of the cubs; of who would get the owl spoon and of who would get the loon spoon.

As dawn broke, the twins were again at the longhouse of Guiding Star. At first, they were pleased to peek in and see that his arms were not shaking. But it was an unnatural stillness. On a closer look, his eyes stared empty, not following their movement. The once nimble hands that lay across his chest were cold. The twins did not need words to tell each other that their grandfather no longer belonged to the same world.

Hearing the news, Morning Blossom turned her head away from her daughters. There followed a long, quiet moment. When she turned back to them, her eyes were tearful, but her face was peaceful and her voice steady. "During the night, his spirit traveled on the light from Grandmother Moon into the star world. His body is at total peace now as his spirit and soul go forward into the After Life beyond the Great Star Belt." She turned away to wipe a long-running tear with the back of her hand.

No one spoke for a long time. Finally, Morning Blossom shared one of her most enduring thoughts, "Your grandfather always seemed to know the right thing to do, the right thing to say. My smallest problem as a child was his problem, and he always helped me to find the answer. He helped you in the same way."

"We know, Mother."

"The Clan Mother gave him his name long ago. The name meant that he always helped everyone find the right path. We must go to him now."

Morning Blossom led a small, silent procession toward the longhouse of Guiding Star. She stood for a moment before the body of her father, then reached forward. With a light touch, she closed the eyes that would never look out again. She lowered her head in prayer without words, then stepped back. Meadow Bird Singing came forward and gave her silent prayer.

Laughing Rain and Awakens Corn in turn stood beside the body of their grandfather. There, they sobbed until the arms of their mother closed around them, slowly drawing them away.

"Come," Morning Blossom said quietly. "A time has come when you must be brave. Follow me."

The twins gathered their strength. Their mother led them back to their longhouse. There, Morning Blossom reached high overhead to a hanging basket. She took from it a long belt of wampum. The twins gasped on sight of the stunning belt, an intricate pattern of purple running through a brilliant field of white.

Turning to Laughing Rain, Morning Blossom asked, "Has Awakens Corn told you about Wolf-With-Night-Eyes, my first husband?"

Laughing Rain nodded as if to say, "Yes."

"I made this string of shells in his memory. Making it helped me overcome my grief at his loss." The girls fidgeted as their mother explained. "I show you at this time so that you will see how putting the mind to work on a remembrance helps ease the sorrow of a great loss."

"What can we do?" the twins asked.

"You can help me wash and prepare his body for its final rest within Mother Earth. We will sing songs of the spirit as we work together. When we have finished, you may wish to paint the elk hide that will cover him for all time."[67]

It was afternoon before they returned to the bedside. They came with baskets of fragrant lotions and oils that were needed to prepare the body for burial. Their faces were coated in white ash, as was the custom for those in the family of the deceased. Even

Sky Flower shared this sign of respect. She looked out from her cradleboard with a smudge of ashes on her forehead and cheeks.

The look-the-same girls saw the face of their grandfather. The face that wasted so in illness was now peaceful. Even in death, there was a trace of his easy smile. The twins glanced at their mother and sensed the pride in her face.

First, Meadow Bird Singing and Morning Blossom brushed the body with tufts of long grass. They washed the body with the oils from yarrow and mint. His hands and feet, arms and legs were rubbed lightly with powdered hazelnut and sunflower seeds mixed in bear grease. Meadow Bird Singing carefully placed a headband trimmed in seashell beads around his head. In it, she tucked the stem of an eagle feather that her father had earned as a young man. Beneath his head, Morning Blossom laid leaves of tobacco to help shape his dreams in the afterworld. Last, the body was wrapped from head to foot with deerskins. Over these went mats of long cattails. On top, they stretched out the elk hide that had hung above his bed.

The elk hide had been there a long, long time. In fact, the sisters could not remember a time when it was not there! From time to time, a new image appeared on it. Guiding Star painted them to stand for events, both good and bad, that were important in his life. On it, there were two girls holding hands: one much bigger than the other. There was a man falling, a canoe under construction, a woman with deformed hands, a lake with a snow-topped mountain behind. No one knew or ever thought to ask what the human figure with bear-like features stood for.

By nightfall, the shaman laid the body of Guiding Star atop a mound that held the earthly remains of others now passed on. The body lay on a great slab of elm bark surrounded by logs of pine. Next to the body were the tools that had now become sacred: a medicine pouch, snowshoes, duck decoys, and a flint knife. There, too, was a long bowl decorated with the leaves of corn; many small wood-carved animals looked out over the rim.

For three days and three nights, as was the custom, someone of the family and others who requested the honor sat by the body. It was a time that a watchful eye had to guard against any mischief that evil-minded spirits might cause. The spirit of the deceased would leave the body and find its way into the sky. Then, the body would be laid to rest in burial.

Laughing Rain and Awakens Corn chose to be night-watchers. Sitting together through the long night, they followed the stars on their slow journey across the sky. The twins spoke softly and reverently about their grandfather and about their memories of growing up in his shadow. They sang the songs that they remembered from childhood. Some were songs that their grandfather had taught them. Sometimes one of them slept but there was always one wide-awake set of eyes.

Still, the twins wanted to do more. At last, Awakens Corn came up with a reminder. "Remember? Mother said we could paint on BaBa's elk hide. There is still room for more on the bottom."

"And around the edges," added Laughing Rain, her voice raised in excitement. She and her sister could hardly wait for the light of morning. There then followed a flurry of activity to bring together some pigments and brushes. They made yellow from goldenrod, blue from blueberries, and green from mixing them. Red came from dried raspberries and powder of cinnabar and black from blackberries. Brushes were the tufted ends of sassafras twigs.

When the girls finally arrived at the gravesite with all their things for painting, Laughing Rain asked of her sister, "What are you going to paint?"

"I haven't thought of anything worthy enough. What are you going to paint?"

"I am having the same trouble. Can we paint something together?"

"Hah! That would be good. What are you thinking of?"

"Well, what if we paint everything in double?" Laughing Rain explained. "That way, BaBa will better think of us in the After-life."

"Perfect. You start."

Laughing Rain carefully painted a big circle in yellow that took up the lower part of the hide. Awakens Corn then made an overlapping blue circle that was just as big.

"Now what?" one asked.

The answer, "You make a tree on that side, I will make one on this side."

"Good. Pine trees will be fine. BaBa was fond of their feathery look and their pleasing scent."

The trees done, the girls painted two streams that came from behind and joined in front. A deer drank from each of the streams. The sky was that of twilight, and the two earliest stars of the night were out. In front of the scene were two box turtles facing each other. The details so painstakingly put into the paintings even showed the thirteen panels on the top shell of each turtle.[68]

After three days and nights of constant watching over the body, a ring of people stood, at nightfall, around the burial mound. There were tears and sniffles.

Chief Red Sun appeared, wearing his antler headdress and his long robe of turkey feathers. He stood by the small fire that blazed nearby. Chief Red Sun spoke with a voice even more solemn than was his custom. "Now all listen to what needs to be said. Now, we stand before a man, the fiber of oak. Yet, a man able to bend for the good of all, the way a birch bends in the wind. Now we gather to honor a life well lived. The Creator has made it so that death comes to all, that no one will live forever. Now, we gather at the wood's edge to mingle our tears. Now, we lay the deceased on the mound of earth where those who have passed on before have begun their final journey to the sky world."

Chief Red Sun paused, then turned toward the family of Guiding Star, saying, "This we know. It is a belief told by our parents who learned it from their parents and they from their parents—the body of the dead has thoughts and knows what is happening around it. This saying is true. Then, the spirit will leave the body and rise toward the little stars." The reflection from the fire sparkled on tears as they rolled down the cheeks of those standing around. "His spirit will join those of his ancestors; it will wander for all time in harmony among them. One day, we will all return to our home among the stars. Today, we can journey with the dead only as far as the grave. Now, we circle around this mortal body."

The silent mourners followed Chief Red Sun as he slowly walked around the burial mound. As they moved around the grave, they let fall gently petals of ox-eye, wild geranium, and lobelia on the stilled body. All minds were on the joy that Guiding Star had brought them in his long and honorable life.

"As we walk about you," Chief Red Sun spoke directly to Guiding Star, "we cover your earthly remains with the flowers that arise from the earth. Your soul is now free to begin its journey to the Spirit World. Now, we sprinkle tobacco leaves into the fire. The sparks will guide your soul along the pathway of stars. The smoke rising carries our prayers to the Creator."

After three times walking around and three times sprinkling tobacco leaves, Chief Red Sun came toward the end of his speech, "Now, we look on this lifeless man one last time. Now, I pull the hide to cover him forever. He will lie in this place, protected from heavy wind, rainstorm, and heaping snow. Now, we say and do."

With these words, Chief Red Sun spread his arms wide and lifted his head up toward the sky. His silhouette stood bold against the full moon. "Oh, Great One who made us, let the soul of this man roam among the star people for all time to come."

The Chief turned to all to say, "When ten days have gone by, we must lay our grief aside. It will be a time for a great feast in honor of the dead. By then, the soul of Guiding Star will return from the sky world to partake of the feast with us. This, it may do in dreams and visions." With these words, he left the mourners with their own thoughts.

There followed songs sung softly over the steady beat of water drums and rattles. Before the last song was sung, full darkness bathed the singers. A low-lying, round moon graced the burial mound with its rich glow.

One by one, the mourners left the gravesite. The last ones to leave were the two girls. They turned to look at the outline of their grandfather's body against the moonlight.

With both hands Laughing Rain grasped one hand of her sister saying, "Awakens Corn, I ask you to make a promise to me."

"Oh, and what is that?" her voice revealing more than a little curiosity.

"I want you to promise that we will keep the memory of BaBa bright in our minds for as long as we live."

"Yes, yes. That I promise."

CHAPTER 20

Tail Feather

IT WAS THE DAY before the Feast for the Dead. Chief Red Sun appeared at the compartment of Morning Blossom and her girls. He wore no headdress, no finery and no other symbol of his position. His voice, however, was stately. "Today, it is nine days since the death of your father and your grandfather. By now, his Soul has followed the pathway to the stars. Tomorrow his spirit will return to share the bounty of our garden, the fruits of the trees, and the meat from the forest. He will hear our happy songs and see our dance. We will honor his life with our messages. After that, our tears will dry and the minds of those who mourn for him will be rested for all time."

Everyone in the village worked feverishly to prepare for the event. There was sweetened corn, puddings of strawberries, and venison. The festival would last all day. There was much to do.

As the work of preparation for the festival went on into the afternoon, a full-voiced chorus of shouts came from outside the wall of wooden stakes. The travelers were returning from their long journey to Water-With-No-End! They entered the village one by one: Two-Bears-Dancing, Round-Wind-Singing, Painted Otter, Turtle Voice, Casts-A-Long-Shadow and, last to appear, Tail Feather.

Everyone looked for Talks-Like-Thunder and Kicking Elk. Anxiety melted away with news that they would arrive within a few days. The travelers explained that an injured leg of Talks-Like-Thunder held him back. Kicking Elk had stayed to help him along the way.

There were great whoops, hugs, and tears of joy. Each family greeting was a high-spirited and noisy affair.

Laughing Rain and Awakens Corn could not hold back their laughing shrieks on seeing their brother again. Tail Feather stood straight and proud, just inside the entryway, smiling and altogether pleased with his returning. He looked leaner, taller, browner.

Tail Feather, through the welcoming, was puzzled that his BaBa and KyKoo were not among the greeters. "Your grandfather will not be with us," said his mother. "He has gone to the Sky World."

With these words, Tail Feather steadied himself, then turned away. His sisters tried to comfort him. "We will go with you to his gravesite," they said.

"No, I must go myself. I will stay there through the night." There followed a long wait before Tail Feather said, "And KyKoo?"

His sisters answered, "You must see for yourself."

"Where is she?"

"In her favorite place."

Tail Feather went straight to the thick pile of brush that KyKoo had long made her home. He was startled to hear his wolf companion growl and snarl as he came close. "Have you have forgotten me, KyKoo? How could you? You were on my mind with every stroke of my paddle, with every step along the way." The growls and snarls got worse as Tail Feather came closer.

Then, Tail Feather's disappointment turned into amazement. He heard some high-pitched squeals coming from deep inside the brush. He soon realized what made the sounds. In the fading light, he could see nothing inside. "Good for you, KyKoo. I will come back in the morning."

At his longhouse, Tail Feather had much to show and much to tell. First, he handed his sisters his gift of a wooden comb. They were delighted to see the figures of themselves that their brother had carved into the handle.

"Mother, your gift will come when Father returns." Morning Blossom's smile barely hid her mask of worry.

Tail Feather carefully turned over his backpack basket. Out spilled many pieces of seashells, most white but some purple and a few pink ones. Some were disk-shaped with holes drilled in their centers. Others were short hollow tubes. Everyone knew that these would become belts and strings for wampum.

"We want to hear about your travels," his sisters pleaded.

Well into the night, the mother and the twin sisters heard about the journey of Tail Feather.[69] He spoke of a river that cannot make up its mind which way to flow. They heard about a fishing village where men pick fish off trees and where their nets held a strange looking fish that was bigger than a man. Tail Feather told about how a terrible storm saved all the travelers from certain capture by a war canoe. He told about trading people who dressed like birds and who had too much to eat. The travel stories seemed to become more and more far-fetched as they went on. But the listeners with their raised eyebrows were hardly prepared for what they were about to hear.

"At Water-With-No-End, I saw something that came in a dream before my journey began. A fish as big as a mountain, well, perhaps a big hill, leaped out of the deep water. The fish had a tiny eye that looked straight at me. I think it was trying to tell me something."

There were, of course, some skeptical looks coming out of this story. "Do you suppose," asked his mother, "that your mountain fish was another dream?"

"No. It was real. Of that, I am sure."

Even this story was not enough to satisfy the appetite of those who had stayed at home. "What else did you see?"

"One morning, we saw a fawn that had just been born. Wolves had chased its mother and almost had her in their grip. She escaped to a little island. Yes, I remember now seeing a great bearded face of stone that looked out of a mountain. Its staring eyes followed us for a long way down river. We saw a game played by a hundred people on each side. Each player carried a stick with a net on one end. With it, he tried to get a small ball into the home of the other players. There was much banging and butting. Talks-Like-Thunder called it the 'Little Brother of War.'"

"What is the strangest happening on your journey?"

"Well, if you cannot believe my story about the Mountain Fish, you will not believe my strangest story."

"Oh yes, we will. We believe it all," were words that came from all voices at once.

"One morning, on the widest part of the River-That-Flows-Two-Ways, a great canoe floated by, carried along on the wind by huge wings. On it were many hairy-faced men wearing strange clothing."

The story was sounding familiar to the twin sisters, remembering about the boyhood story told by Chief Red Sun. Laughing Rain asked, "Did they have red hair?"

Tail Feather thought her question a bit odd. "No, but one of them, who could not have been any older than I was, had long yellow hair, hair as yellow as goldenrod. There was something else about this boy. He held a paddle that burst with lightning and roared like thunder."

By now, the listeners found themselves straining harder and harder to believe the stories from the river. Tail Feather was not put off by the glances of doubt. "Can you imagine what happened next?"

His question was met with silence, but he had to finish the story.

"I looked up at the boy who stood high up on the winged canoe and saw him throw his blue headdress at me."

Some blank faces stared at him. He reached over to his backpack and from the bottom pulled out something blue. This, he placed on his head. Looks of doubt turned into looks of amusement.

The sisters laughed at the absurd headdress, but they did admire its dazzling shade of blue. Even more than the color, its soft feeling impressed them as their brother allowed them to roll it between their fingers and to rub it across their cheeks. Each in turn tried the hat on and posed, making comical faces. Tail Feather's serious expression put a fast end to their antics, however, as his sisters came to realize that the headdress was a treasured keepsake of the journey. "Now, you must tell no one about this headdress. No one. Will you agree?" Both agreed, but with some wonderment.

"Were you ever frightened, Tail Feather?"

"No."

"Not even once?"

"Well, maybe once. It was when a bear chased me. Then twice, when we walked down a roaring cascade at night under the noses of Fire Dancers. If you like, I will tell you these stories someday."

"How many days were you away?" asked Laughing Rain.

"I cannot say."

"Then guess."

"One hundred days?"

"How many days do you guess, Awakens Corn?"

"Eighty days," shot out her reply.

"Well, suppose we find out." With this strange comment, Laughing Rain dashed back to her longhouse. She returned in a moment with a pot that she had designed. This, she carefully tipped over. Out tumbled a heap of pebbles and a few kernels of corn. Awakens Corn and Tail Feather gave each other a baffled look. "Now, count the pebbles."

And count they did. In all, there were ninety-three pebbles.

"Now, what do we do with ninety-three pebbles?" asked the brother.

"They stand for every day that you were away. Every night when I went to bed, I dropped one pebble into the pot."

Awakens Corn laughed, "Hah! So that is the mystery 'plunk' that I heard every night before sleeping."

"Yes. I had to make a new pot, one big enough to hold them all."

What was most on the mind of Tail Feather, however, was not the telling of stories. He spent much of each day sitting by the brush pile den of KyKoo. In time, the wolf's growling lessened. Tail Feather became bolder and every day approached a little closer and stayed a little longer. Then one day, the twins found him there, holding two squirming wolf cubs. KyKoo stood beside him. In their brother's wide grin, they saw the perfect image of their grandfather.

Autumn meant the tedious work of pounding maize and all the other preparations for winter. But the cool days passed happily for the twins. Their brother had returned with many fantastic stories. Their plump and bright-eyed little sister was already standing, even taking a few steps with help.

One day, Laughing Rain stood pounding kernels of corn into a mash in a hollowed-out tree stump. Nearby, Awakens Corn knelt, mindlessly scraping the grease off a deerskin with a stone knife. Then flashed a sudden thought. “Laughing Rain,” she said.

“Yes?”

“Did you count how many days I was away?”

“I did. Those were the kernels of corn mixed in with the pebbles.”

“In your pot?”

“Yes.”

“I saw some kernels but thought nothing more about them.”

“There was one kernel for every day, from the day you left me until the day you came back.”

“How many were there?”

“You must first tell me.”

“Hmmm. Twenty?”

“No. Thirteen. But for me, it seemed as if it were three hundred.”

“For me, too.”

There followed a gap from talking but not for long.

“Awakens Corn. I want to ask you something.”

“You do? Then? Then ask.”

“Do you remember the pond you told me about?” Laughing Rain asked her sister.

“The pond?”

“Yes, the pond where you saw the spider catch the fly in its web.”

“Oh, yes,” answered Awakens Corn, a little puzzled.

“Is that the same pond where you saw your face so clearly in the water?”

“Of course. Why do you ask?”

“Is it far away?”

“It is on the other side of Cloud-Splitter.”

"Do you think that you could find it again?"

"I think so. Yes, I think I can," Awakens Corn replied, becoming ever more curious. "The pond was the first place that I stopped to rest. Why do you ask?"

"Because I want you to take me there."

PART II

Notes About the Story

List of Notes in Book 2, *Laughing Rain and Awakens Corn*

Chapter	Note	Title
1	1	Henderson Lake
	2	Hudson River
	3	The Iroquois
	4	Mount Marcy
	5	Water-With-No-End
	6	Cattails
	7	Coyote
	8	Domesticated Wolf
	9	Roles of Gender
	10	Village
2	11	The Three Sisters
	12	Chief
	13	Tobacco Leaves
	14	Story of Creation
3	15	Tools
	16	Twins
	17	Names
4	18	Loon
	19	Porcupine
	20	Peepers
	21	Woodland Scents
	22	Black Bear
	23	Elk
5	24	Rainbow
6	25	Midden
	26	Wolf
8	27	Missionaries
	28	Religions
	29	Baptism
10	30	Maize

Chapter	Note	Title
12	31	Basketmaking
	32	Clay Pot
13	33	Water Strider
	34	Mirror
	35	Spider Web
	36	Hunting
	37	Beaver / Dam Building
	38	Jewelweed
	39	Bear Cubs
	40	Big Chill
	41	Rattlesnake
	42	Lost in the Woods
	43	Blackberries
14	44	Council House
	45	Dislocated Shoulder
15	46	Marriage
	47	String Beads / Wampum
16	48	Lenapes
17	49	Crooked Tongues
	50	Saint Lawrence River
	51	Hiawatha
	52	Onondagas
	53	Mohawk River
	54	Oneidas
	55	The Iroquois Great League of Peace and Power
	56	Mi'kmaq
	57	Timeline
	58	Canoe
	59	Quebec
18	60	Sky Hunt
	61	Wolf Pup
19	62	Sparkling Stones
	63	Healing Arts
	64	Concept of Death
	65	Milky Way
	66	Cornhusk Doll
	67	Funeral Rites
	68	Turtle Shell Moon Clock

The Notes

CHAPTER 1: THE SECRET

1-1 Henderson Lake

Our story begins at lakeside in the heartland of present-day Adirondack State Park in New York, the largest wilderness forest preserve in the United States. Here, Henderson Lake lies at the foot of surrounding mountains. A small dam at the site, built to support local iron mining, holds back a great volume of water. How large the lake was at the time of this story—perhaps it was little more than a stream then—we will never know.

Here in 1826, a "strapping young Indian," Lewis Elijah, showed David Henderson and his fellow prospectors a rich vein of iron ore at the surface, not the lode of silver first hoped for. In this way began an industry of strip-mining that lasted for more than a century. The drills, carts, and furnaces are quiet now; left remaining are massive, flooded holes in the earth and mountains of gravel debris. The site is slowly regaining its pristine beauty.

1-2 Hudson River

Water spilling over the dam at the southern tip of Henderson Lake forms a narrow stream. Here begins the Hudson River. Gathering water along the way, the river courses beyond New York City where, after 306 miles, it empties into the Atlantic Ocean, a place referred to in this story as "Water-With-No-End." The Hudson River is certainly not one of the longest rivers in the world, but it has more distinct geological features (six, in fact) than any other river. For any impact in history-making, it is secondary to none.

1-3 The Iroquois

The native Americans of the story belong to the Mohawk nation. The Mohawks and other nations speaking a similar language are known as the Iroquois. Their homelands were along the Mohawk River, the Susquehanna River, and the Saint Lawrence River, which now separates Canada and the northeastern states of the United States.

Villages in Iroquoia were mostly spread along the Mohawk River. They were not right on the riverbanks but rather a bit farther back—on hilltops where they were better defended. The village in this story, however, sits near a lake among the Adirondack High Peaks. Countless brooks and streams bring rainwater and snowmelt from the mountainsides to feed the nearby lake.

Our knowledge of life in Iroquoia before the Contact Period is sketchy. Yet, archaeological evidence is plentiful as is the scholarship that makes its interpretation meaningful. Furthermore, descendants of the Iroquois nation treasure their heritage and are making efforts to preserve their memories, traditions, and languages.

1-4 Mount Marcy

Known as the highest point in the State of New York, Mt. Marcy is just a bit over one mile above sea level. It lies within the cluster of the forty-six peaks of the Adirondack Mountains. Native Americans called Mt. Marcy *Tahawus* (meaning "Splits-the-Clouds"). The name was changed in 1837 by the state legislators to honor the then Governor William Learned Marcy. Today, Tahawus is a 'town' with abandoned iron mines and a huge smelting kiln along with a few dilapidated houses. Locals, by the way, now pronounce it "Ta-HAWS."

On the southern shoulder of Mount Marcy is "Lake Tear of the Clouds." The lake is said to be the origin of the Hudson River. Of course, the river originates from every drop of rain and every melted snowdrop that falls within the enormous watershed area of the mountain range.

1-5 Water-With-No-End

As the ocean waters rise and fall in a cycle of 12½ hours, the flow into rivers changes accordingly. The Hudson River drops about one mile from its origin in the Adirondack Mountains to the city of Troy, about 150 miles to the south. From then on, it courses over an almost flat riverbed for another 150 miles until it opens into the ocean in New York Bay.

It is in this lower part that the water flows upriver during the high tide and downriver during low tide, defining it as an "estuary." Exactly where the change from fresh water outflow to brackish water back-and-forth flow depends upon the amount of rain and snow melt coming from the source and the many tributaries along the way.

To early people accustomed to the streams, rivers, ponds, and lakes of forest living, the sight of open water in New York Bay must have been awesome. Ocean-travelers from Europe, on the other hand, saw the bay in a different way. The Dutch explorers and traders eyed it as partially enclosed and, therefore, a haven for ships in severe weather.

Evidence is plentiful that native people in the Adirondacks traveled long distances to trade. Their trading with the people of future New York City on Manhattan Island occurred long before the Europeans came to trade. Book One of The River Quintet—*Tail Feather: Adventures of a Mohawk Paddler on the River-That-Flows-Two-Ways*—is about such a fictional trading mission. The story, taking place in the year 1613, extends from the beginning of the Hudson River to Manhattan Island and beyond. What was traded? Copper and flint for beads made from seashells.

1-6 Cattails

The slender reeds that stand tall in wetlands were very useful to the native people of long ago. Cattails are aptly named for the brown thickened part of the stem near the top. Here, within the "tail" are densely packed seeds.

When ripened in the late spring, the seeds form puffballs, little "parachutes" that float to places for new growth. For the woodland Indians, a wad of puffballs provided an excellent insulator for moccasins and cradleboards. The long, narrow leaves of the cattails could be made into sturdy mats, baskets, and thatch for longhouse roofs. The oozing mucus-like substance from a cut stem was used as a balm to soothe cuts and burns. The densely-packed seeds could be eaten, after boiling, like corn-on-the-cob. The deep-reaching roots, pounded into flour, provided a high starch meal. It was an important source of Indian food.

1-7 Coyote

Somehow, the coyote, to native people across the Americas, developed a reputation as a buffoon or trickster. A person with similar traits was known as a coyote. Why? Perhaps it was due to the animal's habits: of staying out of sight in the bush and foraging for food at night or maybe its stealthy way of sneaking up on prey, then suddenly pouncing on—say—a hapless rabbit. Perhaps the impression came from its crafty and secretive way of finding food at the edge of a human settlement. Possibly to some, its pointed and slender features with a bushy tail, compared with the more robust wolf, suggested a devious personality. But probably the most important source of its clownish image is the coyote's wide repertoire of calls: from a high-pitch bark, wobble, flat howl, series of "yip-yip-yips," quivering cry, and screaming "laugh." The latter is especially eerie when the whole pack forms a chorus late at night and it is enough to freak out most any camper.

A smaller cousin of the wolf and larger cousin of the fox, the coyote lives mostly on rabbits and squirrels caught by expert stalking. A coyote diet also includes birds, frogs, snakes and, when available, berries. Indeed, it is truly resourceful (as many suburbanites discover) and deserves a more respectful reputation.

1-8 Domesticated Wolf

Wolves are highly social animals within a pack. When orphaned and nurtured away from its natural family, a wolf will form a strong bond with its caregiver, shown by many examples of wolves as pets. The wolf so raised becomes highly protective of its keeper, with a touch of jealousy. Yet, the 'wildness' of a wolf cannot be 'bred out' for several generations of domesticated parents and grandparents, after which the wolf becomes a dog.

1-9 Roles of Gender

There was a clear delineation of responsibilities between men and women in the realm of the Iroquois. These roles were accepted and generally inviolate. Men did the hunting and fishing and warring. These activities required great energy and heroic endurance, often in harsh weather and for long periods. They prepared since childhood to endure these hardships. The game of lacrosse (called by the Iroquois the "Little Brother of War") demanded a spirit of competition along with some bruises and hard knocks.

Constructing the longhouses and the palisades around them fell to the men. They peeled the bark off elm trees in huge strips and placed saplings solidly in the ground to frame the longhouse.

Men made the spear points, nets, canoes, and weapons. They were the only ones who attended the tribal councils. Men performed by themselves in dance, prayer, and rituals at the many ceremonies. They also prepared new planting fields by girding trees and burning the underbrush. They traveled long distances to trade or to carry out raids.

Women bore the everyday tasks: preparing meals, keeping up the cookfire, making and mending clothing and tending the gardens. They dressed quarry brought home by the men, scraped and tanned the hides, and stitched from them garments and moccasins.

Women had the additional responsibility of electing a chief and taking away his symbolic antlers (or "dehorning" him), should he prove disappointing in carrying out his duties. In this way, women had much control over the general policymaking of the clan.

In addition, it was the women who bore and raised children. Families, typically in the Iroquois village, were small. After all, a mother had enough to do without caring for babies and toddlers born too close together.

Children, too, helped with the chores in the village, the longhouses, and the fields. Girls learned early the art of making ceramic pots from clay and meal from corn. Boys were exposed to the rigors of the hunt. The youngest ran around naked in what foreign observers called an unruly manner, compared to their strictly disciplined own "seen but not heard" children.

1-10 Village

To surround their village, native people constructed a thick barricade of tall, standing stakes and stuffed brush in between. This defensive wall became known by the French word "palisade." It was meant to keep out pesky critters looking for easy food pickings. It gave some protection, or at least some warning, of an attack on a village.

The iconic dwelling of the Iroquois people is well named. The Iroquois call themselves the "Haudenosaunee," meaning "People of the Longhouse." Framed of bent-over saplings and covered with elm bark, the longhouse may have sheltered a dozen families. Each family lived in a separate but open compartment. Adjacent families shared a cookfire and smoke hole.

Platforms stacked along each wall served as beds. Stuffed in every nook and cranny were the necessities and trappings of everyday life: food, clothing, pots, weapons, and firewood. Floors were mat-covered dirt.

Often crowded with more than a hundred live-in people, the longhouse must have been smoky and probably noisy especially during confinement for long periods in the dead of winter. The longhouse was likely well insulated so that at least it was reasonably warm.

CHAPTER 2: TIME OF THE SQUIRREL'S EARS

2-11 The Three Sisters

Their ways of gardening told much of the ingenuity of the early people. Those of the northeastern woodlands planted their most important crops (corn, beans, and squash) together in small "hills." The time of planting was ushered in with a great ceremony around a fire, including dance, singing, and prayer for a good crop, topped off with the sprinkling of tobacco leaves into the flames.

The corn grew tall, providing a pole upon which the vines of beans could climb into the sunlight. The broad leaves of the squash held down weeds while keeping in-ground moisture.

Corn, beans, and squash, known as "The Three Sisters," were the essential foods in the Indian diet. Growing them required the tribe to have a more or less permanent settlement, at least one that would endure for an entire growing season. This requirement had a profound influence on the evolution of the culture from a "hunter and gatherer" society to an agricultural one. Along with growing these vegetables was the skill to cook them in a never-ending variety of ways. We know the three sisters, when cooked together, as succotash. Most important was their knowledge about preserving them for times when other food sources were scarce, such as winter.

2-12 Chief

The chief of a village or clan led official events wearing certain garments as token of his rank. His headdress featured the antlers of deer, his cloak, the iridescence of turkey feathers. He earned his office by dealing with public issues, morality, eloquence, knowledge of ancient traditions, winning personality and, of course, the ability to lead. He gave speeches at ceremonies, sacred or otherwise. Because the chief had no special voting power and did not have the right of veto, his responsibilities were limited to persuading clan members to accept his advice concerning any action. Understandably, the chief had to be a good diplomat to be an effective chief.

Only the women of a village selected its chief, and it was always a man. The position might be maintained if his performance was acceptable. Tenure depended on action, not heredity or privilege of royal birth, completely opposite to the European model of the time. Should the ability of the chief prove disappointing, the women could replace him by removing his antlers (or dehorning).

2-13 Tobacco Leaves

Tobacco meant something different from what it means today. Indians smoked tobacco in long and decorated wooden pipes only at official functions. A pipe was often passed from one to another for a puff. The smoke from the pipe rose to bring messages to the ancestors wandering along the celestial paths in the sky. Upon receiving the messages, the ancestors would, in one way or another, provide guidance to those who made decisions on earth. Thus, smoking a pipe was reserved for occasions when decisions had to be made.

On other occasions, the crumpled leaves of dried tobacco were sprinkled in a fire. There, they burned with a popping sound and with flying sparks. The rising smoke carried their messages to the Great Spirit above. To the Iroquois, tobacco smoke was deeply embodied into the soul. It provided a sacred communication with the spirits.

2-14 Story of Creation

The legend of how Earth was created was heard in the Iroquois longhouses long before recorded history. References to the story reveal many variations, but the general theme remains intact over at least twenty-five generations. A version written in 1644 by the Dutch pastor in *Beverwijck*, Johannes Megapolensis, describes a dispute between the "Mohawk God" and his brother who together created the earth. After constant conflicts, the brother was eventually killed. Some of the versions that we have today are due to the work of 19th century traditionalists, such as Seth Newhouse; in the 1880s he transcribed oral Iroquois stories and histories into English. Along with the many versions of the Creation legend, there are understandably many spelling variations for the names of characters and places. The Iroquoian languages of the Five Nations, and then of the sixth, the Tuscaroras, may have varied greatly, certainly in terms of pronunciation alone.

The basic story is here quickly told. Twin boys were born from daughter of Sky Woman (or, in another version, from Sky Woman herself), who had fallen from the Sky World where the original supernatural people lived. The earth at that time was all water and had no light. Sky Woman came to a soft landing on the back of a turtle. There, animals of the earth realm saw to her proper nurturing.

Fitting in the tradition of an earth where every good thing has an opposing force, so it was with the creators of Earth. These opposites were personified in twin boys, one good-natured and handsome, the other ugly and evil-minded. Their names were "Sapling" (for a young, healthy tree) and "Flint" (a hard, sharp-edged rock). In one version, the mother (or grandmother) named the twins "Teharonhiawako" (Holder of the Heavens) and "Sawiskera" (Mischievous One).

When Sapling created the sun, Flint drove it westward until it disappeared. Sapling made beautiful mountains and rivers; Flint jumbled the mountains and made the rivers crooked. The brothers continued in this manner as they created plants and animals. One fashioned maize and tobacco, the other, weeds and plant sickness. Sapling gave the world deer and beaver, Flint gave it snakes and mosquitoes. Eventually, Sapling slew Flint in ferocious battle. Flint, however, lived on in spirit. Even today there is always a little sourness that taints the sweetness of everyday life. Thus, the Legend of Creation contains, in the action of contrary forces of nature, the Iroquois principles that governed the cosmos.

CHAPTER 3: THE GOOD LUCK CLOUD

3-15 Tools

How people survived a northeastern winter without cloth or metal tools, depending upon only things found in the forest, is more than the modern mind can fathom. Resourcefulness, perseverance, and tolerance of great discomfort were vital features of the woodland people.

Spear points made of stone or flint required a highly skilled technician. Points of copper (obtained from the Great Lake region) needed high heating to pound into shape. Both the bow and the arrow are remarkable in terms of simplicity and exacting craftsmanship. For digging, the shoulder blade (scapula) of a deer bound to the end of a stick with long tendons from the leg made a hoe. The front upper tooth of a beaver was a fine tool for woodcarving. A hollowed-out tree trunk or natural 'bowl' in a boulder made a mortar for crushing kernels of corn with a wooden pestle. And then, there was the masterpiece of the industrial arts: the bark-covered canoe.

3-16 Twins

The Story of Creation, according to Iroquois of long ago, embodies the conflicting roles of twins who made the earth as it is today (see Note 2-14). Then, the birth of twins was not welcomed by the villagers because no one could decide which one was the good twin and which one was the bad one. Old genealogical records of Iroquois families reveal few twins. It is suspected, alas, that two babies born at the same time by the same mother were not allowed to survive. The mother's heartbreak can hardly be imagined. Certainly, raising two children born at the same time (or even siblings born close together) put a heavy burden on the mother in the early Iroquois village, already struggling to provide for her family.

3-17 Names

Woodland Indians often named a baby to reflect something that may have happened about the time of birth. "Rushing Wind" and "Wandering Moose Calf" could be such names. Sometimes the names were just plain silly. Names may also come from physical or behavioral characteristics of the baby, for example, "Restless Legs" or "The Baby Who Does Not Cry." Long names, by the way, were not a problem for parents and others since, in the language of the Iroquois, many syllables were easily rolled into one singing word.

As they became adolescents, boys took on the name of an event or characteristic. These generally had a heroic spin, such as prowess at hunting, endurance, or strength. Girls, on the other hand, assumed a name of more gentle nature, referring to a waterfall, spring, bird, or, perhaps, a favorable time of day. Another change of name might come as an adult, to commemorate a great feat or significant happening, including injury or impairment.

CHAPTER 4: THE RATTLE

4-18 Loon

No animal speaks more clearly with the voice of the wilderness than the loon. Its resonant call across the lake late at night gives the die-hard camper and fly-rod-caster pause to appreciate his or her surroundings. Seeing a mother loon swimming with her chicks perched on her back is truly unforgettable.

The loon is basically a water bird, coming to land only to nest and hatch chicks. Waddling rather than walking on legs that are "too far back," it is at home in the water where the same legs are placed well for powerful swimming strokes. No fish is safe in a lake that is home to this deep diving predator.

Loons are good flyers, too, migrating from the northeast to the coastal areas of the Carolinas in winter. It is on take-off when they have a problem. To gain enough speed, the loon runs into the wind along the water, its wings flapping madly. The strip of runway required for take-off can be a quarter mile long. Once aloft, the loon proves a fast and enduring flyer.

4-19 Porcupine

One can hardly imagine a better self-defense system in animals than that of the porcupine. Projecting out from the back, sides and tail are thousands of long spikes that are sharp as a needle. The quills are readily dislodged when touched. The myth that a porcupine can project its quills at an approaching adversary is simply that, a myth. Direct contact is necessary.

The quill penetrates the skin of any animal brave enough or curious enough to get close to a porcupine. Tiny barbs along the quill face backward, fixing them in the intruder's flesh. Gradually the quills, if not removed, will work their way deeper into the body and eventually pierce vital organs. Treatment consists of the painful task of pulling out the quills one by one, something that animals cannot do and so are doomed to suffer until they die. Amazing it is to think that when a baby porcupine (known as a porcupette) is born—a wonder in itself—its quills are even then ready for action.

The Great Bard appreciated the porcupine's awesome weapon. In his most famous play, the ghost of Hamlet's recently assassinated father speaks of the horror of the afterlife. Its telling "would harrow up [distress] thy soul, would freeze thy young blood... each particular hair to stand on end like quills upon the fretful porpentine [porcupine]."

Quills readily hold dye from blueberries, raspberries, and other plants. They were sewn into moccasins and other leather apparel and in baskets for colorful decorations.

Native people coveted the porcupine's guard hairs, which were long and stiff although shorter and more pliable than quills. From these, people made strips of standing straight-up guard hairs for headdresses called "porky roaches." They were mounted on a thong or headband and often worn front to back as a narrow, central strip on a shaved head, creating the "Mohawk" hairstyle. (Shaving the head with the edge of a shell or sharpened stone defies the imagination.) Only men wore roaches which were considered sacred and used only for ceremonial dances and in battle. When boys were ready to become warriors, they wore a roach for the first time in a solemn ritual.

Few humans will ever have an opportunity to see or hear the voice of the porcupine. The porcupine is active mostly at night, waddling slowly through the forest in search of sedges, grass, succulent leaves, fruit, and its favorite, pond lilies. Daytime is generally spent resting high up in the forked branches of a tree, safe from predators and away from mosquitoes. Its voice, "*hoo, hoo,*" consisting of moaning, sniffs, snorts, and mews, sometimes sounds like a child's sobbing cry.

4-20 Peepers

Tree frogs are thumb-sized singers that are active at night, calling to other frogs. Whether tan, brown, or green, each one takes on a camouflaging color like its current background. That may be a pond, brook, grassy knoll, or curtain of leaves. An observer requires a keen eye to spot these small creatures. When perched on trees at night for their nocturnal serenading, peepers are even harder to see. Finding them is challenging because they stop singing whenever anyone approaches too closely.

Only the male tree frog can sing. Its vocal sacs expand silently, just as bubbles are blown. The peep then occurs when the "bubble" bursts. The frequency of peeping increases as the temperature goes up. Indeed, a good woodsman can tell the temperature in this way with reasonable accuracy.

The purpose of all the peeping is to attract a member of the opposite sex. In the version of "birds and the bees" for tree frogs, the female deposits her eggs in standing or slow-running water. The male then fertilizes the eggs. They hatch as tadpoles, fish-like creatures with a big head, popping eyes, and a big tail. Tadpoles depend upon surface algae for food. By the end of summer, they sprout legs, switch over to a diet of insects, and attain their adult destiny as frogs.

Tree frogs hibernate in winter just beneath the leaves, not deeply burrowed like most hibernating creatures. Their blood contains a protective "antifreeze" consisting of highly concentrated glucose along with cold-resistant amino acids. This adaptation allows them to maintain a low metabolism throughout the winter without freezing. These amphibians appear after ice melts near the edge of a weedy marsh in the northeastern woodlands, and so are considered early harbingers of spring.

The scientific name of the spring peeper is *pseudocris*, the Greek name for "false locust." The 'cris' part refers to the faint "X" on the back of the tree frog.

4-21 Woodland Scents

Black birch: Scratch the bark or break a twig of the black birch and smell the sweet aroma of wintergreen. It is the mint-like fragrance found in candy, chewing gum, mouthwash, toothpaste, and balsamic vinegar.

Wintergreen has a medical use, as well. A major ingredient of the oil, methyl salicylate, is closely related chemically to aspirin, which is acetylsalicylate. Certainly, black birch in one form of another was useful in the longhouse for easing aches and reducing fever. It is found in many over-the-counter products for topical application, namely *Bengay* and *Thera-gesic.*

Incidentally, the tree, black birch, is not the bushy plant called wintergreen. They share, however, a common scent.

Sassafras: The delicate fragrance of sassafras is not easy to describe. Yet, everyone would recognize it in a tea, perfume, or soap. The fresh smell is best sampled on the twig after scraping off its thin bark with a fingernail. The word "sassafras" comes from the Algonquian, meaning green twig.

Sassafras, when fermented with yeast and combined with carbonated water, become root beer. The smell of sassafras particularly appeals to children, perhaps accounting for the popularity of the cereal, *Fruit Loops.*

The sassafras tree has value in addition to its scent. When the leaves are crushed and mixed into a paste with charred wood and oil, the result becomes a good mosquito repellent. The twig that splits into many fine bristles at the end makes a good toothbrush. Surely, woodland Indians made good use of sassafras for seasoning.

The sassafras tree is of medium size and is the first to grow in cleared land. It is easy to identify by its leaves. Some of these are single and nondescript while others have three lobes of about equal size. The most distinctive version has two lobes, one large, one small, giving the look of a mitten.

Skunk cabbage: This amazing forest plant gets no respect. Its odor is akin to that of the skunk. The best way to sample the aroma is to put one's nose close to the opening between the broad leaves. The leaves form a spiraling sculptured hood. Inside is a round, fleshy knob of berry-like fruits, each one containing a seed. The seeds will not turn into a lovely blossom but, rather, will stay in its cluster and out of sight deep in their protective shell.

The strong odor of skunk cabbage, like rotten meat, attracts carrion-eating insects. Flies, butterflies, beetles, and bees appear during the first stirrings of spring. They, in turn, favor the skunk cabbage by dispersing its pollen throughout the wetland.

During the spring, skunk cabbage also produces something else that is extraordinary: heat! In this way, its biological machinery works in the same way as in animals. That is, it converts stored energy (in this case starch in its roots) to sugar for immediate energy, using oxygen and giving off heat in the process. Ordinary plants, on the other hand, absorb energy from the sun to combine water in air and carbon dioxide in soil, releasing oxygen.

The production of heat begins underground in early spring. The tightly packed, and pointed leaves push up through the frozen ground to announce the coming of spring. Unfurled once above ground, the leaves stand at least a foot high. A ring of ice-melt around the plant testifies to its warmth. To confirm this, put a fingertip inside the hood to feel the "room temperature" of this plant.

Native Americans included skunk cabbage in their pharmacy. Mainly, the leaves were used to control seizures and to treat rheumatism. Wounds from bites were treated with salves made from the leaves. They probably found last-resort nutritional value in the deep-seated roots that are rich in starches and have no odor.

Fern: The hay-scented fern grows in a thick stand. Its delicate leaflets, pinnules, grow on stems that come straight out of the main stem, making a long, feathery triangle. When crushed, the hay-scented fern smells just like that: freshly mown hay.

4-22 Black Bear

The winter home of the black bear is a den. This may be a cave, hollowed-out tree (standing or fallen), or beneath a thicket of underbrush. Here it hibernates through the months of frigid weather, living only on a thick layer of fat stored up in the frenzied gluttony of autumn. Unlike other hibernating animals such as the frog and the turtle, the black bear drops its normal body temperature only a few degrees through the winter; its rate of metabolism slows only slightly. In this state, the bear is readily awakened from its long nap by any intrusion.

Mostly, the black bear is a vegetarian, eating grass and flowering plants in spring, shrubs and fruit in summer, and berries and nuts in autumn, climbing trees to reach them when necessary. The acorn provides a particularly rich food for putting on a good layer of fat before winter.

The black bear's favorite food animals, perhaps surprisingly for such a formidable creature, are ants and wasps that are exposed when the bear claws out rotting tree-trunks. Fishing is seasonal when colossal numbers of herring and other fish swim upriver to spawn. Sometimes the bear will find larger prey such as a deer fawn or a moose calf.

Incidents of attacks on humans by black bears are rare. A mother bear with her young in tow, however, is another story. In any case, the woodland stroller is wise to give any black bear, if spotted, plenty of breathing space.

4-23 Elk

No one meandering through the forest could miss noticing a macho elk with antlers of many points that spread out eight feet. You may hear the grunting squeal he makes as a warning of danger—his danger and that of his harem, not your danger. The magnificent antlers provide a formidable weapon. The elk, however, defends itself mainly by kicking predators with its sharp-hooved front legs.

Males of a higher order of animals become aggressive during periods when females are receptive to mating. During certain seasons, elk, mountain goats, deer, and caribou display such behavior, called "rutting." The changes in disposition often lead to battles between the male rivals in a struggle to win over females.

A prospective bull elk announces his intentions for mating with a screaming bellow, referred to as a bugle-call, that may be heard miles away. A commanding force of the call may keep away potential suitors. More often, perhaps, rival bull elks confront each other by posturing, with stomping and more bellowing. Sometimes the confrontation escalates into physical combat. Then, the match is mostly a show of strength while avoiding injury from the points of sharp antlers. In these shoving matches, there is always a danger of the antlers becoming entangled. When impossible for the bulls to separate themselves, the only outcome is death by starvation for both.

From a genetic point, the winner of these rutting contests proves himself the more fit. His reward is a harem that he must guide valiantly. His genes will be passed on to the offspring, providing them with whatever advantage had won the battle, be it strength, size, agility or just plain courage. One wonders if the elk or his equivalent in nature plays the game by merely lustful instinct or by some sense of responsibility for his inheritance.

The rutting of elk occurs in the autumn, and the calves are born in the spring. This timely order, however, may be upset when a bull elk invades a harem.

The many voices of the elk can be appreciated on internet videos. One site is "Bull Elk sounds: Bugles, Barks, Grunts and More."

CHAPTER 5: SKY FLOWER

5-24 Rainbow

Sunlight passing through a layer of heavily laden moisture breaks up into the individual wavelengths that altogether make "white light." We see this phenomenon as a rainbow when the sun reappears after a rain shower. The shorter wavelengths, that is, the blue end of the spectrum, bend the most, the longer red ones bend the least. The result is an arc with the entire spectrum of colors, the blue band inside, the red outside with the gradations in color between. Who could argue that a rainbow is one of nature's most magnificent sights?

Should one be surprised that this purely optical phenomenon in the sky intrigued people since ancient times throughout the world? For some, it was the unreachable path to unbelievable riches. To others, a rainbow predicted safe or foul weather for sailors (depending upon the time of day). To hunters, a rainbow foretold the prospect of plentiful game. Some traditions held that a rainbow was the sacred pathway to heaven. Others took them for giant serpents left by a violent storm and causing great fear.

We do not know what the twins of this story might have heard about the meaning of rainbows. One Iroquois version, told briefly here, is attributed to handed-down mythology. Thunder God saw Moon getting thinner and thinner with each passing day. He was angered by her withering away. He blamed Sun. Thunder God then formed a great black cloud across the face of Sun. Of course, Sun quickly melted the cloud. There appeared afterwards a rainbow. Earth-bound animals were so attracted by the colorful sight that some of them, against advice of other animals, climbed the rainbow, only to be trapped forever in the sky. It is surely no coincidence that many of the constellations in Iroquoia have the shape of animals.

CHAPTER 6: VOICE OF THE WILDERNESS

6-25 Midden

A trash pile to most, the midden is a treasure trove for archaeologists and anthropologists. Tools, bowls, pots, bones, shells, and other enduring items essential to the way of living in pre-historic times have been found in the middens of the Woodland Indians. To the trained eye and with educated guesswork, these scholars can tell much of life long ago from the discarded stuff of middens.

6-26 Wolf

Wolves hunt in packs, stalking a large animal to the point of its exhaustion. Unrelenting pursuit of a deer, elk, or moose might take a few days, rendering the prey too weary to put their sharp hooves and antlers to a good defensive fight. Within the pack are specialists that may go for the throat of large prey while others attack at the hind end. In deep snow, the pack has it easier because hooved animals run much slower. Broad paws give the wolf overwhelming advantage.

When an adult wolf domesticated in a human world enters the wilderness, there are two possible paths ahead. One is to join a pack, becoming a member and learning the ways of hunting and societal "rules."

An alternate path must be taken if a wolf pack will not accept a newcomer. In that case, the pack members drive the stranger off with whatever aggressive behavior is required. The domesticated wolf-turned-wild must now go it alone.

Without the skill and cooperation of a pack, the "lone wolf" cannot bring down large animals for food. Instead, it must live by wits alone, catching small animals such as rabbits and chipmunks, and by finding edible carrion. Regarding the meal mentioned last, the stomach of the wolf can digest food, including bone, spoiled well beyond that tolerable by humans.

CHAPTER 8: THE MESSAGE OF JOY

8-27 Missionaries

Spanish missionaries came to the Caribbean Islands and to Central America and Florida on the heels of Columbus (or better said, on the stern of Columbus). The first missionaries to arrive in the northeastern shores came a century later.

In 1610, one year after the "discovery" of the Hudson River by Henry Hudson, Jesuit missionaries went to the French fishing colonies of Acadia (present-day Nova Scotia) to minister to the land-bound workers. Here lived the Mi'kmaq, who spoke the language of the Algonquins. The French realized that they now had an opportunity to convert this fresh, "heathen" population to Christianity.

In 1613, the Jesuits began a small colony on the eastern site of Mt. Desert Island in Maine, so called by explorer Samuel de Champlain, meaning "where the mountain summits are all bare and rocky." (It is now the Acadia National Park.) The native people there were the Abenakis, also Algonquian speaking. By 1625, the Jesuits had established themselves along the Saint Lawrence River and well upriver to Quebec. The inhabitants here were the Iroquois-speaking Wyandots (later called the Hurons).

Once in New France, the black robes met stiff resistance to their single-minded purpose. After all, the Indians had their own religion. Although it was far different from the European beliefs, it lay deep inside their psyche. There were, nevertheless, a few communities that eventually adopted the new religion, although it is suspected that there was a more pragmatic reason: to garner protection of the French from other raiding tribes. Some converts spent the remaining days of their lives spreading the "good news" (or gospel) of Christianity. This commitment was not easy because it meant rejecting Indian beliefs that were taught since early childhood.

Even with some success, Jesuit priests faced immense hardships in their pursuit. Some, with unswerving faith in the cause, underwent torture and, for some, death, at the hands of those they tried to "save." Nevertheless, they provide our best descriptions of native life at the time. Their efforts, admittedly, were not focused on cultural anthropology. That was not to come for another 200 years with detailed descriptions of the Senecas by Lewis Henry Morgan of Rochester, New York.

8-28 Religions

NATIVE BELIEF:

All things animate and inanimate have a spirit. If it is a good spirit, that thing brings good fortune. It ministers to the necessities of mankind. If that thing has an evil spirit, it will create mischief, causing the thing to wilt, become ill, and die. The Iroquois called this supernatural force the *Oreda.*

There is a Creator of the World who shares some powers with all the other spirits of nature. These spirits have no definite shape or form but are simply mystic energies. Each of the commonest plants, animals and stones has a spiritual essence that must be revered. Further, the Creator does not judge a person in this world or the next as good or bad.

A fundamental part of the Iroquois religion was recognition of the moral fiber of the individual. There was a strong sense of personal commitment to the overall welfare of the tribe, instilled in early childhood in every member. That obligation was held sacred. And always, the spiritual make-up of every Indian was closely related to the events and things of everyday life and to the natural world around him or her.

Leadership within the clan or tribe depended not on birthright but on ability; women decided who that leader would be. The concept of king, emperor, pope and bishop, and nobility by heritage was unknown in Iroquoia. Historical designations such as King Philip and Princess Pocahontas were European inventions.

EUROPEAN BELIEF OF CHRISTIANITY

Based on the Torah or Old Testament, all life was created in this fashion:

> *In the beginning God created the heaven and the earth.*
> *And the earth was without form, and void; and darkness was upon the face of the deep. And the Spirit of God moved upon the face of the waters.*
> *And God said, "Let there be light;" and there was light.*
>
> *[...]*
>
> *21. And God created great whales, and every living creature that moveth, which the waters brought forth abundantly, and after their kind, and every winged fowl after his kind; and god saw that it was good.*
> *25. And God made the beast of the earth after his kind, and cattle of their kind, and everything that creepeth upon the earth after his kind: and God saw that it was good.*
> *27. So God created man in his own image, in the image of God created he him; male and female created he them.*

The Book of Genesis 1, St. James Version / The Torah / Old Testament

The New Testament taught: God, the Supreme Being in the Kingdom of Heaven, judges human beings on morality and good conduct. Good ones would be blessed with eternal life in Heaven, while unrepentant sinners would not. Jesus, the Son of God, was made human just so that he could bring the word of God to mortals on earth and save them from evil. The greatest of his commandants was love. "Thou shalt love the Lord thy God with all thy heart and with all thy soul, and with all thy mind; thou shalt love thy neighbor as thyself."

The spiritual beliefs from two worlds apart were not compatible. Those of native Americans were largely ignored by explorers, traders, and settlers coming from Europe. Those professed by the Europeans must have seemed strange indeed to Indians.

8-29 Baptism

In the Christian faith, baptism to purify both body and soul is a rite that goes back to the time of Jesus. Even before that, Jewish tradition practiced ritual washing in water, oil, or perfumes in the temple to cleanse someone who had touched a sick or otherwise unclean person and make him presentable before the eyes of God. The word *bapto,* in fact, comes from Greek meaning "washing."

Variations in the practice of baptism continue to exist in religious denominations, from total body immersion to the sprinkling of water over the head. According to the Catholic Church in Rome, baptism means acceptance of the church's doctrines and formal entrance into its membership. Martin Luther professed that baptism saved those baptized from sin, death, and the devil, allowing them to enter the Kingdom of Christ and live with Him forever. Some Christian sects (the Salvation Army and the Quakers or the Religious Society of Friends) reject baptism and other outward sacraments, holding that these practices interfere with spiritual attention.

At baptism an infant receives a name. Parents vow to raise the child in the principles of Christianity. Members of Jehovah's Witnesses permit baptism only when the person is old enough to understand fully and accept the true meaning of the vows.

The missionaries in North America during the Contact Period were zealous in their pursuit of natives willing to be baptized and to follow the obligations preached by the church. Resistance came about from a pervasive native attitude that the missionaries were sorcerers, weakening the spiritual strength, and spreading disease. The ritual of baptism, in short, was met with cold skepticism. The successes and failures of the black robes comprise a large place in the history of the early European incursion of North America.

CHAPTER 10: THE ARROW

10-30 Maize

In Iroquoia, subsistence depended mainly on plants. By far, the most important of these was maize. While the name corn may seem synonymous with maize, it has many different meanings depending on where on the globe it is spoken. Maize carries a more specialized meaning; it is the preferred term in scientific references.

Archaeologists discovered that maize was first cultivated in southwestern Mexico. It developed from a grassy plant, looking nothing like what we know today. As it evolved over seven centuries, maize found its way across North America, probably not reaching the woodlands of what would become New York and New England until about a thousand years ago. Its cultivation marked a major change in the way people lived. It required stay-at-home gardeners to tend the crop and no longer to depend solely on hunting and the chancy prospects of gathering eggs, nuts and berries along the way.

Maize as we know it—in large cobs bristling with tightly packed kernels in neat rows—did not exist during the time of our story. Instead, the cobs in pre-historic America were but a few inches long, the kernels, loose and irregular. Though small, these were highly colorful: red, yellow, black, and purple.

At the top of the maize stalk are spikes loaded with pollen. The pollen falls onto the tassel (or silk) that protrudes from the top of the tightly leaf-wrapped cob. Each strand of silk leads to one of the seeds inside that, when fertilized, will become a kernel.

Maize is highly nutritious, containing virtually all the essential amino acids, the building blocks of protein. It is low in one, however: tryptophan. The body converts tryptophan into the important vitamin, niacin. The disease pellagra (with sunburn-like skin, mental changes and intestinal disturbances) occurs from a diet restricted to only maize. Plants grown along with corn, however, provided this missing nutrient. Of course, this advantage of combining plants was practiced by woodland Indians who knew nothing about vitamins, which were not discovered until well into the 20th century. Maize does not contain the protein mixture known as gluten, present in wheat. This fact is of great importance to people who have gluten-sensitive intestinal tracts.

In Iroquoia, the tasks of planting, weeding, and harvesting maize were women's responsibility. They removed the tough cover (the pericap) from the nutritious inside after soaking the kernels with ground-up roots. Women then pounded the meal into flour with a wooden pestle. From the flour, they made a large assortment of food for immediate consumption, for long-distance travel, and for storage in bark casks or underground in pits lined with grass to prevent mildew.

Today's supermarket may have more than a thousand different products made of corn. In addition, corn has become a major additive to gasoline; it is the basic constituent of some alcohols. No plant has been under such intense scientific scrutiny as maize.

CHAPTER 12: LAUGHING RAIN

12-31 Basketmaking

The art of weaving fibers into useful items was a highly developed skill among the Iroquois. There were three kinds of approaches to making a good basket.

Coiled: weaving from the center and base, spiraling outward and upward. Both flat reeds and round reeds made equally good baskets, as did grapevines after soaking and boiling. The reeds could be interlaced with porcupine quills for decorations.

Splint: strips of wood, woven into strong and squared baskets. For these, the bark of long submerged trees was scored (while still wet) for the desired strip width. The bark was then stripped along growth rings and pounded for separation. The ash tree was preferred for ease, although the oak provided a more durable splint. Scoring may have been done with a sharpened stone, such as flint, or with the incisor of a beaver.

Sweetgrass: Growing in meadows, it gives off a pleasant vanilla-like scent. The hollow stems can be braided into a strong fiber that is easily woven. Sweetgrass baskets can be not only beautiful, but they retain their scent. "Sweetgrass braided is the hair of our Mother; separately, each strand is not as strong as when the strands are braided together." Mary Ritchie (1995)

Since a clump of sweetgrass could be burned by smoldering, not burning with open flame, the Iroquois used it to open solemn ceremonies and to attract the spirits by its smell.

12-32 Clay Pot

Mountains lose their rocky substance of the millennia by weathering from acid rain and from leaching by lichens. The mineral residue flows downward in run-off from rainwater and snowmelt. The smallest particles fall out where the flow is slow, such as in bays or lakes.

Clay is a colorless silicate. Its color comes from impurities, varying from gray to orange and red. Clay is firm when dry, and easy to mold after wetting. When exposed to high heat, it forms into a ceramic, a totally rigid and fragile substance.

Kilns for curing clay into pots have not been found in Iroquoia. It is assumed that native people made pots by placing them near a fire and frequently turning them to avoid cracking. This task alone was another labor-intensive chore. There is no evidence that cured clay (i.e., bricks) was used as a building material.

Clans and nations had their own special designs of pots. These have proven a godsend for archaeologists trying to understand village life of long ago. Rarely is an intact pot found. A clay pot underground collects water; the water freezes in winter; the ice expands on thawing, bursting the pot. A pot with a hole in the bottom is much more likely to remain intact. Most often, the cultural scientist must work with pieces or shards of a clay pot. Even so, the distinctive shapes and patterns of painstakingly reconstructed pots tell much about their makers.

CHAPTER 13: AWAKENS CORN

13-33 Water Strider

The insect that walks on water is an amazing creature. It has many names, among them pond skater, water spider, and, irreverently, the Jesus bug. Its scientific name is the "gerrid." Supporting it upright are six long, skinny legs.

The reason the water strider can walk on water remained a mystery until recent years. In 2004, entomologists at the Chinese National Academy in Beijing, using a powerful microscope, reported their amazing findings: thousands of ultra-tiny hairs over the entire body. (So, mammals are not the only animals with hair!) Grooves along each hair trap air, thereby repelling water and providing buoyancy. A drop of rainwater quickly runs off the body. Should a big splash dunk the insect under, the creature will only pop right up again.

Antennae and a pair of short legs in front sense ripples caused by a struggling insect that may have fallen into the water. The longer middle legs paddle the water strider toward it, traveling at the sensational speed of a yard in one second in short bursts. The longest legs are in back; these serve for steering.

The front legs grip prey while sharp jaws puncture its shell or skin. A tenderizing enzyme from the mouth pours in. The water strider then sucks out the nutritious juices. This creature can in turn become the prey, mostly to birds but also to fish and frogs.

Some water striders can fly remarkable distances should a pond or stream dry up or become too crowded. Those with partially developed wings can disperse to nearby water, if necessary. Some water striders have no wings. These are generally found where the habitat is relatively unchanging and stable. Wings, in fact, can be a liability; they get wet and can weigh the insects down.

If all these were not enough to give the water strider some distinction, the ritual of courtship, too, must be unique in the animal kingdom. The male water strider creates ripples with its front legs, at one frequency to attract females and at another frequency to stake out his territory as a warning to male competitors.

In temperate climates, water striders get through the cold season beneath leaves, sunken logs and rocks. Ponds enliven with them come spring.

13-34 Mirror

Looking at one's own image in a pool is not new. Narcissus of mythology in ancient Greece pined away his life as he admired his own reflection. A beautiful plant, the narcissus, with white and yellow flowers surrounded by long and graceful, slender leaves, sprang up at the site where he died.

Today, the term "narcissus" refers to someone who is excessively taken by the beauty of his or her own body.

The first mirror was the obsidian, a black rock from volcanic lava having a glassy surface. Of course, its rounded shape gave the face a distorted look. Ancient people made mirrors by polishing smooth sheets of bronze in China or copper in the Near East. At the high points of the Greek and Roman civilizations, metal disks that had been hand-rubbed to a glossy surface were fashionable. There followed in the Middle Ages attempts to bond metals to glass. One method was to blow heat-melted glass into a sphere, pour in hot lead, and after cooling, break the glass to obtain small and jagged but good mirrors.

The technical difficulties and poor reflections attained were disappointing in all these methods. In addition, many believed that the devil looked at the viewer from the opposite side, further discouraging mirror making.

In the 1500s, glassmakers in Venice learned to make a good mirror by getting mercury to adhere to a plate of glass. With strict industrial secrecy, Venetian manufacturers and merchants enjoyed a monopoly on mirror-making for generations. The cost of a small mirror, however, (about that of a large ship) meant that only royalty of the first rank could afford one. Even so, a king in France lined a favorite room with Venetian mirrors.

When the secret of manufacturing mirrors finally leaked out, the price plummeted, and mirrors became popular throughout Europe. Technical improvement came in the mid-1800s with invention of a chemical bonding of metallic silver onto plate glass; it provided an affordable mirror that became a rage despite a lingering notion with religious overtones that mirrors were somehow sinful.

Today most mirrors are made by spraying ("sputtering") aluminum on glass. When done in a partial vacuum, the metallic coat is extremely thin yet effective.

The clear mirror effect on a still pond comes from the image reflecting from the surface. Its black bottom absorbs penetrating sunlight so that the reflected image is even more vivid. A lighter color, typical of a painted swimming pool, would make bottom features visible and so obscure the surface image.

As we look at the image of ourselves in a mirror, we should reflect with admiration on this common household object, so long in development and so important in present-day utility.

13-35 Spider Web

Perhaps the most interesting thing about the spider is its web. And fantastic it is!

A spider with its eight eyes sees rather poorly. The web, however, is an extremely sensitive detection device. The spider will sense the slightest vibrations of a struggling insect caught in the web. From the intensity of quivering, it will even get a good idea of the prey's size and activity.

Of 38,000 species of spiders, about half of them spin webs. Different species build different kinds of webs. For example, hammock spiders (that live in trees) make the familiar wheel-like web with concentric threads. Interspersed are radial threads that hold the complex structure together. Some of the threads are sticky, increasing the chances of the spider snaring something to eat. Spiders, in fact, eat great numbers of insects. They make up an extensive control system against mosquitoes and flies.

It is not only the architecture of the web but also the properties of the individual strands that make it so remarkable. Weight for weight, the thread from a spider's web is much stronger than steel. Furthermore, the thread is elastic, capable of stretching twice its own resting length before breaking. It can be bent drastically without damage.

A single thread of three to five meters long consists of thousands of filaments. The strength comes from the same principle that makes a wire cable strong: the twisting together of many small wires.

Each filament of the thread has a molecular structure in which there are proteins that contain the "silk gene." Raising spiders in colonies to produce webs commercially is impractical owing to their fierce territorial instincts. Instead, fiber scientists have inserted their specialized gene-factor into the recombinant DNA of a goat. The female goat conceived from this altered gene may on maturation produce milk that contains filaments identical to that of the web. After a complex process of harvesting the microfilaments in the milk, then purifying, drying and diluting them with special solvents, they can be spun into a tough thread. When combined with fibers from those of plants (such as the potato, tomato or alfalfa), they have been used to manufacture "Bio-steel®." The result of the Spider-Goat-Connection is an artificial silk with strong and flexible fibers that may find its way into bulletproof clothing, car bumpers, and replacement joints, tendons, and sutures for, say, eye surgery in humans. You can't make this stuff up.

13-36 Hunting

The Native American perspective: In a world without cloth, hunting to obtain animal hides was essential, not a sport. For the woodland Indians the meat derived from game was more of a supplemental part of the diet after corn and other harvested vegetables and gathered berries and nuts.

A family of five needed seventeen deer hides for clothing over one year. It is estimated that there were 8,000 Mohawks living in an area of 10,000 square kilometers. Therefore, about 26,000 deer were needed for garments and other products every year. The area inhabited by the Mohawks supported 76,000 deer. The loss of one third of the herd through hunting would not endanger the survival of the herd at large. These data are taken from *The Iroquois,* a book by anthropologist Dean R. Snow at Pennsylvania State University.

A successful hunt required enormous stealth, speed, and accurate marksmanship. Deer were the main prey. For larger animals, such as elk and moose, the element of danger was added. Bear hunting required all these and in heroic measure. For bear, the 'deadfall' trap provided a safer method.

Turkeys have great speed in flight and running. They have little stamina, however, and tire quickly. An Indian, fleet of foot, could outlast the turkey in a long run. Perhaps, because of this weakness, turkeys may have been considered junk food. The iconic "First Thanksgiving" in the Plymouth Colony in 1621 was without turkey.

In 1609, Robert Juet, the first mate of Henry Hudson and his log-keeper, describes Indians bagging pigeons with bow and arrow. There is probably no truer sign of marksmanship.

The Iroquois hunter would offer a prayer to the spirit of each animal slain, giving thanks for its sacrifice. This tradition reflects the deep reverence native people had for all forms of life.

13-37 **Beaver / Dam Building**

Truly the superb engineers of the animal kingdom, beavers build their domed lodges in the middle of a deep, still pond where they are safe from land predators. They work mostly at night and quietly except for an occasional grunt. (Kits, by contrast, make a sound that reminds one of a duck's quack).

Creating a pond by figuring out exactly where to place a dam on a stream (or on more than one stream) and where water will eventually back up against higher land -- all this requires planning. They fell trees large and small (with their teeth!) to make the crisscross skeleton of the dam and lodge. For the entire project, several hundred trees may be cut. They gather brush, sticks, stone, and mud to fill in a "waddle-and-daub" construction technique. It takes some ingenuity to know when the dam is high enough and strong enough to hold back the desired level of water.

Do animals think? Certainly, the beaver confirms this impression with the planning and implementation of its lodge. Inside is a single room with a small air hole on top. Adult beavers and their kits rest on a platform well above the water. Here in pitch-blackness they spend their winter, entertaining each other with grunts and groans and with grooming each other.

The lodge can be entered only from below water, thus providing another safety measure. Food, consisting of twigs, leaves, inner bark, and small logs, is stored at the bottom of the pond or marsh, where the bark is readily available throughout the iced-over season.

The largest of rodents, beavers have short legs that are webbed behind and a scaly, flat paddle for a tail, making them expert swimmers. To keep warm, even in frigid water; they have a plush underfur. Longer, prickly guard hairs help to protect the inner nap from abrasions while shedding rain and snow. These hairs give the beaver its brown color. Glands near the tail secrete an oily and smelly substance (castor) that the beaver spreads over its fur to render it waterproof.

The working parts of the beaver—its teeth—deserve some mention. The incisors overlap, like a pair of scissors. They continue to grow throughout life but are constantly filed down by this shearing action. The hardness of the enamel and the strong jaws give the beaver the ability to gnaw through wood with ease. The cheek teeth, in contrast, are flattened and made for grinding.

By way of animal adaptation, how's this? The beaver has a serious "overbite" owing to its huge incisors. The furry lips, however, can shut tightly behind the upper teeth, allowing it to swim while carrying branches in its jaw without swallowing water!

The Europeans had no interest in the building skills of the beaver. They found a commercial use for its soft luxurious fur. Once the pelts were shipped back home, the fur was used to make winter coats. When the coarse guard hairs were worn off, the fur was steamed with a mercury vapor and the resulting felt was turned into hats.

In 1624, the first year of the Dutch settlement along the Hudson River, about 1,500 beaver pelts were harvested by Indians, traded with the Dutch for cloth and metal tools, and shipped to Europe. Within the next couple of decades, the beaver population of the area was virtually exterminated. Forays by traders deeper into the heartland were necessary to keep up with demand.

13-38 Jewelweed

In summertime, look for jewelweed, a tall plant growing profusely in thick stands along low-lying, wet soil, such as a streamside. It is not hard to find. It has its inch-long yellow-orange flowers that hang like gems on a green necklace and that glisten in the sunlight! The petals of the flower are conical (or trumpet-like) in shape. Inside is reddish-brown mottling. The flower attracts hummingbirds, butterflies, and long-tongued bees that serve unwittingly as pollinators.

The jewelweed flower develops into a small pod that contains the plant's seeds and provides its most characteristic feature: a mini explosion. When ripened, the pod will burst open, spewing little black seeds many feet around. By carefully squeezing a ripening pod, you will see it unzipping itself along a seam and exploding between your fingers. It will cast out its seeds before curling up into a little ball. It is this bursting that led to the alternative botanical name "impatiens" (that includes other members of the balsam family) and to the common name "touch-me-not." Any safety-conscious woodland hiker should be thankful that the jewelweed pod is not the size of a watermelon.

Wherever jewelweed grows, poison ivy is likely to be close by. Native people used the viscous sap of the jewelweed stem to treat poison ivy. Break the stem and press the juice out and onto the rash. Lotions, salves and sprays made from the sap are obtainable on the Internet.

13-39 Bear Cubs

Cubs of the black bear are born in winter, usually two or three at a time. At birth each is about the size of a fully-grown chipmunk, blind, without fur, and totally helpless. Throughout this time, the mother bear provides milk and warmth. The cubs grow rapidly, becoming teddy bear cute and plenty curious by spring. They will stay close to Mom until the following spring, learning from her the complex task of surviving in the wild. Independent living will not occur for two years.

13-40 Big Chill

Humans keep their body temperature at a remarkably even level at about 98° through ever-changing ambient temperature. The rate of heat transmission between body and water is about thirteen times more than between body and air. Thus, in cold water, the body rapidly loses heat. Shivering is a mechanism that increases metabolism somewhat, providing stepped-up production of heat. With prolonged exposure in water, body temperature will continue to fall. As it falls to the low 90s, serious changes in body functions occur, including impaired mental acuity and muscle power, rendering the person relatively helpless. The condition is known as hypothermia.

13-41 Rattlesnake

In its appearance, the rattlesnake is generally like other snakes that produce venom. It has a triangle-shaped head with jowls that project out well beyond the sides of the "neck." What sets the rattlesnake apart is its rattle. When alarmed, the rattlesnake makes its distinctive, sizzling buzz by shaking modified scales at the hind end. It is a warning to trespassers to stay away.

Like other venomous snakes, the rattlesnake is not gifted with sharp eyes. Instead, it has heat-seeking sensors built into small pits just behind the eyes (hence the name "pit viper"). With these, it can identify potential prey nearby from their body heat. The flickering tongue picks up particles in the air, the tip delivering them back to the roof of the mouth where the sensor for smell is located. In addition, the snake is so extremely sensitive to vibrations that it can detect a small animal walking close at hand.

The venom of the rattlesnake is delivered to a victim through its hollow fangs. The rabbit, squirrel, bird or other recipient is not killed outright but may continue its running or flying escape. Soon, however, the injected toxin affects the blood of the victim and paralyzes its muscles. Digestion begins even before ingestion by the snake. The snake then catches up with the prey and swallows it whole, starting at the head so that limbs and feathers fold the right way. Once inside, the prey forms a bulge where the stomach lies. It will then find a place, such as a rock overhang, cave or hole in the ground where it will quietly complete the digestion over several days or more.

The body temperature of the snake varies according to the temperature of the air. To avoid overheating from direct sunlight, the snake will seek shade. To prevent overcooling, it finds shelter from the steady rain by crawling beneath a stone overhang or a fallen tree.

13-42 Lost in the Woods

It is only too easy to stray off a path in the woodland and find no recognizable landmarks. How quickly one can get lost! If you are without compass, cell phone, matches, and clothes for rain and cold, there are some guidelines that will help.

Don't panic. This oft-repeated advice is not easy on first realizing that you are completely lost. Someone will eventually come looking for you and will be better prepared for a woodland stroll.

Do not continue to walk as dusk comes on. And remember it gets dark quickly. A fall or branch in the eye can change an inconvenience into a survival situation. Instead of walking aimlessly, use the time to make a lean-to shelter.

Preserve body heat as much as possible. Hypothermia can occur in summer as rain drenches the body. Each drop carries away tiny amounts of heat that over time adds up.

Stay out of wind. But if clothes are wet, hang them on the windy side of a shelter.

Rest.

If walking is impossible, make a big "X" with rocks, sticks or scuffing up the ground in an open area and stay nearby.

Keep hydrated. Fresh stream water is relatively safe. The remote possibility of acquiring *giardia* or other intestinal disorders is remote. Food is not necessary for several days in the well-nourished and healthy person. Do not eat anything not certain to be edible.

A simple shelter can be made with a pole leaning against a boulder or tree limb. Along this "spine," lean "ribs" from long sticks. Fill in between with branches and leaves. Cover the ground inside with a thick bed of leaves for insulation.

When walking is possible, follow running water downstream. Eventually, this will lead to people.

13-43 Blackberries

Thick, bushy tangles of blackberry brambles are found in open spaces between leaved trees, not in the high acid soil of conifers. Each plant has three long stems or canes. During the first year, a cane will grow to full length but bear no fruit. In the second year it will bud and, in late spring to early summer, blossom with small white and pink petals. The seeds will cluster at the base of these blossoms and grow into fruit. The cane of the third year is dead. Bees and other insects pollinate the flowers. Birds and mammals (coyotes, fox, pine martens, bear) eat the fruit and in this way spread the seeds.

The blackberry is not the old BlackBerry, the smart-phone device. Nor is it a berry at all. A true berry (like the blueberry and grape) comes from a single ovary that ripens into a fleshy and edible outer layer. Rather the blackberry is—from a strictly botanical point of view—an aggregate fruit. That is, it consists of many tiny fruits that cluster around a central, fibrous core. Picking the blackberry leaves the core behind. The seed is embedded within the juicy flesh, as opposed to a cherry or peach. Nor does the blackberry bush have thorns that are sharp, woody extensions of a branch or stem. Instead, the canes have hardened, hair-like prickles, growing from the "bark," as does the rose. These several qualifications notwithstanding, blackberries make a delicious jam, custard, pie, ice cream, and wine. They are highly nutritious for their fiber, vitamin C, folic acid, minerals and antitoxins.

CHAPTER 14: THE HEALER

14-44 Council House

A typical Iroquois village included an oversized longhouse for sacred rituals and meetings in which only members of the tribe were permitted. Inside, everyone in the village could huddle around a central fire for ceremonies and for the telling of stories.

Surviving illustrations and descriptions suggest that the council house was devoid of anything resembling furniture or other common household items. Only upright poles in the middle to support the roof interrupted the space.

14-45 Dislocated Shoulder

The natural movement of the shoulder provides a greater range of motion than any other joint. Watch a baseball pitcher or cellist to appreciate the shoulder's mobility in the extreme. The anatomy of the shoulder that allows this movement, alas, also renders it more susceptible to injury.

The upper arm has a hemi-spherical shape that fits into the shallow bowl of the shoulder. A tough, fibrous ring at the rim of the socket helps to keep the ball within, as do the strong tendons of muscles, including the rotator cuff.

The socket is an extension of the shoulder blade, the scapula; yes, the same bone used to make a hoe, as already described in an early chapter. The scapula floats freely over and under the powerful muscles of the back. Another extension of the scapula forms a stiff joint with the outer end of the collarbone, the clavicle. The inner end of the clavicle attaches to the upper sternum. It is only at this point that the arm is connected directly bone-to-bone with the main body, not like the leg that attaches directly from femur to pelvis in a deep socket.

There are various methods for treating the dislocated shoulder. With each, there is some danger of injuring a blood vessel or nerve. In nearly all cases, however, a physician or other care-giver skilled in the procedure can put the ball back into the socket safely. Full recovery is generally assured. Sometimes it happens that surgical reduction of the dislocated shoulder is necessary.

CHAPTER 15: MORNING BLOSSOM

15-46 Marriage

In marriage, men generally came from a distant clan or tribe. The custom may have been to promote trade or reduce hostilities. There were also men who had been captured and eventually became husbands after proving worthy of kinship.

In this way, women provided the inherited continuity of the community while men, unwittingly, provided an expanded gene pool. Alas, we know little about the marriage ceremony itself but suspect it was a simple affair. The bond between husband and wife, however, was strong.

15-47 String Beads / Wampum

There is no Indian relic more sacred than a belt in which small shells make a pattern that commemorates treaties and social obligations, such as marriage. One may represent a badge of office or a ceremonial tradition. Perhaps the most famous wampum belt is the "Haudenosaunee Great Law of Peace" that codifies the constitution of the League of the Iroquois. For details on wampum, see Note 1-14 in BOOK 1.

Before metal tools became available, decorative and commemorative articles were made with strings of shells. The central, spiral column of the whelk shell provided small, barrel-shaped white pieces; the outer part of the quahog shell produced purple discs. The arrangement of white and purple on the string signified its purpose.

Breaking and cutting the shells into usable disks and drilling a hole in them with stone tools took perseverance. Craftsmen (including women) drilled holes in shells with a sharp-edged hard stone, such as quartz, mounted on a stick. A bow around the stick allowed drilling with a pumping action.

Inland people had to obtain the shells from coastal nations, mostly those on Long Island. The Mohawks conducted long distance travel along the Hudson River to trade flint, quartz gems, and possibly copper (from the Great Lakes region) for shells at Manhattan Island, Far Rockaway, or Coney Island.

The tubular shell piece used to make broad belts of wampum, by the way, required working with iron tools. Consequently, there were no wampum belts before the Contact Period. With the coming of the Dutch, mass production of glass beads saturated the market. Some with red stripes were prized by the native people. Red symbolized blood and, by extension, life. Wampum in strings found a new role, that of currency. As money, tooled shells continued to be used until the time of American Revolutionary War.

CHAPTER 16: NOISY GOOSE

16-48 Lenapes

Their name meaning "people," the Lenapes were bands of Algonquian speakers living along valleys of the lower Hudson, Raritan, Hackensack, East, and Delaware Rivers and along the coastal areas of New York, New Jersey, and Pennsylvania.

The numerous and mostly peaceful bands of Lenapes maintained distinctive identities including dialects. These were the people of the region who first greeted Giovanni da Verrazzano (1524) and Henry Hudson (1609). Those in the south eventually became known as the Delaware Indians. This designation comes from a river named by the English in honor of Thomas de la Warr, the first governor in 1610 of the large territory called Virginia.

The first mention of Manna-hata was written on October 2, 1609 by Robert Juet, Henry Hudson's first mate on the *Half Moon.* We do not know if he referred to the New Jersey shore of the Upper New York Bay or to the island in it we know as Manhattan. In any case, the native people living on the island were thereafter known as the Manahattoes. They were part of the confederation of Wappingers, extending northward to the Hudson Highlands.

The Dutch and European settlers preserved many of the Lenapes' names for the places they inhabited. Raritan, Tappan, Canarsee, Munsee are but a few.

CHAPTER 17: CHIEF RED SUN

17-49 Crooked Tongues

The people who lived along the St. Lawrence River were called Wyandots (or "Islanders"), referring to the many islands in the river. They spoke one of the dialects of the Iroquois language. Mohawks, their longstanding enemies, referred to them as "Crooked Tongues." Since the name is interpreted widely to mean "the tellers of lies," it appears that the Mohawks distrusted this tribe. There could also be a linguistic reason for the term: "crooked-tongued" may have referred to a speaker of another dialect.

Later the French called the Wyandots the "Hurons," their word for "wild boar," referring unflatteringly to a savage-like appearance. Europeans, by the way, used the term "savage" not to mean ferocious but rather to mean uncivilized or uneducated, at least according to the customs in Europe. The French at the time had no appreciation of the moral principles and the rules of conduct of native people.

17-50 Saint Lawrence River

The Mohawks called it *Kaniatarowanenneh,* meaning The Big Waterway, and they were right on. The St. Lawrence River begins from the overflow of Lake Ontario, courses past Montreal and the impassible Lachine Rapids, past Quebec to empty into the Atlantic Ocean 800 miles away. Its source (or headwaters), that is, where it enters the chain of the Great Lakes, is from Seven Beaver Lake in Minnesota, 2,000 miles from the mouth.

From Quebec City outward, the water becomes brackish (meaning salty and undrinkable). The rising and falling of the ocean water causes a to-and-fro tidal movement river up to that point. And so, the Saint Lawrence River is a long estuary as is the Hudson River.

Certainly, the Vikings had known about the St. Lawrence River centuries before the "discovery" of America by Columbus in 1492. Portuguese sailors had come to "fisherman's heaven" at the mouth of the river in the 1500s. With ships loaded down with cod for sale in Europe, they successfully kept their source a secret, at least for a few decades. The incredible story of fishing in the Grand Banks and its economic and environmental importance on the modern world is masterfully told in a book by Mark Kurlansky. He called it, simply, *Cod.*

Another book— written many years ago for children by Holling Clancy Holling—is mentioned here. In it, we follow a small, carved and painted wooden model of a canoe with rider as it drifts from Lake Nipigon in central Canada into Lake Superior. It travels next through the chain of the Great Lakes and eventually to the Atlantic Ocean. The journey provides a sense of adventure, suspense, geography, and history told along with beautiful paintings and line drawings. This book was this author's inspiration for the story of *Tail Feather,* which, in turn, led to the set of stories called The River Quintet.

17-51 Hiawatha

The "Song of Hiawatha" by Henry Wadsworth Longfellow, published in 1855, was unlike anything written in America before. It put a human face, and indeed a heroic face, on the misunderstood, maligned, and mistreated Indians of the time. It is noteworthy that this change in attitude began closer to our time than to the time of our story.

Longfellow's poem took the young nation by storm, capturing the affection of millions. Who can forget the beautiful imagery: "By the shores of Gitche Gumee, By the shining Big-Sea-Water...?" The poem is told in a meter strange to an American ear but harking back to an exotic rhythm pattern of the folk songs taken from the runes of ancient Finland. No longer required reading in 7th and 8th grade, modern schoolchildren may be missing out on one of life's great treasures.

Hiawatha was a real person, but not the one in the poem. An early version of his name was written as *Ayonhwathah.* Sometime during the 16th century (the best guess is about the 1520s), Hiawatha was the chief of the Onondagas, an Iroquois tribe located along the Mohawk River just west of Mohawk land. Overcome with grief at the loss of his wife and seven daughters in an attack, he was determined to find a way out of the endless cycle of fighting among the Iroquois. His pact with Deganawidah, the Messenger of Peace from the land of the Hurons (Wyandots), lies within the core of Iroquois legends.

Many versions of the founding of the League of the Iroquois have appeared. Oral traditions carried the message with variations around a theme. The legend first saw print in 1892 in the *American Anthropologist.* The book, *The Iroquois,* by Professor Dean R. Snow at Pennsylvania State University, summarizes subsequent publications of other scholarly versions.

The *Song of Hiawatha* is based upon a vast amount of folklore passed down in telling stories through the generations in the tribes of the Ojibways and Chippawas. The collector was Henry Rowe Schoolcraft, an Albany (New York) glass manufacturer turned mid-western mineralogist. In 1822, he became an Indian Agent assigned to Sault Ste. Marie at the mouth of Lake Michigan. Schoolcraft was not successful in popularizing his traditional material in essays or in poems and turned to Longfellow to write a more dramatic epic. Above all, he wanted to preserve the "truth and roughness" of the original. Schoolcraft, however, was not favorably disposed to the name *Manobozoh* of the principle character of the local legends. He chose for their heroic being a more resonate name, that of an historical figure closer to his boyhood home in New York State.

17-52 Onondagas

The continental glacier of 20,000 years ago carved out the Finger Lakes and many other lakes in New York. The tribe of Onondagas lived around a lake of that name to the northeast of the "Fingers" at what is today the City of Syracuse. While the terrain is surely flat there, some small hills do exist. The Indian name for the tribe is *Gana'dagweniio'geh,* meaning People of the Hills.

Of the Iroquois-speaking people, the Onondagas resided between the Oneidas and the Mohawks on the east, and the Cayugas and Senecas on the west. With the creation of the Great Confederation of the Iroquois Nations, the Onondagas took on responsibility as "Keepers of the Fire" in their metaphorical longhouse. The Chiefs of the Confederation (Hiawatha being one of them) met in Onondaga, and still do. Onondaga Lake is, for Native Americans, a sacred place.

17-53 Mohawk River

Follow the Mohawk River upstream past Cohoes Falls, (about a mile inland from its entrance to the Hudson River,) and go about 150 miles to its source at Mohawk Hill, 1,800 feet above sea level. Along the way, you will pass through the only cut between the mountains of the Catskills and the Adirondacks.

It was along this river valley that the Iroquois tribes settled. They called it *Tenonanatche* (the river flowing through mountains). It provided not only ready canoe transportation but also fertile soil for gardens and sufficient land for hunting.

As the number of European settlers increased, Iroquois land along the river became the battlefields of the British and the French. Later it was used by the Rebels against the Redcoats in the War of Independence. In the aftermath of the war, the cities of Schenectady, Amsterdam, Little Falls, Utica, and Rome sprang up. Transportation by river became essential. Yet, the Mohawk was shallow in places and notorious for destructive flooding both from prolonged downpours and from the break-up of ice.

Gaining control of the waterway and extending it to the Great Lakes led to one of the great American achievements of imagination, engineering, and grunt work: the Erie Canal. Waterways built around obstacles in the Mohawk River and locks to raise and lower the water level gently insured the safe passage of barges. The extension of the river from Rome and Syracuse to Lake Erie opened the agricultural and mineral rich heartlands of the United States through the Hudson River to New York City and the Atlantic Ocean. A passageway from the canal to Lake Ontario would have been shorter but the plunge between the two lakes at Niagara posed a bit of a problem.

With great celebration, the country completed the canal in 1825 after eight years of toil by thousands of workers, many from Ireland. Modern transportation gradually eroded the canal's usefulness as railroad tracks and highways took advantage of the near water-level valley. Today, small lengths of the canal, revitalized by intrepid supporters, are open for recreational boating.

17-54 Oneidas

At the end of the year in 1634, Harmen van den Bogaert, the Dutch surgeon from Fort Orange, arrived in the village of the Oneidas. It lay on "a very high hill" from which could be seen the Mohawk River. Although he and his two fellow travelers were making the first recorded visit this far into New York's interior, they found iron hinges and axes, items of clothing, and razors that were either given to the Oneidas as "gifts" by the French or received in trade. There in Oneida on New Year's Eve Bogaert and his companions fired off three musket balls in honor of "Jesu Christo."

A north-flowing river from Oneida Lake (the largest lake within the State of New York) promoted early contact with the French along the Saint Lawrence River. It flows into Lake Ontario at Oswego and enters the Saint Lawrence between Cape Vincent and Wolfe Island. In spring, rainbow trout migrate upstream to Oneida Lake to spawn in freshwater. In autumn, salmon take their turn.

The Oneidas were known as *Onyota'aka* ("People of the Standing Stone"). During the American Revolutionary War, Oneida warriors did battle alongside the continentals. They took food to Valley Forge during the awful winter of 1777-8. Modern Oneidas still live in the vicinity and continue to practice their strong traditions. The *Shako: wi* Cultural Center in downtown Oneida exhibits important Oneida relics and memorabilia; dance, song, and skills are often performed at the Center.

17-55 Iroquois Great League of Peace and Power

The Iroquois League was likened to the longhouse in a culture rich in imagery and symbolism. They called themselves the *Haudenosaunees* ("People of the Longhouse").

The Nation of Mohawks resided at the eastern door of the Iroquois League, that is, nearest the Hudson River where the sun rises. The Mohawks *Gomiengehaka,* ("People of the Flint") were regarded as "keepers of the eastern door." Guardians of the western door, facing the setting sun and Lake Erie, were the Senecas. The Mohawk River connected these nations and the other three between them: the Onondaga, the Oneida, and the Cayuga.

A wampum belt represented the five nations of the League in the form of a longhouse. A heart (or pine tree, the "Tree of Peace") was at the center. It symbolized the Onondaga Nation, the "Keepers of the Central Fire." Two squares on each end stood for the other nations. These belts were made after the Contact Period when iron tools for shaping and drilling became available.

It is estimated that the five-member Iroquois pact was established about 1525, long before Europeans could have had any influence. This date fits best with oral traditions and by evidence from regional battles. In practice, the Great League did not solidify a political authority. Rather it promoted a spiritual unity. With the agreement, each of the Five Nations promised to keep peace among themselves.

With nations outside of the league, however, The Great League of Peace did not reduce hostility. Feuding continued against tribes on all sides, including the Hurons who spoke the Iroquoian language but who refused to join the League. Raids and warfare continued for revenge, spoils, captives for adoption, and adventure.

17-56 Mi'kmaq

Native people living near the outlet of the Saint Lawrence River were among the first to greet European explorers and fishermen. These were the

Mi'kmaq (pronounced Micmac). The tribe was scattered among the many coves and islands in what is now coastal Maine and southeastern Canada. The relationship with the newcomers, mostly French, was generally cordial. In 1610, the priest baptized their Chief, *Membertou.* Eventually, the tribe suffered terribly from European infections and, of course, the unstoppable grab for land.

17-57 Timeline

The European incursion into the northeastern continent begins not long after Columbus's "discovery" of the New World. A timeline of the rapidly unfolding events helps keep them in mind. Here, focus is on two major northeast rivers and their outlets: the Saint Lawrence and the Hudson.

1497: John Cabot (Giovanni Caboto), was an Italian navigator, employed by the English to find a waterway to the spices and jewels of the Far East. He is credited with "discovering" the mainland of North America, sighting Breton Island and Nova Scotia, thus establishing ownership of the land for England. He noted that fish were so thick in the Bay that they impeded his progress (they "stayed his shippe").

1520: Following up on Cabot's description of plentiful fish, fisherman from the Basque region of Spain and from Normandy in France went to coastal Newfoundland. There they conducted a long, thriving, and secretive codfish harvest, extending their nets southward into the Gulf of Saint Lawrence and to Nova Scotia and Maine.

They knew that getting the fish all the way back to France without spoiling was impossible, and, because western Europe was salt-poor, food preservation by salt was always prohibitively expensive. Instead, the fishermen created settlements on land where they could gut and dry the fish by fire and exposure to sun. Only then would it be ready for sale in France.

1534-1542: Jacques Cartier, a French navigator made three voyages. In the first voyage, he explored the bays and capes of Newfoundland. The second took him farther up the river to the rapids at Montreal, where further ship progress was impeded. On his last voyage, Cartier returned with quartz crystals and iron pyrites, thinking that these were diamonds and gold. To the end, he was convinced that riches in gems awaited the French in the new-found land.

These voyages were the basis for the French territorial claim. Cartier came to the river on August 10, the feast-day celebrating the Catholic martyr Saint Lawrence, of centuries before. Cartier named the mouth of the river in his honor. *Canada* is an Iroquois word meaning village. Cartier used the name for all the land along the river. These names, of course, have come to mean a lot more.

1603: Samuel de Champlain began a series of explorations along the eastern coast of Canada over the next several years. During this time, the trade of axes, knives, kettles, and blankets for pelts (mostly of beavers) was well underway.

1608: The settlement at Quebec, founded by de Champlain on a former Indian village, stood on the high cliffs where the Saint Lawrence River narrows abruptly. It is about 800 miles upriver from its outlet into the Atlantic Ocean.

1609: Samuel de Champlain and his men paddled southward on a long body of water, now called Lake Champlain, where they confronted Mohawk warriors wearing wooden armor. The explorers demonstrated the lethal power of their firearms with one shot that killed three warriors. The incident instantly set the Mohawks and French as long-term enemies.

1609: Henry Hudson, an English navigator on a Dutch ship, the *Half Moon,* entered New York Bay and sailed as far as present-day Albany, the upper reach of the estuary. His men rowed their small boat farther upriver to Troy, confirming it to be a river by its continuous downstream flow, not a strait leading to the riches of the Orient. The voyage was marked by hostility in the lower Hudson among the Lenape tribes but friendliness among the astonished Mohicans who lived upriver.

1612: On the advice of Queen Marie de' Medici, the mother of Louis XIII, the nine-year old King of France gave a gift to Madame Antoinette de Pons, Marquise de Guercheville, the Queen's Lady of Honor. Madame de Pons was a young and radiant widow, known for her grace and beauty, and wooed by the young king's recently deceased father.

The gift was all the land from Florida to the Gulf of Saint Lawrence (then called Northern Paraguay). How far inland was left vague. Occupancy by European tradition was a fundamental rule of land ownership, and the French failed to populate the whole coastal northeastern continent. Other European powers, it seems, simply ignored the gift.

1613: Jesuit priests set up a small colony on Mt. Desert Island, off southeastern Maine (and now the Acadia National Park). They arrived in Quebec in 1625.

1614: The Dutch built a trading post at Fort Nassau, a small island just south of present-day Albany. In 1617, a spring flood swept away the post.

1624: The Dutch tried again, this time constructing another place for trading and for settlers to establish a foothold in the New World. Called Fort Orange, it began about a mile to the north of the former Fort Nassau. Over time, the name was changed to Beverwyck (*Beverwijck* in Dutch) and finally—with the British take-over in 1664—Albany, to honor King Charles's brother James, the Duke of York and Albany.

1634-1635: Harmen van den Bogaert, a youthful barber-surgeon at Fort Orange ventured into the hinterland of the Mohawks, keeping a long-lost journal of his observations of the palisaded villages, customs, healing rituals, and ceremonial battle. In this, the first recorded journey into Iroquoia, van den Bogaert and his two companions sought the cause of the crash in the beaver pelt supply, not considering that beavers had been almost exterminated along the Mohawk River but rather suspecting that the Mohawks were trading them with the French. What the adventurers discovered was that December was not a good time to start off on a long walk through the forest and wetlands of New York. Iron hinges on swing doors of a longhouse confirmed suspicion of Mohawk and French trade. A fascinating translation of the journal can be found in "A Journey into Mohawk and Oneida Country 1634-1635," translated and edited by C.T. Gehring and W. A. Starna.

1637: In April of 1637, thirty-seven people arrived on the ship *Rensselaerswijck* to try their luck in the wilds of the New World. Kiliaen van Rensselaer, a merchant in diamonds and pearls in Amsterdam, had acquired a patroonship around Fort Orange with a commitment to establish more settlements. He then purchased land from the local Mohicans, who in 1629, had lost a devastating battle with the Mohawks. The land covered twenty-four miles along the North River (the early Dutch name for the Hudson River) and forty miles in breadth. Rensselaer, who never went to America, ran his extensive and rapidly growing enterprise with a tight fist.

These incursions of Europeans explorers along the major rivers went deep into the northeastern territory of the Northern Hemisphere. Of course, the explorers encountered native people all along the way. They did not overlook the opportunity for trading. Iron axes, copper kettles, glass beads, cloth, sundry metal goods, and alcohol soon changed the lives of woodland dwellers.

Having given up thoughts of acquiring untold amounts of gold and silver in the New World, the European traders settled for more humble prizes: fur, fish, and marine ivory (of walrus tusks). Pelts were highly profitable, providing material for coats and hats back home. The animals providing the pelt were available in inexhaustible supply (or so they thought until beavers were virtually extinguished within a couple of decades). It is in a more modern time that we are finding codfish disappearing from the Grand Banks caused by over-fishing.

Conflicts between Indians and settler/traders, too, were inevitable, considering the cultural insensitivity and the rush for living space by an ever-increasing flow of immigrants. But the most devastating blow of all was brought to the native population by children: disease. Smallpox and measles soon wiped out most of the Indians who were highly susceptible to these unfamiliar infections.

17-58 Canoe

The early visitors from Europe thought of the canoe as a flimsy and primitive craft. They soon learned otherwise. The light-weight boat, made from the bark of trees, provided easy and versatile transportation on the great waterways of the New World. A canoe, fully loaded, with a strong paddler at each end, can cover up to sixty miles a day. It can be carried overland between waterways with relative ease. They say that a skilled boat builder can put a canoe together from native materials using native tools in two weeks.

17-59 Quebec

The Saint Lawrence River abruptly narrows about six hundred miles inland from the Atlantic Ocean. The Algonquian word *Kebec* refers to this narrowing. On the north side, the riverbank rises steeply to a plateau, called the Plains of Abraham. In 1608, the explorer and military leader, Samuel de Champlain, chose to establish a permanent settlement here atop an abandoned Indian village. De Champlain envisioned the beginning of a continental empire that he called "New France."

The settlement rapidly developed into a walled fortress, the City of Quebec *(Québec)*. From here, traders, trappers, craftsmen, and settlers soon spread along the entire Saint Lawrence River.

Continued conflict with the English farther south eventually led to a struggle for domination. Here in Quebec on September 13, 1659 on the Plains of Abraham, the destiny of North America was defined in battle that lasted about fifteen minutes. Invading British troops defeated the French. Within four years, the King of France ceded all of Canada to Great Britain, keeping instead the Island of Guadeloupe where growing and processing sugar cane was a profitable business.

The people of the City of Quebec and, indeed, the entire Province of Quebec, avidly cherish their French traditions, language, and culture. A constant reminder is the automobile license plate that reads: *Je me souviens,* meaning "I remember," alongside the fleur de lys, the symbol of France.

CHAPTER 18: KYKOO

18-60 Sky Hunt

Orion and Ursa Major are two prominent constellations that move together across the sky. Since ancient times throughout the world people have told stories about them. These narratives provided something familiar yet always mysterious to the listeners throughout the pitch-dark nights.

There were many variations of the mythology among the Iroquois of long ago. In one version Orion was a hunter and Ursa Major, a Bear. The hunt of the bear began in spring (when Orion appeared) and went on through the whole summer. By autumn, the hunter found its mark. The blood of the bear spilled out of the heavens and turned the leaves red. Later, in winter, its fat became snow. The snow melted in spring, and the heat caused the fat to become the sap that ran in the trees.

Instead of Orion as the hunter, the Mohicans used the constellation Pleiades, which is closer to Ursa Major. The hunters were the seven stars that make up Pleiades. In another version, this of the Blackfoot Indians of the western Plains, Ursa Major is a grizzly bear, and it chases the hunters.

18-61 Wolf Pup

It is hard to imagine anything more cuddlesome than a wolf pup with its long and soft grayish brown fur, floppy ears, its housecat-like squeaks and need to snuggle up for warmth.

Two senses, hearing and smell, are outstanding. Deaf at birth, the wolf pup will hear within a few days and eventually develop hearing perception many times more acute than humans. The ears, by the way, will stand up by one month and face forward. Smell is certainly the wolf's most acute sense, a hundred times that of humans. What is inborn and what is learned, we do not know

Eyes tightly shut at birth will open in a week or two to show them blue. The irises will become deep yellow over the next eight to sixteen weeks. The black lids around them add to the wolf's piercing stare. While the wolf has limited frontal vision, it has keen side vision, especially at night..

For the first month, the pup is entirely dependent upon its mother's milk but thereafter can begin to eat. Solid food at first is partially digested meat that the mother regurgitates. To say that the wolf pup is hungry is an understatement. It will increase its weight about three pounds every week, perhaps gaining thirty pounds in the first few months.

The wolf pup begins to walk at about two weeks. By four weeks, it is truly rambunctious, play-fighting almost continuously with its litter mates when not sleeping. It will venture out of the den in about a month's time, there to bond with other members of the pack who seem to delight in pup-care. A too-mischievous pup may be picked up by the scruff of its neck and shaken.

A wolf pup raised by a person will accept the caregiver as a member of the pack though staying very wary of other humans. The older wolf taken in by humans will not bond with the same intensity.

Wolves communicate with a wide repertoire of yips, yaps, grunts, growls, and barks. But perhaps the most endearing feature of the wolf—at least to nature-lovers—is the howl, a talent that the pup begins within its first month of life. While the wolf may howl at any time of day, it is the howl at night that gives the woodlands its soul-revealing character. The howl is a sliding pitch, high to low or low to high that often breaks into distinctive overtones. Howling is meant to indicate the wolf's location, but it appears that it is also made just for fun.

CHAPTER 19: GUIDING STAR

19-62 Sparkling Stones

"Herkimer diamonds" are clear gemstones with natural facets and pointed ends. They are almost pure quartz and are clear and hard, easily passing as true diamonds. Formed from magnesium-hardened sandstone half a million years ago, they lie in cavities with dolostone. In Mohawk territory, the gemstones appeared in streams after release from the weathering of rocks. Today they are quarried in local mines in Herkimer County after some hard digging.

The Iroquois people treasured these gemstones as symbols of good health and long life. The findings of archaeologists confirm their use as decorations and as amulets.

19-63 Healing Arts

Medical care as practiced by the Iroquois in the 17th century depended upon intimate knowledge of a wide variety of natural substances. The herbal pharmacopoeia was based upon an admixture of favorable results and superstition. The many natural remedies were meant to restore the order of the sick person that had been disturbed by a mysterious force.

Perhaps the most useful of herbal remedies was willow bark, a bitter astringent 'salicin' with aspirin-like properties. For fever and pain, it was as utilitarian as aspirin is today. Honey was helpful for dressing wounds. When mixed with beeswax, honey soothed scratches and burns. It may also act as an antiseptic.

Responsibility for healing fell within the realm of the shaman. The Iroquois considered the shaman a holy person with supernatural power, able to communicate with higher beings. Surely, the shaman knew his herbal remedies. Perhaps, even more, he prescribed sweat baths for many illnesses. He set bones and treated wounds. He interpreted dreams (that may in some way have caused the illness).

The Iroquois rationale for treating a disease meant restoring the balance of the body that had been put out of sort by some adversity, even by a dream, however little understood. This was accomplished by coaxing the Spirit of Sickness out of the body where it would follow the smoke that wound its way up through the rooftop hole. Treatment in the pre-scientific age may seem based largely on superstition to the modern healer, but the practices of the shaman were not harmful. European physicians, on the other hand, often got it all wrong, treating their patients in ways that were actually dangerous. Their concept held that there was something in the body that caused the illness and that getting rid of it was entirely rationale. From the time of Galen in the 2nd century to the early 20th century, Western medical practice favored withdrawing body fluids through venesection (letting blood), emetics (causing vomiting), clysis (enemas), diuretics (increasing urine flow), sudorifics (sweat-inducing drugs) and cupping (raising giant fluid-filled welts)—all to draw out the toxins that made a person sick.

Treatment in Iroquoia often took on a highly ritualistic performance. Van den Bogaert described such a session, observed in a Mohawk village on December 24, 1634, before a large fire. The shaman (actually, there were two, but the plural form of shaman does not seem to exist) placed a snakeskin around the heads and proceeded with much singing, shouting, and clapping of hands. We are not told of the diagnosis or the outcome of the treatment.

Iroquois healers often wore masks and carried a stick in one hand and a turtle shell rattle in another. The mask was not intended to hide the identity of the wearer but rather portray spiritual forces. Braided husks of maize made the 'bushy head' mask. The rattle was a turtle shell hollowed out and with pebbles placed inside, with the head and neck used as a handle. It was an important symbol because of the turtle's long life (though not for the donor of the rattle). Masks and rattles are among the most sacred of Iroquois relics, and modern Indigenous sensitivities restrain museums and other public venues from displaying or illustrating them.

19-64 Concept of Death

The brave and worthy person crosses over into a land of shade where it is never bright and never dark. It is a land where life continues with endless festivals, where strawberries are always ripe, where animals to hunt are abundant and where fish fill the rivers. There, the deceased will live in peace for all time.

Persons who are lazy or cowardly dwell in the same celestial space. They are destined, however, to wander restlessly forever. They will live in eternal darkness and eat snakes and ashes.

19-65 Milky Way

The hazy, faintly lit band that extends across the night sky is the Milky Way. It is a galaxy consisting of 200 to 400 billion stars, none of which can be distinguished with the naked eye. The first person to make out individual stars was Galileo Galilei, using a crude telescope (crude by today's standards) at almost the same time that our story takes place.

To give some perspective of the size of the Milky Way, think of the known universe as the size of a football field. Our solar system, that is, the sun and all the planets, including the Earth, would be a grain of sand in that field.

The Milky Way is best seen far away from the nightglow of cities and towns. One can be certain that the Indians of long ago had a good view, especially when the moon was well below the horizon. Sky watching and wondering led pre-scientific people throughout the world to contemplate the Milky Way and create myths as to its meaning. Of the Iroquois legends, we know of one, that is ascribed to the Senecas and dates back to about AD 1800, almost 200 years after this story.

By the late 1700s the Senecas had already been dislodged from their ancestral home in central New York State. At their new home along the Allegheny River in Pennsylvania, life proved very difficult. One man of the tribe, Handsome Lake, had a vision during a terrible illness. One vision was of a guide with bow and arrow who led human souls on a path that crossed the sky. On this "Great Sky Road" the good people went to the lands of the Creator.

19-66 Cornhusk Doll

A child was taught early to place value on character or spiritual beauty rather than on physical beauty. A cornhusk doll remains faceless until its spirit can create its own character or other evidence of uniqueness. Although the doll can still be dressed and decorated in any number of ways depending on the child's preferences, its spirit remains free to develop. The child, in turn, can find joy in such creative play.

Following this concept of simplicity are the notions of conceit and self-importance. If a face were to be drawn on a doll, the child would learn to focus on physical appearance, entirely neglecting the importance of selflessness and humility. An Iroquois story tells of a doll who was supposed to teach others the lessons of good character, but she forgot to do this. She became so obsessed with her own beautiful reflection on passing a puddle or a pond that the Creator erased her face forever.

19-67 Funeral Rites

Native Americans held deep respect for those who have passed on, believing the spirits of the departed will continue forever. Yet, without proper attention by the living, deceased persons would be unable to find a resting place in the afterworld. They would spend eternity as a restless spirit, perhaps returning to haunt their neglectful relatives.

At Iroquois funerals, around the washed, oiled, and perfumed body, grieving relatives and friends sang, chanted, danced, and prayed to blend the path of life and death. Relatives covered their faces and clothes with ashes. There followed a feast of the deceased's favorite food. Tobacco, as flaked leaves, was offered to the spirits according to sacred protocol.

Burials occurred in earthen mounds after a mourning period of ten days. Good luck items were placed beside the body: food, beads, combs, and gourds all to promote a successful journey to the land of the dead. Archaeologists have also found more precious items such as clay pots, spearheads, and stone and metal jewelry, thus representing a sacrifice of the living to those passing to the next world. Most elaborately gifted of all were the graves of children.

After one year, there was another festival to honor the departed. With that, the mourning came to an end.

19-68 Turtle Shell Moon Clock

The turtle plays a central role in the Legend of Creation. The turtle also provided a way in which humans could measure time.

On every carapace (upper shell) of the turtle, there is an outer border of twenty-eight small plates. To the Iroquois, each plate represented one day of the twenty-eight days lapsing between full moons. Inside is a mosaic of thirteen plates. These represent all the new moons coming in one year. This handy calendar was not accurate—there are 29.53 days between full moons—but it was in a world in which the times for planting, harvest, fish migration, and picking berries did not need to be precisely conducted. The turtle shell was a good enough guide.

The Iroquois gave each of the thirteen plates timely recognition: Maple Sugar Moon, Strawberry Moon, Harvest Moon, and so forth. And so, the turtle held the key to the passage of time according to the new moons.

CHAPTER 20: TAIL FEATHER

20-69 Stories from the Journey-to-the-Water-With-No-End

From Book I of The River Quintet, *Tail Feather: Adventures of A Mohawk Paddler on the River-That-Flows-Two-Ways*

Locations of the Book 1 references are identified in brackets.

The River That Flows Two Ways [The Lower Hudson River].

The Hudson River falls one mile from its origin in the Adirondack Mountains to its halfway point at Troy, New York. From this point on, the riverbed falls only a few more feet to New York Harbor at Manhattan Island. The tides of the ocean cause the river to rise and fall, and the water to go back and forth all the way to Troy. This behavior defines an estuary, so that for its lower half it is an estuary and not a river at all.

Shad fishing [Bear Mountain – Iona Island].

Shad do not eat on their spring migration from the Atlantic Ocean to the upstream wetlands of the Hudson River. For hundreds of years, fishermen have caught shad in nets suspended from poles in the river. The nets are submerged at high tide when the shad catch their gills in the nets. At low tide, the nets are exposed above water level. The shad are then picked as if ripened apples on a tree.

Bird-People [Manhattan Island]

Giovanni da Verrazzano, an Italian captain commanding a French ship, came into the Upper New York Bay in 1524. In a letter, he noted the "nude" Indians encountered along the coast of Maryland and Virginia. On Manhattan Island, however, those who came out to meet him and his crew were "dressed out with feathers of birds of various colours."

Trading people living on Manhattan Island were a tribe of Lenapes. They kept up a lively trade with people who traveled great distances to obtain their tooled seashells. These pieces were the units that went into wampum-making. Other Lenapes on seaside beaches (the Canarsees of

Coney Island, the Rack-a-wak-e on the Rockaways and the Raritans on Staten Island) all contributed to the supply and tooling of shells.

The Europeans who first encountered Native Americans on Manhattan Island described them as ornate and adorned with feathers and other decorations. On the southern shore (near present-day Wall Street), the islanders traded seashells for items brought from inland by long distance travelers.

The War Canoe [West Point]

Dugout canoes are seen in the earliest known drawings of the New York Harbor scene, dating back to the mid-1600s. Paddlers are depicted in these canoes, standing and holding shovel-like paddles.

The Sperm Whale [Outer New York Harbor]

A long time ago, whales were frequently sighted in New York's Lower Bay. The sperm whale, for example, swam past Long Island and Far Rockaway in its long, migratory journey.

Birth of a fawn [Castle Island]

The sighting of the newborn deer is placed on a small island just south of the capital city of Albany. It was on Castle Island in 1614 (a year after the *Tail Feather* story) that the Dutch established a trading post called Fort Nassau. Their post, modest as it was, was the first European building in what would become the State of New York.

Turk's Head [Breakneck Mountain]

Until the mid-1800s, a stone formation in the Hudson Valley strongly resembled a human face. This imposing figure looked out from the side of a mountain onto the river. Evergreen trees standing on the chin made an upturned beard. Kegs of gunpowder placed on the mountain by a construction engineer took down the mountainside to fill the ever-increasing need for granite building blocks. Today, Breakneck Mountain's rough terrain makes it a premier site for the rugged hiker bent on having a great view.

Lacrosse [Fishkill]

Lacrosse is the quintessential game of Native Americans. It was certainly played long before the Contact Period with the Europeans (although its common name is French). The game was placed with large numbers of stick-wielding players. The daylong bruising contest was meant to prepare young men for battle.

The Tall Ship [Tappan Zee]

The meeting of the canoes and a sailing ship of Adriaen Block from Holland sets the *Tail Feather* story in 1613. A yellow-haired boy on the ship offers a salute to the paddlers by firing his matchlock gun. The age of gunpowder is thereby introduced to the astonished spectators. (The boy is the main character in Book 3 of The River Quintet, *Johannes van der Zee: The Journey of a Dutch Sailor to a Trading Post in New Netherland.)*

The blue hat that the boy on the boat threw to Tail Feather was made of cloth. Cloth was new to the Native Americans at this time. The Mohawks referred to white people as *Assyreoni* or cloth-makers, according to writings of the Dutch preacher, Megapolensis, in 1644.

Chase by a Bear [Palmer Falls, Corinth]

A solitary bear cub in the story causes a lapse in good judgment. The episode nearly ends in disaster. Today, a huge hydroelectric plant is at the site where it diverts water and exposes the rocky drop-off.

The Fire Dance [Rockwood Falls, Lake Luzerne]

Travel here in hostile land required portaging canoes down a roaring cascade at night. It happened beneath a rocky overhang upon which masked Mohican dancers, close to the edge, were celebrating a festival. The dancers cast eerie shadows on the travelers below.

www.ingramcontent.com/pod-product-compliance
Ingram Content Group UK Ltd.
Pitfield, Milton Keynes, MK11 3LW, UK
UKHW041636190726
13854UKWH00006B/2518